of PRYD[A]IN

D0352114

STRONGHOLDS

NORTHERN
REALMS

EAGLE
MOUNTAINS

REALM OF
THE FAIR
FOLK

S

CAER
DATHYL

LLAWGADARN
MOUNTAINS

RUINED
WALL

MEDWYN'S
VALLEY

MERIN

ISAV

GWENITH

VALLEY
CANTREVS

FREE COMMOTS

SMALL AVREN

CENARTH

CAER
ADARN

HILL
CANTREVS

RIVER YSTRAD

CAER
DALLBEN

KING

THE CHRONICLES *of* PRYDAIN

The High King

LLOYD ALEXANDER

USBORNE

For the boys who might have been Taran
and the girls who will always be Eilonwy

First published in this edition in 2006 by Usborne Publishing Ltd.,
Usborne House, 83,85 Saffron Hill, London EC1N 8RT, England.
www.usborne.com

A CIP catalogue record for this book is available from
the British Library.

J MAMJJASOND/06
ISBN 0 7460 6838 7

Printed in Great Britain.

CHAPTER ONE

Homecomings

Under a chill, grey sky, two riders jogged across the turf. Taran, the taller horseman, set his face against the wind and leaned forwards in the saddle, his eyes on the distant hills. At his belt hung a sword, and from his shoulder a silver-bound battle horn. His companion Gurgi, shaggier than the pony he rode, pulled his weathered cloak around him, rubbed his frost-nipped ears, and began groaning so wretchedly that Taran at last reined up the stallion.

"No, no!" Gurgi cried. "Faithful Gurgi will keep on!

He follows kindly master, oh yes, as he has always done. Never mind his shakings and achings! Never mind the droopings of his poor tender head!"

Taran smiled, seeing that Gurgi, despite his bold words, was eyeing a sheltering grove of ash trees. "There is time to spare," he answered. "I long to be home, but not at the cost of that poor tender head of yours. We camp here and go no farther until morning."

They tethered their mounts and built a small fire in a ring of stones. Gurgi curled up and was snoring almost before he had finished swallowing his food. Though as weary as his companion, Taran set about mending the harness leathers. Suddenly he stopped and jumped to his feet. Overhead, a winged shape plunged swiftly towards him.

"Look!" Taran cried, as Gurgi, still heavy with sleep, sat up and blinked. "It's Kaw! Dallben must have sent him to find us."

The crow beat his wings, clacked his beak, and began squawking loudly even before he landed on Taran's outstretched wrist.

"Eilonwy!" Kaw croaked at the top of his voice. "Eilonwy! Princess! Home!"

Taran's weariness fell from him like a cloak. Gurgi, wide awake and shouting joyfully, scurried to unloose the steeds. Taran leaped astride Melynlas, spun the grey stallion about, and galloped from the grove, with Kaw perched on his shoulder and Gurgi and the pony pounding at his heels.

Day and night they rode, hardly halting for a mouthful of food or a moment of sleep, urging all speed and strength from their mounts and from themselves, ever southwards, down from the mountain valley and across Great Avren until, on a bright morning, the fields of Caer Dallben lay before them once again.

From the instant Taran set foot across the threshold, such a commotion filled the cottage that he scarcely knew which way to turn. Kaw had immediately begun jabbering and flapping his wings; Coll, whose great bald crown and broad face shone with delight, was clapping Taran on the back; while Gurgi shouted in glee and leaped up and down in a cloud of shedding hair. Even the ancient enchanter Dallben, who seldom let anything disturb his meditations, hobbled out of his chamber to observe the welcomings. In the midst of it all, Taran could hardly glimpse Eilonwy, though he heard the voice of the princess very clearly above the din.

"Taran of Caer Dallben," she cried, as he strove to draw near her, "I've been waiting to see you for days! After all the time I've been away learning to be a young lady – as if

I weren't one before I left — when I'm home at last, you're not even here!"

In another moment he was at her side. The slender princess still wore at her throat the crescent moon of silver, and on her finger the ring crafted by the Fair Folk. But now a band of gold circled her brow, and the richness of her apparel made Taran suddenly aware of his travel-stained cloak and muddy boots.

"And if you think living in a castle is pleasant," Eilonwy went on, without a pause for breath, "I can tell you it isn't. It's weary and dreary! They've made me sleep in beds with goosefeather pillows enough to stifle you; I'm sure the geese needed them more than I did — the feathers, that is, not the pillows. And servitors to bring you exactly what you don't want to eat. And washing your hair whether it needs it or not. And sewing and weaving and curtsying and all such I don't even want to think about. I've not drawn a sword for I don't know how long. . ."

Eilonwy stopped abruptly and looked curiously at Taran. "That's odd," she said. "There's something different about you. It's not your hair, though it does look as if you'd cropped it yourself with your eyes shut. It's — well, I can't quite say. I mean, unless you told someone they'd never guess you were an Assistant Pig-Keeper."

Taran laughed fondly at Eilonwy's puzzled frown. "Alas, it's been long since last I tended Hen Wen. Indeed, when

we journeyed among the folk of the Free Commots, Gurgi
and I toiled at nearly everything but pig-keeping. This
cloak I wove at the loom of Dwyvach the Weaver-Woman;
this sword – Hevydd the Smith taught me the forging of it.
And this," he said with a trace of sadness, drawing an
earthen bowl from his jacket, "such as it is, I made at the
wheel of Annlaw Clay-Shaper." He put the bowl in her
hands. "If it pleases you, it is yours."

"It's lovely," answered Eilonwy. "Yes, I shall treasure it.
But that's what I mean, too. I'm not saying you aren't a good
Assistant Pig-Keeper, because I'm sure you're the best in
Prydain, but there's something more –"

"You speak truth, Princess," put in Coll. "He left us a
pig-keeper and comes back looking as if he could do all he
set his hand to, whatever."

Taran shook his head. "I learned I was neither
swordsmith nor weaver. Nor, alas, a shaper of clay. Gurgi
and I were already homeward bound when Kaw found us,
and here shall we stay."

"I'm glad of that," replied Eilonwy. "All anyone knew
about you was that you were wandering every which where.
Dallben told me you were seeking your parents. Then you
met someone you thought was your father but wasn't. Or was
it the other way round? I didn't altogether understand it."

"There is little to understand," Taran said. "What I
sought, I found. Though it was not what I had hoped."

"No, it was not," murmured Dallben, who had been watching Taran closely. "You found more than you sought, and gained perhaps more than you know."

"I still don't see why you wanted to leave Caer Dallben," Eilonwy began.

Taran had no chance to reply, for now his hand was seized and shaken vigorously.

"Hullo, hullo!" cried a young man with pale blue eyes and straw-coloured hair. His handsomely embroidered cloak looked as though it had been water-soaked, then wrung out to dry. His bootlacings, broken in several places, had been retied in large, straggling knots.

"Prince Rhun!" Taran had almost failed to recognize him. Rhun had grown taller and leaner, though his grin was as broad as it had ever been.

"King Rhun, actually," the young man answered, "since my father died last summer. That's one of the reasons why Princess Eilonwy is here now. My mother wanted to keep her with us on Mona to finish her education. And you know my mother! She'd never have left off with it, even though Dallben had sent word Eilonwy was to come home. And so," he proudly added, "I finally put my foot down. I ordered a ship fitted out, and off we sailed from Mona Haven. Amazing what a king can do when he sets his mind to it!"

"We've brought someone else along, too," Rhun continued, gesturing towards the fireside where Taran for the first time noticed a pudgy little man sitting with a cook-pot between his knees. The stranger licked his fingers and wrinkled a flabby nose at Taran. He made no attempt to rise, but only nodded curtly while the scraggly fringe of hair around his bulbous head stirred like weeds under water.

Taran stared, not believing what he saw. The little man drew himself up and sniffed with a mixture of haughtiness and wounded feelings.

"One should have no trouble remembering a giant," he said testily.

"Remember you?" replied Taran. "How could I not! The cavern on Mona! Last time I saw you, though, you were – bigger, to say the least. But it is you, nevertheless. It is, indeed! Glew!"

"When I was a giant," Glew said, "few would have forgotten me so quickly. Unfortunate that things worked out as they did. Now, in the cavern –"

"You've started him off again," Eilonwy whispered to Taran. "He'll go on like that until you're fairly wilted, about the glorious days when he used to be a giant. He'll only stop talking to eat, and only stop eating to talk. I can understand his eating, since he lived on nothing but mushrooms for so long. But he must have been wretched as a giant, and you'd think he'd want to forget it."

"I knew Dallben sent Kaw with a potion to shrink Glew

back to size," Taran answered. "Of what happened to him since then, I've had no word."

"*That's* what happened to him," said Eilonwy. "As soon as he got free of the cavern, he made his way to Rhun's castle. No one had the heart to turn him away, though he bored us all to tears with those endless pointless tales of his. We took him with us when we sailed, thinking he'd be grateful to Dallben and want to thank him properly. Not a bit of it! We almost had to twist his ears to get him aboard. Now that he's here, I wish we'd left him where he was."

"But three of our companions are missing," Taran said, glancing around the cottage. "Good old Doli, and Fflewddur Fflam. And I had hoped Prince Gwydion might have come to welcome Eilonwy."

"Doli sends his best wishes," said Coll, "but we shall have to do without his company. Our dwarf friend is harder to root out of the Fair Folk realm than a stump out of a field. He'll not budge. As for Fflewddur Fflam, nothing can keep him and his harp from any merry-making, whatever. He should have been here long since."

"Prince Gwydion as well," Dallben added. "He and I have matters to discuss. Though you young people may doubt it, some of them are even weightier than the homecomings of a princess and an Assistant Pig-Keeper."

"Well, I shall put this on again when Fflewddur and Prince Gwydion arrive," said Eilonwy, taking the golden circlet from her brow, "just so they can see how it looks. But I won't wear it a moment longer. It's rubbed a blister and it makes my head ache — like someone squeezing your neck, only higher up."

"Ah, Princess," Dallben said, with a furrowed smile, "a crown is more discomfort than adornment. If you have learned that, you have already learned much."

"Learning!" Eilonwy declared. "I've been up to my ears in learning. It doesn't show, so it's hard to believe it's there. Wait, that's not quite true, either. Here, I've learned this." From her cloak she drew a large square of folded cloth and almost shyly handed it to Taran. "I embroidered it for you. It's not finished yet, but I wanted you to have it, even so. Though I admit it's not as handsome as the things you've made."

Taran spread out the fabric. As broad as his outstretched arms, the somewhat straggle-threaded embroidery showed a white, blue-eyed pig against a field of green.

"It's meant to be Hen Wen," Eilonwy explained as Rhun and Gurgi pressed forwards to study the handiwork more closely.

"At first, I tried to embroider you into it, too," Eilonwy said to Taran. "Because you're so fond of Hen and because — because I was thinking of you. But you came out looking like sticks with a bird's nest on top, not yourself at all.

So I had to start over with Hen alone. You'll just have to make believe you're standing beside her, a little to the left. Otherwise, I'd never have got this much done, and I did work the summer on it."

"If I was in your thoughts then," Taran said, "your work gladdens me all the more. No matter that Hen's eyes are really brown."

Eilonwy looked at him in sudden dismay. "You don't like it."

"I do, in all truth," Taran assured her. "Brown or blue makes no difference. It will be useful —"

"Useful!" cried Eilonwy. "Useful's not the point! It's a keepsake, not a horse blanket! Taran of Caer Dallben, you don't understand anything at all."

"At least," Taran replied, with a good-natured grin, "I know the colour of Hen Wen's eyes."

Eilonwy tossed her red-gold hair and put her chin in the air. "Humph!" she said. "And very likely forgotten the colour of mine."

"Not so, Princess," Taran answered quietly. "Nor have I forgotten when you gave me this," he added, taking up the battle horn. "Its powers were greater than either of us knew. They are gone now, but I treasure it still because it came from your hands.

"You asked why I sought to know my parentage," Taran went on. "Because I hoped it would prove noble, and give me the right to ask what I dared not ask before. My hope was mistaken. Yet even without it —"

Taran hesitated, searching for the most fitting words. Before he could speak again, the cottage door burst open, and Taran cried out in alarm.

At the threshold stood Fflewddur Fflam. The bard's face was ashen, his ragged yellow hair clung to his forehead. On his shoulder he bore the limp body of a man.

Taran, with Rhun behind him, sprang to help. Gurgi and Eilonwy followed as they lowered the still figure to the ground. Glew, his pudgy cheeks quivering, stared speechless. At the first instant, Taran had nearly staggered at the shock. Now his hands worked quickly, almost of themselves, to unclasp the cloak and loosen the torn jacket. Before him, on the hard-packed earth, lay Gwydion Prince of Don.

Blood crusted the warrior's wolf-grey hair and stained his weathered face. His lips were drawn back, his teeth set in battle rage. Gwydion's cloak muffled one arm as though at the last he had sought to defend himself with this alone.

"Lord Gwydion is slain!" Eilonwy cried.

"He lives — though barely," Taran said. "Fetch medicines," he ordered Gurgi. "The healing herbs from my saddlebags —" He stopped short and turned to Dallben. "Forgive me. It is not for me to command under my master's roof. But the herbs are of great power. Adaon Son of

Taliesin gave them to me long ago. They are yours if you wish them."

"I know their nature and have none that will serve better," Dallben answered. "Nor should you fear to command under any roof, since you have learned to command yourself. I trust your skill as I see you trust it. Do as you see fit."

Coll was already hurrying from the scullery with water in a basin. Dallben, who had kneeled at Gwydion's side, rose and turned to the bard.

"What evil deed is this?" The old enchanter spoke hardly above a whisper, yet his voice rang through the cottage and his eyes blazed in anger. "Whose hand dared strike him?"

"The Huntsmen of Annuvin," replied Fflewddur. "Two lives they almost claimed. How did you fare?" he urgently asked Taran. "How did you outride them so quickly? Be thankful it went no worse for you."

Taran, puzzled, glanced up at the distraught bard. "Your words have no meaning, Fflewddur."

"Meaning?" answered the bard. "They mean what they say. Gwydion would have traded his life for yours when the Huntsmen set upon you not an hour ago."

"Set upon me?" Taran's perplexity grew. "How can that be? Gurgi and I saw no Huntsmen. And we have been at Caer Dallben this hour past."

"Great Belin, a Fflam sees what he sees!" cried Fflewddur.

"A fever is working in you," Taran said. "You, too, may be wounded more grievously than you know. Rest easy. We shall give you all the help we can." He turned again to Gwydion, opened the packet of herbs which Gurgi had brought, and set them to steep in the basin.

Dallben's face was clouded. "Let the bard speak," he said. "There is much in his words that troubles me."

"Lord Gwydion and I rode together from the northern lands," Fflewddur began. "We'd crossed Avren and were well on our way here. A little distance ahead of us, in a clearing. . ." The bard paused and looked directly at Taran. "I saw you with my own eyes! You were hard pressed. You shouted to us for help and waved us onwards.

"Gwydion outdistanced me," Fflewddur went on. "You'd already galloped beyond the clearing. Gwydion rode after you like the wind. Llyan carried me swiftly, but by the time I caught up there was no sign of you at all, yet Huntsmen a-plenty. They had dragged Gwydion from his saddle. They would have paid with their own lives had they stood against me," cried Fflewddur. "But they fled when I rode up. Gwydion was close to death and I dared not leave him."

Fflewddur bowed his head. "His hurt was beyond my skill to treat. I could do no more than bring him here as you see him."

"You saved his life, my friend," Taran said.

"And lost what Gwydion would have given his life to keep!" cried the bard. "The Huntsmen failed to slay him, but a greater evil has befallen him. They've stripped him of his sword — blade and scabbard!"

Taran caught his breath. Concerned only for his companion's wounds, he had not seen that Dyrnwyn, the black sword, hung no longer at Gwydion's side. Terror filled him. Dyrnwyn, the enchanted blade, the flaming weapon of ancient power, was in the Huntsmen's hands. They would bear it to their master: to Arawn Death-Lord, in the dark realm of Annuvin.

Fflewddur sank to the ground and put his head in his hands. "And my own wits are lost, since you tell me it was not yourself who called out to us."

"What you saw I cannot judge," Taran said. "Gwydion's life is our first care. We will talk of these things when your memory is clearer."

"The harper's memory is clear enough." A black-robed woman moved from the dark corner where she had been silently listening, and stepped slowly into the midst of the company. Her long, unbound hair glittered like pale silver; the deadly beauty of her face had not altogether vanished, though now it seemed shadowy, worn away, lingering as a dream only half-recalled.

"Ill fortune mars our meeting, Assistant Pig-Keeper,"

Achren said. "But welcome, nonetheless. What, then, do you still fear me?" she added, seeing Taran's uneasy glance. She smiled. Her teeth were sharp. "Neither has Eilonwy Daughter of Angharad forgotten my powers, though it was she who destroyed them at the Castle of Llyr. Yet, since I have dwelled here, have I not served Dallben as well as any of you?"

Achren strode to the outstretched form of Gwydion. Taran saw a look almost of pity in her cold eyes. "Lord Gwydion will live," she said. "But he may find life a crueller fate than death." She bent and with her fingertips lightly touched the warrior's brow, then drew her hand away and faced the bard.

"Your eyes did not play you false, harper," Achren said. "You saw what was meant for you to see. A pig-keeper? Why not, if thus he chose to appear? Only one wields such power: Arawn himself, Lord of Annuvin, Land of the Dead."

CHAPTER TWO

The Letter Sticks

Taran could not stifle a gasp of fear. The black-robed woman glanced at him coldly.

"Arawn dares not pass the borders of Annuvin in his true form," Achren said. "To do so would mean his death. But he commands all shapes, and they are both shield and mask. To the harper and Lord Gwydion, he showed himself as a pig-keeper. He could as well have appeared as a fox in the forest, an eagle, even a blind worm if he deemed that would best serve his ends. Yes, Pig-Keeper, with no less ease could he have chosen the form and features of any creature living. For Lord Gwydion, what better lure than the sight of a companion in danger — one who had fought often at his side, known to him, and trusted. Gwydion is too shrewd a warrior to be taken in a weaker snare."

"Then all of us are lost," Taran said, dismayed. "The Lord of Annuvin can move among us as he pleases, and we are without defence against him."

"You have reason to fear, Pig-Keeper," replied Achren. "Now you glimpse one of Arawn's subtlest powers. But it is a power used only when none other will serve him. Never will he leave his stronghold, save in the press of mortal danger; or, as today, when what he sought to gain far outweighed the risk." Achren's voice lowered. "Arawn has many secrets, but this one is most deeply guarded. Once he assumes a shape, his strength and skill are no greater than that of the guise he wears. Then can he be slain, like any mortal thing."

"Oh, Fflewddur, if I'd only been with you!" Eilonwy cried in despair. "Arawn wouldn't have deceived me, no matter how much he looked like Taran. Don't tell me I couldn't have told the difference between a real Assistant Pig-Keeper and a false one!"

"Foolish pride, Daughter of Angharad," Achren answered scornfully. "No eyes can see behind the mask of Arawn Death-Lord. No eyes," she added, "but mine. Do you doubt me?" Achren went on quickly, seeing Eilonwy's surprise.

The woman's ravaged features held shreds of an old pride, and her voice sharpened with haughtiness and anger.

"Long before the Sons of Don came to dwell in Prydain, long before the lords of the cantrevs swore allegiance to Math, High King, and Gwydion, his war-leader, it was I who commanded obedience to my rule, I who wore the Iron Crown of Annuvin.

"Arawn was my consort, who served me and did my bidding," Achren said. "And he betrayed me." Her voice was low and harsh, and rage glittered in her eyes. "He robbed me of my throne and cast me aside. Yet his powers are no secret to me, for it was I who taught them to him. Let him cloud your sight with whatever guise he chooses. From me, never can the face of Arawn be hidden."

Gwydion stirred and groaned faintly. Taran turned again to the basin of healing herbs, while Eilonwy raised the warrior's head.

"Bear Prince Gwydion to my chamber," Dallben ordered. The enchanter's careworn face was drawn, and the lines had deepened in his withered cheeks. "Your skill has helped keep him from death," he said to Taran. "Now I must see if mine may help him to life."

Coll lifted Gwydion in his burly arms.

Achren made to follow after him. "I have little need of

sleep and can best keep a vigil," Achren said. "I shall watch the night over Lord Gwydion."

"I shall watch over him," Eilonwy said, stepping to the side of Coll.

"Fear me not, Daughter of Angharad," Achren said. "I bear no ill will against Lord Gwydion." She bowed deeply, half-humble and half-mocking. "The stable is my castle and the scullery my realm. I seek no other."

"Come," Dallben said, "both of you shall help me. Wait — the others. Be patient and hopeful."

Darkness had blinded the windows of the cottage. To Taran, it seemed the fire had lost its warmth and cast only cold shadows among the silent companions.

"At first I thought somehow we could overtake the Huntsmen and keep them from reaching Annuvin," Taran said at last. "But if Achren speaks truth, Arawn himself commanded them, and Gwydion's sword is already in his hands. I do not know his purpose, but I am deeply afraid."

"I can't forgive myself," Fflewddur said. "The loss is my fault. I should have seen the trap instantly."

Taran shook his head. "Arawn worked a bitter ruse on you. Gwydion himself was deceived."

"But not I!" cried the bard. "A Fflam is keen-eyed! From the first moment, I saw differences. The way he sat his steed, the way..." The harp, slung at the bard's shoulder, tensed suddenly and a string snapped with such a twang that Gurgi, crouched near the hearth, started bolt upright. Fflewddur choked and swallowed. "There it goes again," he muttered. "Will it never leave off? The slightest...ah, colouring of the facts, and the beastly strings break! Believe me, I meant no exaggeration. As I thought back it did seem that I could notice...no, the truth of it is: the guise was perfect. I could be snared again — and as easily."

"Amazing!" murmured the King of Mona, who had been watching wide-eyed. "I say, I wish I could do that sort of shape-changing myself. Unbelievable! I've always thought: how interesting to be a badger, or an ant. I should love to know how to build as well as they do. Since I've been king, I've tried to improve things here and there. I mean to put up a new seawall at Mona Haven. I've begun once already. My idea was to start from both ends at the same time and thus be done twice as quickly. I can't understand what went wrong, for I took charge of all the work myself, but somehow we didn't meet in the middle and I'll have to find a better way of going at it. Then I've planned a road to Glew's old cavern. It's an amazing place and I think the folk of Dinas Rhydnant will enjoy visiting it. Surprising how easy it is," Rhun said, beaming proudly. "The planning, at any rate. The doing, for some reason, always seems a little harder."

Glew, hearing his name spoken, pricked up his ears. He had not left his place in the chimney corner; nor had his alarm at the happenings in the cottage made him loosen his hold on the cook-pot. "When I was a giant," he began.

"I see the little weasel is with you," said Fflewddur to King Rhun, recognizing Glew immediately despite the former giant's present stature. "When he was a giant," the bard muttered, giving Glew a look of ill-concealed vexation, "he was a paltry one. He'd have done anything to be free of that cavern — even to popping us into that foul stew he'd cooked up. A Fflam is forgiving! But I think he went a little too far."

"When I was a giant," Glew continued, either ignoring or not hearing the bard's remarks, "no one would have humiliated me by taking me by the ears and hustling me aboard a smelly boat. I had no wish to come here. After what's happened today, I have less wish to stay." Glew pursed his lips. "Dallben shall see that I'm taken back to Mona without delay."

"I'm sure he will," Taran replied. "But Dallben has graver concerns now, and so do we all."

Mumbling something about shabby treatment and lack of consideration, Glew scraped a finger along the bottom of the pot and sucked his teeth with indignant satisfaction. The companions said no more, but settled down to wait out the night.

The fire burned to ashes. A night wind rose outside the cottage. Taran rested his head on his arms. At this homecoming he had longed to stand before Eilonwy, forgetting rank and birth, as any man before any woman, and ask her to wed. But now the disaster that had overtaken Gwydion made Taran's own wishes unimportant. Though he still did not know Eilonwy's heart, nor what her answer to him might be, he could not bring himself to learn it until all hearts were at peace again. He closed his eyes. The wind screamed as if it would rip to tatters the quiet meadows and orchards of Caer Dallben.

A hand on his shoulder aroused him. It was Eilonwy.

"Gwydion has wakened," she said. "He would speak with us."

In Dallben's chamber the Prince of Don half-raised himself from the couch. His features were pale under their weathering, and tightly drawn, though more in anger than pain. His mouth was set, bitter, his green eyes burned with dark flashes, and his glance was that of a proud wolf scornful of his hurt, and scornful all the more of those who had given him his wounds. Achren was a silent shadow in the corner. The old enchanter stood anxiously beside the book-strewn table near the wooden bench where Taran, throughout boyhood, had sat for lessons. *The Book of Three*, the huge, leather-bound tome of secret lore forbidden to all but Dallben himself, lay closed atop a pile of other ancient volumes.

Taran, with Eilonwy, Fflewddur, and King Rhun behind him, strode to Gwydion and clasped the warrior's hand. The Prince of Don smiled grimly.

"No merry meeting, and no long one, Assistant PigKeeper," Gwydion said. "Dallben has told me of the DeathLord's ruse. Dyrnwyn must be regained at all cost, and without delay. He spoke, too, of your wanderings," Gwydion added. "I would hear more of them from yourself, but that must wait another time. I ride to Annuvin before the day is out."

Taran looked at the Prince of Don in surprise and concern. "Your wounds are still fresh. You cannot make such a journey."

"Neither can I stay here," Gwydion answered. "Since Dyrnwyn first came into my hands, I have learned more of its nature. Only a little more," he added, "but enough to know its loss is fatal.

"Dyrnwyn's lineage is as ancient as Prydain itself," Gwydion continued, "and much of its history has been forgotten or destroyed. For long, the blade was thought no more than legend, and matter for a harper's song. Taliesin Chief Bard is wisest in the lore of Prydain, but even he could tell me only that Govannion the Lame, a master craftsman, forged and tempered Dyrnwyn at the behest of

King Rhydderch Hael, as a weapon of greatest power and protection for the land. To safeguard it, a spell was cast upon the blade and a warning graven on the scabbard."

"I remember the Old Writing," Eilonwy said. "Indeed, I shall never forget it, for I had an impossible time keeping Taran from meddling with things he didn't understand. '*Draw Dyrnwyn only thou of royal blood...*'"

"Closer to its true meaning is '*noble worth*'," said Gwydion. "The enchantment forbade the sword to all but those who would use it wisely and well. The flame of Dyrnwyn would destroy any other who sought to draw it. But the writing on the scabbard has been marred. The full message, which might have told more of the sword's purpose, is unknown.

"King Rhydderch bore the blade throughout his life," Gwydion continued, "and his sons after him. Their reigns were peaceful and prosperous. But here Dyrnwyn's history ends. King Rhitta, grandson of Rhydderch, was the last to hold the blade. He was lord of Spiral Castle before it became the stronghold of Queen Achren. He met his death, in a way unknown, with Dyrnwyn clutched in his hands. From that time on the sword was seen no more, forgotten as it lay buried with him in Spiral Castle's deepest chamber." Gwydion turned to Eilonwy. "Where you, Princess, found it. You gave it to me willingly; but it was not willingly that it left my hands. The blade is worth more than my life, or the lives of any of us. In Arawn's grasp, it can bring doom upon Prydain."

"Do you believe Arawn can unsheathe the sword?" Taran asked hurriedly. "Can he turn the weapon against us? Can he make it serve some evil end?"

"This I do not know," replied Gwydion. The warrior's face was troubled. "It may be that Arawn Death-Lord has found means to break the enchantment. Or, unable to use it himself, his purpose may be to keep the blade from any other use. He would have taken my life as well as the sword. Thanks to Fflewddur Fflam, I still have the one. Now I must find the other, though the path lead me to the depths of Annuvin itself."

Achren, silent until now, raised her head and spoke to Gwydion. "Let me seek Dyrnwyn in your stead. I know the ways of Annuvin; no stranger am I to its secret hoards, and where and how they are guarded. If the sword is hidden, I will find it. If Arawn himself bears it, Dyrnwyn will be taken from him. More than that. I swear by every oath to destroy him. Thus have I sworn already to myself, and swear it again to you. You forced life upon me, Gwydion, when I begged for death. Now give me what I live for. Give me my vengeance."

Gwydion did not answer immediately. His green-flecked eyes searched the woman's face. He said, "Vengeance is not a gift I may bestow, Achren."

Achren stiffened. Her hands twisted into claws and Taran feared she would fling herself upon Gwydion. She did not move. "You will not trust me," Achren said hoarsely. Her bloodless lips turned in a smile of contempt. "So be it, Prince of Don. Once you scorned to share a kingdom with me. Scorn me again to your own loss."

"I do not scorn you," Gwydion said. "I only urge you to accept Dallben's protection. Stay here in safety. Among all of us, your hope of finding the sword is the least. Arawn's hatred of you can be no less than yours of him. He or his servants would slay you at sight, even before you set foot in Annuvin. No, Achren, what you offer is not possible." He thought a moment. "There may be another way to learn how Dyrnwyn shall be found."

Gwydion turned to Dallben, but the enchanter sorrowfully shook his head.

"Alas," Dallben said, "*The Book of Three* cannot tell us what we most need to know. I have searched carefully, every page, to understand its hidden meanings. They are dark, even to me. Fetch the letter sticks," the enchanter said to Coll. "Hen Wen alone can help us."

From her enclosure the white pig watched the silent procession. On his bony shoulders Dallben bore the letter sticks, the ash-wood rods carved with ancient symbols. Glew, interested only in the provisions of the scullery, remained behind, as did Gurgi, who well remembered the former giant and chose to keep an eye on him. Achren had spoken no further, but hooded her face and sat motionless in the cottage.

Usually, at the sight of Taran, the oracular pig would squeal joyously and trot to the railing to have her chin scratched. Now she cowered in a far corner of the pen, her little eyes wide and her cheeks trembling. As Dallben entered the enclosure and planted the letter sticks upright in the earth, Hen Wen snuffled and crouched closer against the bars.

Dallben, murmuring inaudibly, moved to stand beside the ash-wood rods. Outside the enclosure, the companions waited. Hen Wen whimpered and did not stir.

"What does she fear?" Eilonwy whispered. Taran made no answer; his eyes were fixed on the aged enchanter in his wind-whipped robe, on the letter sticks, and the unmoving form of Hen Wen. Against the dull sky they seemed to him frozen together in their own moment, far beyond the silent watchers. This was the first time Taran had seen the enchanter seek a prophecy from the oracular pig. Of Dallben's powers he could only guess; but he knew Hen Wen, and knew she was too terrified to move. He waited what felt an age. Even Rhun sensed something amiss;

the King of Mona's cheerful face was darkly clouded.

Dallben glanced uneasily at Gwydion. "Never before has Hen Wen refused to answer when the letter sticks were shown her."

Again he murmured words Taran could not distinguish. The oracular pig shuddered violently, shut her eyes, and sank her head between her stubby trotters.

"Perhaps a few notes on my harp?" Fflewddur suggested. "I've had excellent success. . ."

The enchanter motioned the bard to be silent. Once more he spoke, softly yet commandingly. Hen Wen shrank into herself and moaned as though in pain.

"Her fear blinds her powers," Dallben said gravely. "Even my spells do not reach her. I have failed."

Despair filled the faces of the watching companions.

Gwydion bowed his head, and his eyes were deeply troubled. "We, too, shall fail," he said, "if we do not learn whatever she can tell us."

Quickly and without a word Taran climbed the railing, walked steadily towards the frightened pig, and dropped to his knees beside her. He scratched her chin and gently stroked her neck. "Don't be afraid, Hen. Nothing will harm you here."

Dallben, surprised, started forwards, then halted. Hearing Taran's voice, the pig had cautiously opened one eye.

Her snout twitched, she raised her head slightly and gave a faint "Hwoinch!"

"Hen, listen to me," Taran pleaded, "I have no power to command you. But we need your help, all of us who love you."

Taran spoke on; as he did, the oracular pig ceased her trembling. Though she did not attempt to rise, Hen Wen grunted fondly, wheezed, and made affectionate muttering sounds in her throat. She blinked her eyes and her wide face seemed nearly to grin.

"Tell us, Hen," Taran urged. "Please. Tell us what you can."

Hen Wen moved uneasily. Slowly she climbed to her feet. The white pig snorted and glanced at the letter sticks. Step by step, on her short legs, she moved closer to them.

The enchanter nodded to Taran. "Well done," he murmured. "This day, the power of an Assistant Pig-Keeper is greater than my own."

As Taran stared, not daring to speak, Hen Wen paused at the first rod. Still hesitant, she pointed with her snout at one of the carved symbols, then at another. Dallben, watching intently, quickly wrote on a scrap of parchment the signs the oracular pig had indicated. Hen Wen continued a few moments, then suddenly left off and backed anxiously from the stick.

Dallben's face was grave. "Can this be so?" he murmured,

his voice filled with alarm. "No. . .no. We must learn more than that." He glanced at Taran.

"Please, Hen," Taran whispered, coming to the side of the pig, who had begun to shudder again. "Help us."

Despite his words, Taran feared Hen Wen would turn away. She shook her head, squinted her eyes, and grunted piteously. Nevertheless, at his pleading, she cautiously trotted to the second rod. There, in desperate haste, as if to make an end of it quickly, she pointed to other symbols.

The enchanter's hand trembled as he wrote. "Now the third one," he said urgently.

Hen Wen, stiff-legged, reared back and sank to her haunches. All of Taran's soothing words would not budge her for several moments. At last, however, she rose and more fearfully than ever trotted to the final ash-wood rod.

Even as Hen Wen approached and before she could point to the first letter, the ash-wood rods shook and swayed like living things. They twisted as though to uproot themselves, and with a sound that ripped the air like a thunder clap, they split, shattered, and fell to earth in splinters.

Hen Wen, squealing in terror, flung herself backwards and fled to a corner of the enclosure. As Taran hurried to her, Dallben bent, picked up the fragments of wood, and studied them hopelessly.

"They are destroyed beyond repair, and useless now," Dallben said in a heavy voice. "The cause is dark to me, and Hen Wen's prophecy remains unfinished. Even so, I doubt its end could bode less ill than its beginning. She must have sensed this herself."

The enchanter turned and walked slowly from the enclosure. Eilonwy had joined Taran, who strove to calm the terrified pig. Hen Wen still gasped and shook, and pressed her head between her forelegs.

"No wonder she didn't want to prophesy," Eilonwy cried. "And yet," she added to Taran, "Hen would have told nothing at all if it hadn't been for you."

Dallben, with the parchment in his hand, had gone to the side of Gwydion. Coll, Fflewddur, and King Rhun gathered anxiously around them. Sure that Hen Wen was unharmed and wanted only to be left in peace, Taran and Eilonwy hurried to the companions.

"Help! Oh, help!"

Yelling, waving his arms frantically, Gurgi raced across the turf. He dashed into their midst and pointed towards the stables.

"Gurgi could do nothing!" he cried. "He tried, oh yes, but there were only smackings and whackings for his poor tender head! Gone!" Gurgi shouted. "With fast and speedful gallopings! Wicked queen is gone!"

CHAPTER THREE

The Prophecy

The companions hastened to the stable. As Gurgi had told them, one of King Rhun's horses was missing. Of Achren, there was no trace.

"Let me saddle Melynlas," Taran urged Gwydion. "I shall try to overtake her."

"She's going straight to Annuvin," burst out Fflewddur. "I never trusted that woman. Great Belin, who knows what treachery she plans! She's off to feather her own nest, you can be sure of it."

"Achren goes more likely to her death," answered Gwydion, his face grim as he looked towards the hills and the leafless trees. "There is no safety for her beyond Caer Dallben. I would protect her, but dare not delay my quest to seek her now." He turned to Dallben. "I must know Hen Wen's prophecy. It is my only guide."

The enchanter nodded and led the companions to the cottage. The aged man still held the parchment and the splintered letter sticks. Now he cast them on the table and gazed at them for a long moment before he spoke.

"Hen Wen has told us what she can. All, I fear, that we shall ever learn from her. I have again studied the symbols she pointed out, hoping against hope I had misread them." His expression was withdrawn, his eyes lowered, and he spoke with difficulty, as if each word wrenched his heart. "I asked how Dyrnwyn might be recovered. Hear the answer given us:

Ask, sooner, mute stone and voiceless rock to speak.

"Such is Hen Wen's message as I have read it from the first letter stick," Dallben said. "Whether it is a refusal to speak, a prophecy in itself, or a warning to ask no further, I cannot be sure. But the symbols of the second letter stick spell out the fate of Dyrnwyn itself."

Dallben continued, and the enchanter's words filled

Taran with cold anguish that struck deep as a sword thrust:

> *Quenched will be Dyrnwyn's flame;*
> *Vanished, its power.*
> *Night turn to noon*
> *And rivers burn with frozen fire*
> *Ere Dyrnwyn be regained.*

The ancient man bowed his head then and was silent for a time. "The third stick," he said at last, "was destroyed before Hen Wen could complete her message. She might have told us more; but, judging from the first two, we would have cause for no more hope than we have now."

"The prophecies mock us," Taran said. "Hen told us truly. We could as well have asked stones for help."

"And got as much sense from them!" cried Eilonwy. "Hen could have come straight out and said we'll never get Dyrnwyn back. Night can't be noon, and that's the end of it."

"In all my travels," added Fflewddur, "I've never noticed even a small creek burning, not to mention a river. The prophecy is doubly impossible."

"And yet," said King Rhun, with innocent eagerness, "it would be an amazing thing to see. I wish it could happen!"

"I fear you shall not see it come to pass, King of Mona," Dallben said heavily.

Gwydion, who had been sitting thoughtfully at the

table and turning the splintered rods back and forth in his hands, rose and spoke to the companions. "Hen Wen's prophecy is disheartening," he said, "and far from what I had hoped. But when prophecies give no help, men must find it of themselves." His hands clenched and snapped the fragment of ash wood. "As long as life and breath are mine, I will seek Dyrnwyn. The prophecy does not change my plans, but makes them only more urgent."

"Then let us go with you," Taran said, rising to face Gwydion. "Take our strength until your own returns."

"Exactly so!" Fflewddur jumped to his feet. "I'll pay no heed whether rivers burn or not. Ask stones to speak? I'll ask Arawn himself. He'll keep no secrets from a Fflam!"

Gwydion shook his head. "In this task, the more men the greater risk. It is done best alone. If any life be staked against Arawn Death-Lord, it must be mine."

Taran bowed, for Gwydion's tone forbade dispute. "If such is your will," he said. "But what if Kaw were to fly ahead to Annuvin? Send him first. He will go swiftly and bring back whatever knowledge he can gain."

Gwydion looked shrewdly at Taran and nodded approval. "You have found some wisdom in your wanderings, Assistant Pig-Keeper. Your plan is sound. Kaw may serve me better than all your swords. But I shall not await him here. To do so would cost me too much time. Let him spy out Annuvin as far as he is able, then find me at

King Smoit's castle in Cantrev Cadiffor. Smoit's realm lies on my path to Annuvin, and thus my journey will be half accomplished when Kaw rejoins me."

"At least we can ride with you as far as King Smoit's castle," Taran said, "and guard you until you are well on your way. Between here and Cantrev Cadiffor, Arawn's Huntsmen may be abroad, still seeking your death."

"The foul villains!" cried the bard. "Treacherous murderers! They'll have a taste of my sword this time. Let them attack us. I hope they do!" A harp string snapped with a loud crack that set the instrument a jangling. "Ah, yes — well — that's only a manner of speaking," Fflewddur said sheepishly. "I hope we don't come upon them at all. They could be troublesome and delay our journey."

"No one has considered the inconvenience to *me*," said Glew. The former giant had come out of the scullery and looked peevishly around him.

"Weasel!" muttered Fflewddur. "Dyrnwyn is gone, we don't know if our lives are at stake, and he frets about inconvenience. He's a little man indeed, and always was."

"Since no one has mentioned it," said Eilonwy, "it seems I'm not being asked to come along. Very well, I shan't insist."

"You, too, have gained wisdom, Princess," said Dallben. "Your days on Mona were not ill spent."

"Of course," Eilonwy went on, "after you leave, the thought may strike me that it's a pleasant day for a short ride to go picking wildflowers, which might be hard to find, especially since it's almost winter. Not that I'd be following you, you understand. But I might, by accident, lose my way, and mistakenly happen to catch up with you. By then, it would be too late for me to come home, through no fault of my own."

Gwydion's haggard face broke into a smile. "So be it, Princess. What I cannot prevent, I accept. Ride with me, all those who choose, but no farther than Smoit's stronghold at Caer Cadarn."

"Ah, Princess," Coll sighed, shaking his head. "I will not gainsay Lord Gwydion, whatever. But it is hardly the conduct of a young lady to force her own way thus."

"Certainly not," Eilonwy agreed. "That's the first thing Queen Teleria taught me: a lady doesn't insist on having her own way. Then, next thing you know, it all works out somehow, without one's even trying. I thought I'd never learn, though it's really quite easy once you get the knack."

Without further delay, Taran lifted Kaw from his fireside perch and carried him to the dooryard. This time the crow did not clack his beak or gabble impudently. Instead of his customary scoldings, hoarse quackings, and mischievous foolery, Kaw hunched on Taran's wrist and cocked a beady, attentive eye, listening closely while Taran carefully explained the task.

Taran raised his arm and Kaw flapped his glossy wings in farewell.

"Annuvin!" Kaw croaked. "Dyrnwyn!"

The crow flew aloft. Within moments Kaw was high over Caer Dallben. The wind bore him like a leaf, and he hung poised above the watching companions. Then, with a roguish flirt of his wings, Kaw sped northwestwards. Taran strained his eyes to follow his flight until the crow vanished into the looming clouds. In sadness and disquiet, Taran at last turned away. Kaw, he was sure, would be alert to the perils of the journey: the arrows of the Huntsmen; the cruel talons and slashing beaks of the gwythaints, Arawn's fierce winged messengers. More than once had gwythaints attacked the companions, and even the fledglings could be dangerous.

Taran recalled, from his boyhood, the young gwythaint whose life he had saved, and he well remembered the bird's sharp claws. Despite Kaw's gallant heart and sharp wits, Taran feared for the safety of the crow; and feared, still more, for Gwydion's quest. And to him came the foreboding that an even heavier fate might ride on Kaw's outspread wings.

It had been agreed that when the travellers neared Great Avren, King Rhun would escort the disgruntled Glew to the ship anchored in the river, there to await his return, for Rhun was determined to ride with Gwydion to Caer Cadarn. Glew liked neither cooling his heels on the swaying vessel nor sleeping on the hard pebbles of the shore; but the protests of the former giant could not move the King of Mona to change his plan.

While Gwydion held a last, hurried council with Dallben, the companions began leading the horses from the stable. The wise Melyngar, Gwydion's white, golden-maned steed, waited calmly for her master. Melynlas, Taran's stallion, snorted and impatiently pawed the ground.

Eilonwy was already mounted on her favourite, the bay mare Lluagor. In a fold of her cloak the Princess carried her most treasured possession: the golden sphere that glowed brightly when she cupped it in her hands.

"I'm leaving that uncomfortable crown behind," Eilonwy declared. "There's no use for it at all, except to hold down your hair, and that's hardly worth the blisters. But I'd sooner walk on my hands than go without my bauble. Besides, if we need a light, we shall have one. That's much more practical than a hoop on top of your head." In a saddlebag, she had packed the embroidery made for Taran, intending to finish it along the way. "Perhaps," Eilonwy added, "I might fix the colour of Hen Wen's eyes while I'm at it."

Fflewddur's mount was the huge, tawny cat, Llyan, herself tall as a horse. Seeing the bard, she purred loudly, and Fflewddur could barely keep the powerful animal from knocking him down with her nuzzling.

"Gently, old girl," cried the bard, as Llyan thrust her great head between his neck and shoulder. "I know you want a tune on my harp. I shall play one later, I promise you."

Glew had recognized Llyan immediately. "That's not fair," he sniffed. "By all rights she belongs to me."

"Yes," replied Fflewddur, "if you count feeding her those vile potions you once brewed to make her grow bigger. If you care to ride her, you're welcome to try. Though I warn you — Llyan has a memory longer than her tail."

Llyan, indeed, had begun lashing her tail at the sight of Glew. She towered over the pudgy little man, her yellow eyes blazed, her whiskers twitched, her tufted ears went flat against her head; and from her throat came a sound quite unlike her greeting to the bard.

Fflewddur quickly strummed a melody on his harp. Llyan turned her eyes from Glew and her mouth curved in an enormous smile and she blinked fondly at the bard.

However, Glew's pale face had gone paler and he edged away from the cat. "When I was a giant," Glew muttered, "things were considerably better managed."

King Rhun saddled his dapple grey steed. Since Coll, who had also decided to accompany Gwydion, would ride the sorrel mare Llamrei, foal of Melynlas and Lluagor, Glew had no choice but to climb up behind Gurgi on his shaggy pony — a companionship unwelcome to all three.

Taran, meanwhile, helped Coll rummage in the stables, forge and tool sheds for weapons.

"Few enough of them there are," said Coll. "These spears have served me well as beanpoles," the stout warrior added. "I had hoped never to use them for another purpose. Alas, the only blade I can give Gwydion is rusted from propping up one of the apple trees. As for helmets, there are none save my leather cap; and the sparrows have a nest in it. I shall not disturb them. But my own old pate is tough as leather," Coll said, winking. "It can last me to Caer Cadarn and back.

"And you, my lad," Coll went on cheerfully, though he had not failed to notice Taran's troubled frown, "I remember a day when an Assistant Pig-Keeper would have been all flash and fire to ride with Lord Gwydion. Now you look as glum as a frostbitten turnip."

Taran smiled. "I myself would ride to Annuvin, if Gwydion allowed me. What you say is true, old friend. For the boy I was, this would have been a bold adventure, full of glory. This much have I learned: a man's life weighs more than glory, and a price paid in blood is a heavy reckoning.

"My heart is not easy," Taran added. "Long ago, you made your way to Annuvin, to rescue Hen Wen after she had been stolen from you. Tell me: what chance has Gwydion alone in Arawn's realm?"

"No man has better," said Coll, shouldering the spears.

And he was gone from the shed before Taran realized the old warrior had not really answered him at all.

Caer Dallben lay far behind them and the day was darkening when the companions made camp deep in the shadows of the forest.

Eilonwy happily flung herself to the ground. "It's been long since I've slept on comfortable roots and rocks!" she cried. "What a pleasant change from goosefeathers!"

Gwydion allowed a fire to be built; and while Coll saw to the mounts, Gurgi opened his wallet of food to share out provisions. For the most part the companions were silent, chilled, and stiff after the long day's journey. King Rhun, however, had lost none of his good spirits. As the travellers huddled closer to the pale flames, Rhun picked up a twig and scratched busily in the earth, covering the ground before him with a spiderweb of lines.

"About that seawall," said Rhun. "I think I see how it went wrong. Yes, exactly so. Now, here's the way to do it."

From across the fire Taran saw Rhun's eyes brightly eager and on his face the familiar boyish grin. But Rhun, Taran sensed, was no longer the feckless princeling he had known on the Isle of Mona. As Rhun was absorbed in the tasks he had planned, so Taran had been caught up in his own labours at forge, loom, and potter's wheel. And if Rhun had found manhood in ruling a kingdom, Taran had found the same in toiling among the staunch folk of the Free Commots. He watched Rhun with new affection. The King of Mona spoke on and Taran's interest was drawn to the scratchings on the ground. He studied them as Rhun continued. Taran smiled. One thing had not changed, he realized; as usual, the King of Mona's intentions went somewhat beyond the King of Mona's skill.

"I fear your wall may tumble if you build it thus," Taran said with a kindly laugh. "See this part here." He pointed. "The heavier stones must be sunk deeper. And here. . ."

"Amazing!" exclaimed Rhun, snapping his fingers. "Quite right! You shall come to Mona and help me finish it!" He began scratching new lines so vigorously he nearly pitched himself headlong into the fire.

"Oh, great and kindly master!" cried Gurgi, who had been listening closely without altogether understanding what the two comrades had been discussing. "Oh, clever scannings and plannings! Gurgi wishes he, too, had wisdom of wise speakings!"

Gwydion warned them to silence. "Our fire is risk enough, without adding noise to it. I can only hope Arawn's Huntsmen are not abroad. We are too few to withstand even a handful of them. They are not common warriors," Gwydion added, seeing Rhun's questioning expression, "but an evil brotherhood. Slay one of their band, and the strength of the others grows that much greater."

Taran nodded. "They are as much to be feared as the Cauldron-Born," he cautioned Rhun, "the deathless, voiceless creatures that guard Annuvin. Perhaps more to be feared. The Cauldron-Born cannot be slain, yet their power dwindles if they journey too far, or stay too long beyond Arawn's realm."

Rhun blinked and Gurgi fell silent, glancing behind him uncomfortably. Memory of the ruthless Cauldron-Born turned Taran's thoughts once more to Hen Wen's prophecy. "The flame of Dyrnwyn quenched," Taran murmured. "Yet how shall Arawn achieve this? For all his power, I will not believe he can even draw the blade."

"Prophecy is more than words that shape it," Gwydion said. "Seek the meaning that underlies it. For us, the flame of Dyrnwyn will be as good as quenched if Arawn keeps it from my hands. Its power will indeed vanish, for all it may avail us, should the blade be locked for ever in his treasure hoard."

"Treasure?" said Glew, stopping his munching only long enough to speak the word.

"The Death-Lord's domain is as much a treasure-house as a stronghold of evil," Gwydion said. "Long has it been filled with all the fair and useful things Arawn has stolen from Prydain. These treasures do not serve him; his purpose is to deprive, to keep their use from men, to sap our strength by denying us what might yield a richer harvest than any of us here has known." Gwydion paused. "Is this not death in but another guise?"

"I have been told," Taran said, "the treasure troves of Annuvin hold all that men could wish for. Ploughs, there are said to be, that work of themselves, scythes that reap with no hand to guide them, magical tools, and more," Taran went on. "For Arawn stole the craft secrets of metalsmiths and potters, the lore of herdsmen and farmers. This knowledge, too, lies locked for ever in his hoard."

Glew sucked his teeth. The morsel of food stayed untouched in his chubby fingers. For a long while he said nothing. At last he cleared his throat. "I mean to forgive your slights and humiliations. It would not have happened when I was a giant, I assure you. But no matter. I pardon you all. In token of my good will, I too shall journey with you."

Gwydion looked at him sharply. "Perhaps you shall," he said quietly after a time.

"No question of it now!" Fflewddur snorted. "The little weasel hopes to sniff out something for himself. I can see his nose trembling! I never thought the day would come when I should want him at our side. But I think that's safer than having him at our backs."

Glew smiled blandly. "I forgive you, too," he said.

CHAPTER FOUR

King Smoit's Castle

At dawn, King Rhun made ready to part from the companions and ride farther westwards to Avren harbour, where he would advise his shipmaster of the change in plans. Fflewddur was to accompany him, for the bard knew the shallow fording places across the river and the swiftest paths on the opposite bank.

Eilonwy had decided to go with them. "I've forgotten half my embroidery thread in Rhun's ship, and must have it if I'm to finish Hen Wen properly. Neither of you can find it, for I'm not sure myself where it might be. I believe I've left a warmer travelling cloak, too; and a few other things — I don't remember what they are right now, but I'm bound to think of them once I get there."

Coll grinned and rubbed his bald crown. "The princess," he remarked, "becomes more the lady in every way."

"Since I'm not staying on the ship," said Glew, whose decision of the night before remained unshaken, "I see no reason to be taken out of my way. I shall follow with Lord Gwydion."

"That, my puny giant, is where you're wrong," the bard replied. "Mount up behind the King of Mona, if he can stand your company, and be quick about it. Don't think I'll let you out of my sight for a moment. Where I go, you go. And the other way around, too, for the matter of that."

"Surely, Fflewddur," Taran said, drawing the bard aside, "Glew can't trouble us. I myself shall watch over him."

The bard shook his tousled, yellow head. "No, my friend. I'll be easier in my mind if I see him with my own eyes. And at all times. No, the little weasel is in my charge. Ride on ahead, and we'll catch up with you on the other side of Avren well before midday.

"I'll be glad to see Smoit again," Fflewddur added. "That red-bearded old bear is dear to my heart. We shall feast well at Caer Cadarn, for Smoit eats as bravely as he fights."

Gwydion had already mounted Melyngar and signalled them to hasten. Fflewddur clapped Taran on the shoulder and ran to climb astride Llyan, who was frisking gaily in the bright, cold sun and pouncing at the tip of her own tail.

King Rhun, Fflewddur, Eilonwy, and Glew soon were out of sight. Bearing westwards, Taran rode between Gwydion and Coll, while Gurgi, on his pony, trotted at the rear.

They halted on the far bank of Great Avren. Midday passed without a sign of the other companions. Though Taran was anxious about them, he preferred to believe they had not come to harm. "Rhun has likely stopped to look at a badger tunnel or anthill," he said. "I hope it is no more than that."

"Never fear," said Coll. "Fflewddur will jog him along. They'll be here at any moment."

Taran sounded his horn, hoping the signal would guide the bard in case Fflewddur had mistaken the path. Still they did not come. Gwydion, having waited as long as he dared, chose to press on to Caer Cadarn. They continued at a brisk pace for the rest of the day.

Taran turned often in his saddle, expecting always to glimpse Rhun and the other companions galloping up behind them, or suddenly to hear the King of Mona's cheerful "Hullo, hullo!" However, as the day waned, Taran realized that Rhun, a slow horseman at best, was by now outdistanced. Fflewddur, he was sure, would not travel after nightfall.

"They have camped somewhere behind us," Coll assured Taran. "Were aught amiss, one of them would have reached us. Fflewddur Fflam knows the way to Smoit's castle. We shall all meet there. And if they seem too long delayed, Smoit will raise a searching party." The stout warrior put a hand on Taran's shoulder. "Ease your spirit until there is clear cause for alarm. Or," he added, with a wink, "is it the company of Princess Eilonwy you long for?"

"She should not have come with us," Taran replied, half angrily.

"No doubt." Coll grinned. "Yet you were not the one to speak against her."

Taran grinned back at him. "As for doing that," he said, "I have given it up long since."

At mid-morning of the following day, Caer Cadarn rose before them, and from a stone tower Smoit's crimson banner with its emblem of a black bear snapped in the wind. The stronghold had been built in a clearing, and the heavy walls jutted like the bearded king's own brows, scarred and pitted by many a battle. Coll, urging Llamrei ahead, shouted to the guards in the name of Gwydion Prince of Don. The massive gates opened and the companions galloped into the courtyard, where men-at-arms tethered the horses and a party of warriors led the way to Smoit's Great Hall.

Gwydion strode quickly down the corridor. Flanked by the guards, Taran, Coll, and Gurgi followed. "Smoit will be at his meat," Taran said. "His breakfast lasts till high noon." He laughed. "He says it whets his appetite for the rest of his meals. Gwydion will get no word out of him until we ourselves are stuffed."

"Yes, yes!" Gurgi cried. "Gurgi longs for tasty crunchings and munchings!"

"You shall have them, old friend," Taran answered. "Be sure of it."

They entered the Great Hall. At one end stood Smoit's huge throne, cut from half an oak tree and carved in the shape of a bear with paws upraised on either side.

The man seated there was not King Smoit.

"Magg!" Taran gasped.

Guards fell upon them instantly. Taran's sword was ripped from his belt. With a great cry, Gwydion flung himself against the warriors, but they pressed about him and bore the Prince of Don to his knees. Coll, too, was borne down and a spear pressed against his back. Gurgi yelled in rage and terror. A guard seized him by the scruff of his shaggy neck, buffeting him until the poor creature could barely stagger to his feet.

Magg grinned like a skull. With a slight movement of his skinny fingers, he gestured the warriors to stand away. His grey, pinched face twitched with pleasure. "Our meeting, Lord Gwydion, is one I did not foresee. My warriors hold Caer Cadarn, but this is an added prize, and a richer one than I had hoped."

Gwydion's green eyes blazed. "Have you dared even to enter King Smoit's cantrev? Begone from here before he returns. He shall deal with you less gently than I."

"You will join King Smoit," Magg replied. "Though king I scorn to call this rude cantrev lord." Magg's thin lips curled. Caressingly he put a hand to his embroidered cloak. Taran saw that Magg's garments were even richer than those the lank-haired man had worn as Chief Steward to the Court of Mona.

"More powerful than Smoit or the King of Mona, more powerful than Queen Achren is my liege lord," Magg said with a yellow smile. "And mightier now than the Prince of Don." He touched the iron chain hanging from his neck and fondled the heavy badge of office. In horror Taran saw it bore the same symbol that was branded on the foreheads of the Huntsmen.

"I serve no lesser liege," Magg said haughtily, "than the King of Annuvin, Arawn Death-Lord himself."

Gwydion's glance did not falter. "You have found your true master, Magg."

"When last we parted, Lord Gwydion," said Magg, "I believed you dead. It was my joy, later, to learn that you were not." The Chief Steward licked his lips. "Seldom is one given to savour his revenge twice, and I was patient until the day we should meet again.

"Patient, yes," Magg hissed. "Long I wandered after I sailed from the Isle of Mona. There were those I served humbly, biding my time. One sought even to cast me in a dungeon – I, Magg, who once held a kingdom in his grasp." The voice of the Chief Steward rose shrilly. His face had gone livid and his eyes started from their sockets. But in a moment he gained control of his trembling hands and sank back on Smoit's throne. Now the words came from his lips as if he were tasting each one.

"At length, I made my way to Annuvin," Magg said, "to the very threshold of Dark Gate. Lord Arawn did not know me then, as he knows me now." Magg nodded in satisfaction. "There was much he learned from me.

"Lord Arawn knew the history of Dyrnwyn," Magg continued. "He knew it had been lost and found again, and that Gwydion Son of Don bore it. But it was I, Magg, who told him how best to gain it."

"Even your treachery is paltry," Taran said. "Late or soon, with or without you, Arawn would have struck on that evil scheme himself."

"Perhaps," Magg said slyly. "Perhaps what he learned from me was less than what I learned from him. For I soon discovered that his power was dangerously balanced. His champion, the Horned King, had long been defeated. Even the Black Crochan, the cauldron that gave him the deathless Cauldron-Born, was shattered.

"Lord Arawn has many secret liege men among the cantrev kings," Magg went on. "He has promised them great riches and domains, and they are sworn to serve him. But his defeats turned them restive. It was I who showed him the means to win stronger allegiance. It was my plan, mine alone that put Dyrnwyn in his hands!

"Word now spreads throughout the cantrevs that Arawn Death-Lord holds the mightiest weapon in Prydain. He knows its secrets, far better than you do, Lord Gwydion, and knows he cannot be defeated. His liege men rejoice, for they will soon taste victory. Other war lords will rally to his banner and his host of warriors will grow.

"I, Magg, have wrought this!" the Chief Steward cried. "I, Magg, second only to the Death-Lord! I, Magg, speak in his name. I am his trusted emissary, and I ride from realm to realm, gathering armies to destroy the Sons of Don and those who give them allegiance. All Prydain will be his dominion. And those who stand against him — if Lord Arawn chooses to be merciful, he will slay them. His

Huntsmen will drink their blood. The others will grovel in bondage for ever!"

Magg's eyes gleamed, his pale brow glistened, and his cheeks quivered violently. "For this," he hissed, "for this, Lord Arawn has sworn to me by every oath: one day I, Magg, will wear the Iron Crown of Annuvin!"

"You are as much a fool as a traitor," Gwydion said, in a hard voice. "And doubly so. First, to believe Arawn. Then to believe King Smoit would heed your serpent's words. Have you slain him? Only dead would he listen to you."

"Smoit lives," answered Magg. "I care nothing for his allegiance. I seek the fealty of the liege men in his cantrev. Smoit shall order them, in his name, to serve my cause."

"King Smoit would sooner have his tongue ripped out," Taran cried.

"And so perhaps he shall," replied Magg. "Mute, he will serve me as well. He will ride with me and I will speak on his behalf better than he would speak on his own. Yet," he mused, "I would prefer the commands to come from his lips rather than mine. There are ways to loosen his tongue instead of cutting it from his head. Some have already been tried."

Magg narrowed his eyes. "The best means stand before me now. You, Lord Gwydion. And you, Pig-Keeper. Speak with him. Let Smoit see that he must yield to me." Magg smiled crookedly. "Your lives hang on it."

The Chief Steward moved his head slightly. The guards stepped forward.

Roughly the companions were prodded from the Great Hall. Shock and despair so filled Taran that he was hardly aware of the passages they were led down. The warriors halted. One flung open a heavy door. Others thrust the companions into a narrow chamber. The door grated shut and darkness swallowed them.

As they groped blindly Taran stumbled on a prostrate form that stirred and bellowed loudly.

"My body and blood!" roared the voice of King Smoit, and Taran was grappled by a pair of bone-cracking arms. "Are you come again, Magg? You'll not take me alive!"

Taran was nearly smothered and crushed before Gwydion called out his own name and the names of the companions. Smoit's grip loosened and Taran felt a huge hand on his face.

"My pulse, and so it is!" cried Smoit, as the companions gathered around him. "The Pig-Keeper! Lord Gwydion! Coll! I'd know that bald pate of yours anywhere!" His hand fell on Gurgi's dishevelled head. "And the little — whatever-it-is! Well met, my friends." Smoit groaned heavily. "And ill met, too. How has that simpering sop trapped you? The lard-lipped, squirming lackey has snared us all!"

Gwydion quickly told Smoit what had befallen them.

The red-bearded king growled furiously. "Magg caught

me as easily as he did you. Yesterday I was at breakfast, and had barely set myself to my meat, when my steward brought tidings that a messenger from Lord Goryon sought words with me. Now then, I knew Goryon was at odds with Lord Gast. A matter of cow-stealing, as usual. Ah, will the cantrev lords of Prydain ever stop their endless bickering! However, since I'd heard Gast's side of it, I deemed I should listen to Goryon's."

Smoit snorted and struck his massive thigh. "Before I could swallow another mouthful, Magg's warriors were about me. My heart and liver! Some of them will remember Smoit! Another troop had lain in ambush and stormed through the gate." Smoit put his head in his hands. "Of my own men those not slain are prisoned in the guardrooms and armouries."

"And you," Taran asked anxiously, "are you in pain? Magg spoke of torture."

"Pain!" Smoit bellowed so loudly the chamber echoed. "Torture? I suffer till I sweat. But not at the hands of that long-nosed worm! My skin's thick enough. Let Magg break his teeth on my bones! He troubles me no more than a fleabite or bramble scratch. Why, I've taken worse in a friendly scuffle!

"Do you speak of pain?" Smoit stormed on. "By every hair of my beard, I swear it pains me more than hot iron to be mewed up in my own castle! My own stronghold, and a captive in it! Gulled in my own Great Hall! My own food and drink snatched from my lips, and my breakfast ruined. Torment? Worse than that! It's enough to sour a man out of his appetite!"

Gwydion and Coll, meantime, had made their way to the walls and, as far as the dim light allowed, were hastily examining them for any sign of weakness. Taran, now that his eyes had grown a little more used to the gloom, feared that his companions were wasting their labours. The cell was windowless; what little air reached them came only from the tiny, heavily barred grating of the door. The floor was not of hard-packed earth, but of flagstones joined with barely a crack.

Smoit himself, realizing the purpose of Gwydion's efforts, shook his head and pounded his iron-shod boots on the floor. "Solid as a mountain," he cried. "I know, for I built it myself. Spare yourself pains, my friends. It will crack no sooner than I!"

"How far below ground is this dungeon?" Taran asked, though his hope for escape was fading with each moment. "Is there no way we can dig upwards?"

"Dungeon?" cried Smoit. "I've no more dungeons in Caer Cadarn. When last we met, you called my dungeons useless. Right you were, and so I walled them up. Now there's no wrongdoing in my cantrev that I can't settle quicker and easier with a few words. Who hears my voice will mend his ways – or mend his head. Dungeon indeed! It's a spare larder.

"Would that I had stocked it as solidly as I built it," groaned Smoit. "Let Magg bring his irons and lashes. I'll heed them not a bit in the midst of this other fiendish torment. The larder lies beside my scullery! I've not lined my belly for two days. Two years, it feels! The vile traitor has not left off his feasting! And for me? No more than the sniff of it! Oh, he shall pay for this," Smoit cried. "I'll beg him one thing only: a moment with my paws about his skinny neck. I'll squeeze out all the puddings and pastries he's ever gobbled!"

Gwydion had come to crouch beside the furious Smoit. "Your larder may be our tomb," he said grimly. "Not only for ourselves," he added. "Fflewddur Fflam leads our companions here. Magg's jaws will close on them as tightly as they are closed on us."

CHAPTER FIVE

The Watcher

Although Fflewddur Fflam quickly led Eilonwy, King Rhun, and Glew to Avren harbour, their return from the ship was less rapid. First, the King of Mona managed, against all likelihood, to tumble over his horse's neck when the dapple grey halted to drink at the riverbank. The ducking thoroughly soaked the unlucky king but did not dampen his spirits. However, Rhun's sword belt had come undone and the blade had sunk in the shallows. Rhun being unable to fish it out again because he had also got himself tangled in the steed's harness, Fflewddur was obliged to plunge into the river for the weapon. Glew now protested bitterly against riding behind the sopping king.

"Walk, then, little weasel!" cried Fflewddur, shivering and beating his arms against his sides. "By my choice, in the opposite direction!"

Glew only sniffed haughtily and refused to budge.

Eilonwy stamped her foot with impatience. "Will you make haste, all of you! We came to look after Lord Gwydion, and we can hardly look after ourselves."

The former giant consented to ride behind the princess on Lluagor, and they set out once more. Llyan, however, had suddenly taken it into her head to be playful. She lunged forwards on her huge padded paws and spun joyfully about while the desperate bard clung to her tawny neck. It was all Fflewddur could do to keep Llyan from rolling onto her back with himself astride her.

"She — seldom does this," shouted the breathless bard, while Llyan, with great leaps, circled the companions. "She's really been — quite well — behaved! No use — scolding her. Makes no — difference!"

At last Fflewddur was forced, with difficulty, to unsling his harp and pluck out a melody until Llyan grew calm again.

Soon after midday the bard heard the faint, distant notes of Taran's horn. "They're worried over us," Fflewddur said. "I hope we shall soon rejoin them."

The companions pressed on as quickly as they could, but the distance between the two bands increased rather than dwindled, and at nightfall they wearily halted and slept.

A fresh morning start brought them, according to Fflewddur's reckoning, less than half a day behind the others. King Rhun, more than ever eager to reach Caer Cadarn, urged all speed from the dapple grey; but the mare's pace was much slower than Llyan's and Lluagor's; Eilonwy and Fflewddur continually had to rein in their mounts.

Midway through the afternoon, King Rhun gave a glad cry. Caer Cadarn lay only a little distance off. They saw Smoit's crimson banner clearly beyond the trees. The companions were about to hasten onwards, but Eilonwy frowned and looked once more at the fluttering standard.

"How odd," the princess remarked. "I see King Smoit's jolly old bear. But Gwydion surely must be there by now, and I don't see the banner of the House of Don. Queen Teleria taught me it is courtesy for a cantrev noble to fly the Golden Sunburst of Don when one of the Royal House visits him."

"True enough in ordinary circumstances," agreed Fflewddur. "But I doubt, at this point, that Gwydion wants anyone to know where he is. He's told Smoit to put aside the formalities. A most sensible precaution."

"Yes, of course," Eilonwy replied. "I shouldn't have thought of that. How clever of you, Fflewddur."

The bard beamed happily. "Experience, Princess. Long experience. But never fear. Such wisdom will come to you, in time."

"Even so," Eilonwy said, as they rode farther. "It's curious the gates are closed. Knowing King Smoit, you might suppose they'd be flung wide open and a guard of honour waiting for us, with King Smoit himself at their head."

Fflewddur waved the girl's remark aside. "Not a bit of it. Lord Gwydion follows a path of danger, not a round of festivals. I understand how such things are done. I've been on a thousand secret missions – ah, well, perhaps one or two," he added hastily. "I fully expected Caer Cadarn would be buckled, bolted, and shut tight as an oyster."

"Yes," Eilonwy said, "I'm sure you know more about such things than I." She hesitated, straining her eyes to take in the castle, which the companions were now rapidly approaching. "But King Smoit isn't at war with his neighbours, as far as I've heard. Two watchmen on the walls would be more than enough. Does he need a whole party of bowmen?"

"Naturally," replied Fflewddur, "to protect Lord Gwydion."

"But if no one is to know Gwydion's there –" Eilonwy persisted.

"Great Belin!" cried the bard, reining up Llyan. "Now you make my head spin. Are you trying to say Gwydion's not at Caer Cadarn? If he's not, we shall soon find out. And if he is, we shall find that out as well." Fflewddur scratched his spiky yellow head. "But if he's not, then, why not? What could have happened? And if he is, then there's nothing to worry about. Yet, if he isn't. . . Oh, drat and blast, you've turned me queasy. I don't understand. . ."

"I don't understand, either," Eilonwy answered. "All I know — and I don't even *know* it — is that, well, I can't explain. I — I see the castle all crooked-wise — no, not *see*. Taste? No. . . Well, no matter," she burst out, "I've come all over chills and creeps and I don't like it. You've had experience, I don't doubt. But my ancestors were enchantresses, every one. And so should I have been, if I hadn't chosen to be a young lady."

"Enchantments!" the bard muttered uncomfortably. "Stay away from them. Don't meddle. It's also been my experience they never turn out well."

"I say," put in Rhun, "if the princess feels there's something amiss, I'll be glad to ride ahead and find out. I shall frankly rap on the gates and demand to know."

"Nonsense," replied Fflewddur. "I'm quite sure all is well." A harp string broke and twanged loudly. The bard cleared his throat. "No, I'm not sure at all. Oh, bother it! The girl has put an idea in my head and I can't shake it out.

One way, everything looks all right; the other way, it looks all wrong.

"Just to ease your mind — ah, *my* mind, that is," Fflewddur told the princess, "I shall be the one to find out. As a wandering bard I can go and come as I please. If anything's wrong, none will suspect me. If not, there's no harm done. Stay here. I'll be back directly. We shall laugh over this at King Smoit's table," he added, but without great assurance.

The bard dismounted, considering it wiser not to draw attention by riding Llyan. "And you try no mischief," he warned Glew. "I hate to let you out of my sight, but Llyan will keep an eye on you. Hers are sharper than mine. So are her teeth."

On foot, the bard made his way to the castle. After a time, Eilonwy saw the gates swing open and Fflewddur disappear within. Then all was silent.

By nightfall the girl had grown seriously alarmed, for there had been no further sign from the bard. The companions had concealed themselves in a thicket, awaiting Fflewddur's return, but now Eilonwy rose and anxiously faced the castle. "It *is* all wrong!" she cried, taking an impatient stride forwards.

King Rhun drew her back. "Perhaps not," he said. "Why, he'd have come back immediately to warn us if there was. No doubt Smoit's giving him supper, or. . ." Rhun loosened his sword in its sheath. "I'll go and see."

"No, you shall not!" Eilonwy cried. "I should have gone in the first place. Oh, I should have known better than to let myself be put off by anyone."

Rhun, however, insisted. Eilonwy refused. The heated, although whispered, dispute that followed was interrupted by the sudden arrival of the bard himself. Breathless and gasping, he stumbled into the thicket.

"It's Magg! He has them all!" Fflewddur's voice was pale as his face in the moonlight. "Caught! Trapped!"

Eilonwy and Rhun listened aghast at what Fflewddur had learned. "The warriors themselves don't know who the prisoners are, only that there are four with Smoit locked up for treachery. Treachery indeed! They've been made to swallow some kind of tale! The game goes deeper than that. What it is, I couldn't discover. I think the guards had orders to lay hold of everybody entering the castle. Luckily, those orders didn't seem to apply to wandering bards. It's so usual for a bard to drift in and sing for his supper that the warriors never gave it a second thought, though they did keep an eye on me and wouldn't let me near Smoit's Great Hall or the larder where they've put the prisoners. But I caught a glimpse of Magg. Oh, the sneering, smirking spider! If only I could have run him through then and there!

"The warriors kept me harping until I thought my fingers would drop off," he hurriedly concluded. "Otherwise, I should have been back long ago. I didn't dare stop, or they'd have smelled a rat. And there's a rat to be smelled!" he cried furiously.

"How shall we rescue them?" Eilonwy demanded. "I don't care *why* they're locked up. Ask later. First get them out."

"We can't," Fflewddur answered in despair. "Impossible. Not with only four of us. And that's four counting Glew, who can't be counted at all."

Glew snorted. Usually the little man took no interest in anything not bearing directly on himself; now, his face was agitated. "When I was a giant I could have torn the walls down."

"Bother when you were a giant," snapped Fflewddur. "You're not one now. Our only hope is to go farther into the cantrev, tell one of the cantrev lords what's happened, and have him rally an attack force."

"It will take too long," cried Eilonwy. "Oh, do be quiet and let me think!"

The girl strode again to the clearing, and turned her eyes defiantly towards the castle which flung its own dark defiance against her. Her mind raced, but with no clear plan. With half a sob and half a cry of anger she was about to turn away. A movement against a nearby tree caught her glance. She halted a moment. Not daring to turn her head, from a corner of her eye she grew aware of a strange, humped shadow, motionless now. As if to continue on her path she walked seemingly in the direction of Fflewddur and Rhun, but edged little by little towards the tree.

Suddenly, quick as Llyan, she leaped upon the humped figure. Part of it went rolling in one direction, and the rest of it set up a muffled shrieking. Eilonwy pummelled, kicked, and scratched. Fflewddur and King Rhun were at her side in an instant. The bard seized one end of the flailing shape, King Rhun the other.

Eilonwy drew back and quickly took the bauble from her cloak. As she cupped it in her hand the sphere began to glow. She held it closer to the struggling form. Her jaw dropped. The golden beams shone on a pale, wrinkled face with a long, drooping nose and mournful mouth. Wild wisps of cobweb-like hair floated above a pair of eyes that blinked wretchedly and tearfully.

"Gwystyl!" Eilonwy cried. "Gwystyl of the Fair Folk!"

The bard loosened his grasp. Gwystyl sat up, rubbed his skinny arms, then climbed to his feet and pulled his cloak defensively about him.

"How nice to see you again," he mumbled. "A pleasure, believe me. I've thought of you often. Goodbye. Now I really must be on my way."

"Help us!" Eilonwy pleaded. "Gwystyl, we beg you. Our companions are prisoned in Smoit's castle."

Gwystyl clapped his hands to his head. His face puckered miserably. "Please, please," he moaned, "don't shout. I'm not well, I'm not up to being shouted at this evening. And would you mind not shining that light in my eyes? No, no, it's really too much. It's more than enough to be pulled down and sat on, without people picking at you and bellowing and half-blinding you. As I was saying — yes, it's been delightful running into you. Of course I'll be glad to help. But perhaps another time. When we're not feeling so upset."

"Gwystyl, don't you understand?" Eilonwy cried. "Have you been listening to me at all? Another time? You must help us *now*. Gwydion's sword is stolen. Dyrnwyn is gone! Arawn has it! Don't you see what that means? This is the most terrible thing that could ever happen. How can Gwydion get the sword back if he's locked up, with his own life in danger? And Taran — and Coll and Gurgi. . ."

"Some days are like that," Gwystyl sighed. "And what's to be done about it? Nothing, alas, but hope things will brighten, which they very likely won't. But, there you are, it's all one can do. Yes, I know Dyrnwyn is stolen. A sad misfortune, a disheartening state of affairs."

"You already know?" exclaimed the bard. "Great Belin, speak up! Where is it?"

"No idea whatever," Gwystyl gasped in such desperation that Eilonwy believed the melancholy creature indeed spoke the truth. "But that's the least of my concerns. What's happening around Annuvin —" He shuddered and patted his pale forehead with a trembling hand. "The Huntsmen are gathering. The Cauldron-Born have come out, whole troops of them. I've never seen so many Cauldron-Born all together in my life. It's enough to make a decent person take to his bed.

"And that's not the half of it," Gwystyl choked. "Some of the cantrev lords are rallying their battle hosts, and their war-leaders hold council in Annuvin. The place is thick with warriors, inside, outside, wherever you look. I was even afraid they'd discover my tunnels and spy holes. These days, I'm the Fair Folk's only watcher close to Annuvin — more's the pity, for the work piles up so.

"Believe me," Gwystyl hurried on, "your friends are better off where they are. Much safer. No matter what's being done to them, it can't be worse than stumbling into that hornet's nest. If, by chance, you do see them again, give them all my fondest greetings. I'm sorry, terribly sorry I can't stay longer. I'm on my way to the realm of the Fair Folk; King Eiddileg should learn of these matters without delay."

"If King Eiddileg learns you wouldn't help us," Eilonwy indignantly burst out, "you'll wish you'd never left your way post."

"It's a long, hard journey." Gwystyl sighed and shook his cobwebby head, completely ignoring Eilonwy's remark. "I shall have to go above ground every step. Eiddileg will want to know all that's stirring along the way. I'm not up to journeying, not in my condition, not in this weather, least of all. Summer would have been much more agreeable. But – there's nothing to be done about that. Goodbye, farewell. Always a pleasure."

Gwystyl stooped to pick up a bundle almost as large as himself. Eilonwy clutched him by the arm.

"Oh, no you don't!" she cried. "You'll warn King Eiddileg after we free our companions. Don't try to deceive me, Gwystyl of the Fair Folk. You're cleverer than you care to let on. But if you won't give us your help, I know how to get it. I'll squeeze it out of you!"

The girl made a movement to seize the creature about his neck. Gwystyl gave a heartrending sob and feebly endeavoured to defend himself.

"No squeezing! No, please. I couldn't face up to it. Not now. Goodbye. Really, this is hardly the moment..."

Fflewddur, meanwhile, was staring curiously at the bundle. The large, lumpy pack had rolled near a bush when Eilonwy had first set upon Gwystyl and it lay partly undone on the ground.

"Great Belin," murmured the bard, "what a tangle of oddments. Worse than a snail with his household on his back."

"It's nothing, nothing at all," Gwystyl said hurriedly. "A few little comforts to ease the journey."

"We might do better squeezing this pack instead of Gwystyl's neck," remarked Fflewddur, who had dropped to his knees and had begun to rummage through the bundle. "There may be something here more useful than Gwystyl himself."

"Take whatever you please," Gwystyl urged, as Eilonwy turned the bauble's glow upon the heap. "Have it all, if you like. It makes no difference. I shall manage without it. Painfully, but I shall manage."

King Rhun kneeled beside the bard, who thus far had pulled out a few mended sheepskin-lined jackets and several ragged cloaks. "Amazing!" Rhun cried. "Here's a bird's nest!"

"Yes," Gwystyl sighed. "Take it. It's something I've been saving; you never know when the need for one might arise. But it's yours now."

"No thank you," muttered the bard. "I shouldn't want to deprive you."

Their hasty search next revealed water flasks both empty and full, a walking staff in jointed sections allowing it to be folded up, a cushion with an extra bag of feathers, two lengths of rope, some fishing lines and large hooks, two tents, a number of iron wedges and a crooked iron bar, a wide piece of soft leather – which, as Gwystyl reluctantly explained, could be set about a willow frame to serve as a small boat — several large bunches of dried vegetables and herbs, and numerous bags of lichens in all colours.

"For my condition," Gwystyl mumbled, indicating the latter. "The dampness and clamminess around Annuvin is dreadful. These don't help at all, but they're better than nothing. However, you're welcome. . ."

The bard shook his head in despair. "Useless rubbish. We might borrow the ropes and fish hooks. But, for whatever good they may do us. . ."

"Gwystyl," Eilonwy cried angrily, "all your tents and boats and walking staves won't answer! Oh, I could squeeze you anyway, for I'm out of patience with you. Begone! Yes, goodbye indeed!"

Gwystyl, heaving huge sighs of relief, rapidly began packing his bundle. As he hoisted it to his shoulder, from his cloak fell a small sack which he tried desperately to recover.

"I say, what's this?" asked Rhun, who had already gathered up the bag and was about to hand it to the agitated creature.

"Eggs," mumbled Gwystyl.

"Lucky they weren't smashed when you took your tumble," said Rhun cheerfully. "Perhaps we'd better have a look," he added, untying the string around the mouth of the bag.

"Eggs!" said Fflewddur, brightening somewhat. "I shouldn't mind eating one or two of them. I've had no food since midday – those warriors kept me harping, but they took no pains to feed me. Come, old fellow, I'm starved enough to crack one now and swallow it raw!"

"No, no!" squealed Gwystyl, snatching for the bag. "Don't do it! They're not eggs. Not eggs, at all!"

"I say, they surely look like it," remarked Rhun, peering into the sack. "If they aren't, then what are they?"

Gwystyl choked, then went into a fit of violent coughing and sighing before he answered. "Smoke," he gasped.

CHAPTER SIX

A Clutch of Eggs

"Amazing!" cried King Rhun. "Smoke made of egg! Or is it egg made of smoke?"

"The smoke is inside," Gwystyl muttered, drawing his shabby cloak about him. "Goodbye. Crack the shell and the smoke comes out – in considerable quantity. Keep them. A gift. If you should ever see Lord Gwydion, warn him to shun Annuvin at all cost. For myself, I'm glad to leave the place behind me and hope never to return. Goodbye."

"Gwystyl," Eilonwy said sharply, gripping the melancholy creature's arm, "something tells me there's more to that cloak of yours than meets the eye. What else have you hidden away? The truth, now. Or I promise you such squeezing. . ."

"Nothing!" Gwystyl choked. Despite the chill wind, he had begun perspiring heavily. His cobwebby hair hung limp and his brow dripped as if he had been caught in a downpour. "Nothing, that is, but a few little personal things of my own. Odds and ends. If they interest you, by all means. . ."

Gwystyl raised his arms and spread his cloak on either side, a gesture which made him resemble a long-nosed and dismal bat. He sighed and groaned miserably while the companions stared in surprise.

"Odd indeed!" said Fflewddur. "And, Great Belin, there's no end of them!"

Neatly attached within the folds of the cloak hung a dozen cloth sacks, mesh bags, and carefully wrapped packets. Most of them seemed to contain clutches of eggs of the sort Fflewddur had narrowly avoided eating. Gwystyl pulled off one of the mesh bags and handed it to Eilonwy.

"I say," exclaimed Rhun. "First eggs, now mushrooms!"

As far as the princess could see, the mesh bag held nothing more than a few large, brown-speckled toadstools; but Gwystyl waved his arms desperately, and moaned.

"Beware, beware! Break them and they'll singe your hair off! They make a handsome puff of flame, if you should ever need such a thing. Take them all. I'm well pleased to be rid of them."

"It is what we need!" Eilonwy cried. "Gwystyl, forgive me for threatening to squeeze you." She turned to the bard who was examining the sacks with an air of uneasiness. "Yes! These will help us. Now, if we can find a way into the castle..."

"My dear Princess," replied Fflewddur, "a Fflam is dauntless, but I hardly think it practical, overcoming a stronghold with little more than eggs and mushrooms in our hands, even eggs and mushrooms of this particular sort. And yet..." He hesitated, then snapped his fingers. "Great Belin, we might pull it off at that! Wait! I'm beginning to see the possibilities."

Gwystyl, meantime, had unfastened the remaining packets from his voluminous cloak. "Here," he sighed, "since you have most of them, you might as well have the rest. All of it. Go on, it makes no difference to me now."

The packets which Gwystyl held out in a trembling hand were filled with a quantity of what appeared to be dark, powdery earth. "Put this on your feet, and no one can see your tracks — that is, if someone's looking for your tracks. That's really what it's for. But if you throw it into someone's eyes, they can't see anything at all — for a short while at least."

"Better and better!" cried Fflewddur. "We'll have our friends out of the spider's clutches in no time. A daring deed! Clouds of smoke! Billows of fire! Blinding powder! And a Fflam to the rescue! That will give the bards something to sing about. Ah — tell me, old fellow," he added uneasily to Gwystyl, "you're quite sure those mushrooms work?"

The companions hurriedly returned to the cover of the thicket to set their plans. Gwystyl, after much coaxing and cajoling, as well as hints of further squeezing and suggestions of King Eiddileg's displeasure, at last agreed — with many a racking sigh and moan — to help in the rescue. The bard was eager to begin immediately.

"In my long experience," Fflewddur said, "I've found it best to go at this kind of business head-on. First, I shall return to the castle. Since the warriors know me, they'll open the gates without a second thought. Under my cloak I'll have Gwystyl's eggs and mushrooms. Directly the gates are open — clouds of smoke, a blast of fire! The rest of you will be lurking behind me in the shadows. At my signal, we all rush in, swords drawn, shouting at the top of our voices!"

"Amazing!" put in Rhun. "It can't fail." The King of Mona frowned. "On the other hand, it would almost seem — not that I know anything about these matters — we'd be rushing into our own smoke and fire. I mean to say, the warriors couldn't see us; but neither could we see them."

Fflewddur shook his head in disagreement. "Believe me, my friend, this is the best and quickest way. I've rescued more captives than I have fingers on my hands." The harp tensed and shuddered, and a number of strings would have given way had not Fflewddur added in the same breath: "*Planned* to rescue, that is. I've never, in strict point of fact, actually done so."

"Rhun is right," Eilonwy declared. "It would be worse than stumbling over your own feet. Besides, we'd be risking everything at one go. No, we must have a better plan than that."

King Rhun beamed, surprised and delighted that his words had found agreement. He blinked his pale blue eyes, grinned shyly, and ventured to raise his voice once more. "I suddenly think of the seawall I've been rebuilding," he began, in some hesitation. "I mean, starting it from both ends. Unfortunately, it didn't turn out quite as I had hoped. But the *idea* was a good one. Now, if we might try the same kind of thing. Not building a wall, of course. I mean going at Caer Cadarn from different ways."

Fflewddur shrugged, not a little crestfallen that his own suggestion had been dismissed.

But Eilonwy nodded. "Yes. It's the only sensible thing."

Glew snorted. "The only sensible thing is to get an army behind you. When I was a giant, I'd have been willing to help you. But I mean to have no part in this scheme."

The little man was about to say more, but a glance from the bard silenced him. "Never fear," said Fflewddur. "You and I will be together at every moment. You'll be in good hands."

"Now then," broke in Rhun, impatient to speak again. "There are five of us. Some should climb over the rear wall, the others enter at the gate." The young king rose to his feet and his eyes flashed eagerly. "Fflewddur Fflam shall have the gates opened. Then, while the others attack from the far wall, I shall ride straight through the gates."

Rhun's hand had gone to his sword. His head was thrown back and he stood before the companions as proudly as if all the Kings of Mona were at his side. He spoke on, firmly and clearly, with such joyful enthusiasm that Eilonwy had no heart to stop him.

But at last she interrupted. "Rhun, I'm sorry," Eilonwy said. "But – and I think Fflewddur will agree with me – you will serve better if you stay out of the actual fighting unless it's absolutely necessary. That way, you'll be on hand when you're needed, but it won't be quite so dangerous for you."

Rhun's face clouded with disappointment and dismay. "But, I say. . ."

"You're not a prince any more," Eilonwy added, before Rhun could continue his protest. "You're King of Mona. Your life isn't altogether your own, don't you see? You have a whole realm of people to think of, and we shan't let you take any more risks than you have to. You'll be in far too much danger as it is. If Queen Teleria could have guessed the way things would turn out," Eilonwy added, "you wouldn't have sailed to Caer Dallben in the first place."

"I don't see what my mother has to do with it," cried Rhun. "I'm sure my father would have wanted. . ."

"Your father understood what it means to be a king," Eilonwy said gently. "You must learn as well as he did."

"Taran of Caer Dallben saved my life on Mona," Rhun said urgently. "I am in his debt, and it is a debt that I alone can pay."

"You owe another kind of debt to the fisher folk of Mona," Eilonwy replied. "And theirs is the greater claim."

Rhun turned away and sat dejectedly on a hummock, his sword trailing at his side. Fflewddur gave him an encouraging clap on the shoulder.

"Don't despair," said the bard. "If our friend Gwystyl's eggs and mushrooms fail, you'll have more than your share of trouble. So will we all."

It was nearly dawn and bitter cold when the little band left the concealment of the thicket and moved stealthily towards the lightless castle. Each carried a share of Gwystyl's mushrooms and eggs, and a packet of his black, loamy powder. Making a wide circle, they now approached Caer Cadarn from its darkest, most shadowed side.

"Remember the plan," Fflewddur warned under his breath. "It must go exactly as we set it. When we are all in position, Gwystyl is to pop open one of those famous mushrooms of his; the fire should draw the guards to the rear of the courtyard. That will be your signal," he said to Eilonwy and Rhun. "Then – and not before, mind you – be ready to force the gates open as soon as possible, for I imagine we shall be rather in a hurry to get out. At the same time, I'll free Smoit's men locked up in the guardroom. They'll help you if you need them, while I make my way to the larder and loose our friends. We must hope that villainous spider hasn't already taken them away somewhere. If he has, well, we shall have to make new plans on the spot.

"And you, old fellow," Fflewddur added to Gwystyl, as the dark walls loomed ahead, "I think it's time for you to do as you promised."

Gwystyl sighed heavily and his mouth drooped more wretchedly than ever. "I'm not up to climbing, not today. If only you could have waited. Next week, perhaps. Or when the weather turns better. Well, no matter. There's little a person can do about it."

Still shaking his head dubiously, the gloomy creature set down the coils of rope he carried over his shoulder. The large fish hooks, taken from his bundle, he now attached at various angles to the end of a slender line. Fascinated, King Rhun watched as Gwystyl with a deft movement flung the line into the air. From the parapet high above came a faint rasping sound, then a dry click as the hooks caught on a projecting stone. Gwystyl tugged at the cord and slung the remaining coils of rope about his neck.

"I say," Rhun whispered, "will that fishing line hold you?"

Gwystyl sighed and looked mournfully at him. "I doubt it."

Nevertheless, mumbling and moaning, he quickly hoisted himself into the air, hanging an instant before his feet found the stones of the wall. Pulling himself up on the line and scrabbling with his feet against the sheer side of the castle, Gwystyl was soon out of sight.

"Amazing!" cried Rhun.

The bard frantically cautioned him to silence.

A moment later the fishing line was hauled up and the end of one of the heavier ropes came swinging down. The bard lifted Glew, who was protesting as loudly as he dared, and boosted him onto the dangling cord.

"Up you go," Fflewddur muttered. "I'll be right behind you."

Rhun followed, as the bard and the former giant

disappeared into the shadows. Eilonwy seized the rope and felt herself rapidly drawn aloft. She swung herself over the parapet and dropped to a projecting ledge. Gwystyl had already scuttled towards the rear of the castle. Fflewddur and Glew slid into the darkness below. King Rhun grinned at Eilonwy and crouched against the cold stones.

The moon was down; the sky had turned black. Amid the shadows of the silent buildings, the stables, and the long dark mass which Eilonwy guessed to be Smoit's Great Hall, the low flames of a watch fire gleamed. Farther along the parapet, in the direction of the gates, the figures of the guards stood motionless, drowsing.

"I say, it's dark enough!" Rhun whispered cheerfully. "We shan't need Gwystyl's powder, at this rate. I can hardly see as it is."

Eilonwy turned her eyes in the direction Gwystyl had taken, waiting from one endless moment to the next for the signal. Rhun was tensed, ready to fling himself down the rope.

A shout rang from the courtyard. At the same instant, a cloud of crimson flame burst in the shadows of the Great Hall.

Eilonwy jumped to her feet. "Something's amiss!" she cried. "Fflewddur attacks too soon!"

It was only then that she saw a burst of fire at the far end of the castle. More shouts of alarm rose above the clatter of racing footsteps. But the warriors, Eilonwy saw with sinking heart, ran not to Gwystyl's false attack but to the Great Hall. The courtyard seethed with shadows. Torches sprang to light.

"Quickly!" Eilonwy shouted. "The gates!"

Rhun swung from the ledge. Eilonwy was about to follow him when she glimpsed a bowman at one of the guard posts on the wall. He raced towards her, then halted to take aim.

Hastily, Eilonwy drew a mushroom from her cloak and flung it at the warrior. It fell short and split against the stones; fire spurted, blinding her. The flames leaped in a roaring, searing cloud. The bowman shouted in terror and staggered back. His arrow whistled past her head.

The girl seized the rope and dropped into the courtyard below.

CHAPTER SEVEN

The King of Mona

In the larder which had become a prison, Gurgi was first to hear the shouts of alarm. Though muffled by the heavy walls, the cries brought him to his feet before the other companions were aware of the tumult beyond their cell. All night, fearing the arrival of Magg from one moment to the next, they had vainly sought escape. Exhausted from their efforts, they dozed fitfully by turns; hoping only to sell their lives dearly when the guards at last came for them.

"Fightings and smitings!" Gurgi cried. "Is it for weary

tired captives? Yes, yes, it must be! Yes, we are here!" He ran to the door and began shouting through the iron grating.

Now Taran heard what seemed to be a clash of swords. Coll and King Smoit were quickly beside him. Gwydion had already reached the door in two strides and drew away the excited Gurgi.

"Beware," Gwydion sharply warned. "Fflewddur Fflam may have found a way to free us, but if the castle is aroused, Magg may take our lives before our comrades can save us."

Footsteps rang outside, the lock of the heavy door began to rattle, and the companions fell back, crouched and ready to set upon their captors. The door was flung open. Into the cell burst Eilonwy.

"Follow me!" she cried. In one upraised hand she held the brightly glowing bauble; and with the other, pulled a sack from her belt. "Take these. The mushrooms are fire, the eggs are smoke. Throw them at anyone who attacks you. And this powder – it will blind them.

"I couldn't find weapons," she hurried on. "I've set Smoit's warriors free, but Fflewddur's trapped in the courtyard. Everything's gone wrong. Our plan has failed!"

Smoit, bellowing in rage, dashed to the door. "Away with your toadstools and rooster eggs!" he roared. "My hands are all I need to wring a traitor's neck!"

Gwydion sprang through the doorway. With Coll and Gurgi behind him, Taran sped after Eilonwy. From the corridors of the Great Hall, Taran raced into what was neither daylight nor darkness. Huge billows of dense, white smoke rose in the courtyard, blotting out the dawn sky. Like swaying, twisting waves, they shifted as the wind caught them, lifted a moment to show a struggling knot of warriors, then flooded back in an impenetrable tide. Here and there roaring columns of fire writhed through the smoke.

Losing sight of Eilonwy, Taran plunged into the swirling clouds. A warrior brought up his sword and slashed at him. Taran stumbled to escape the blow. With outflung hand he cast his small store of powder in the man's face. The warrior fell back as if stunned; his wide-open eyes stared blankly at nothing. Taran snatched the blade from the baffled guard and raced on.

"A Smoit! A Smoit!" The red-bearded king's war cry rang from the stables. Before smoke filled his eyes again, Taran caught a fleeting glimpse of the furious Smoit, armed with a huge scythe and laying about him like a bear turned harvester.

The luckless Gurgi, however, had stumbled with his eggs still clutched in his hands. Smoke poured over him. For an instant all Taran could see of him was a pair of waving, hairy arms before these, too, vanished in the billows. Yelling at the top of his voice, Gurgi spun about and dashed frantically wherever his feet led him. Warriors shouted and fled from this fearsome whirlwind.

King Smoit, Taran realized, was trying to rally his own men around him, and Taran attempted to fight his way towards the stables. Coll, briefly, was at his side. The stout warrior had just gained a blade from a fallen opponent. Flinging aside the hoe which, until then, had served him as a weapon, Coll threw his bulk against the press of swordsmen besetting Fflewddur Fflam. Taran leaped into the fray, striking left and right with telling blows.

Magg's warriors fell back. The bard joined Taran as they raced across the court.

"Where is Rhun?" Taran cried.

"I don't know!" Fflewddur gasped. "He and Eilonwy were to open the gates for us. But, Great Belin, what's happened since then I can't guess. Everything has changed. One of Magg's men trod on Glew, and we were discovered before we could go another step. From then on the fat was in the fire. Where Glew is now I have no idea — though the little weasel gave a fair account of himself, I must say. So did Gwystyl."

"Gwystyl?" Taran stammered. "How. . ."

"Never mind," replied Fflewddur. "We'll tell you later. If there is a later."

They had nearly reached the stables. Taran caught sight of Gwydion. The Prince of Don's wolf-grey head towered above the milling warriors. But Taran's relief at Gwydion's safety turned to despair. He saw, through the shifting clouds, the tide of battle was turning against the companions. Only a handful of Smoit's men had been able to rally for an attack; the others were cut off, locked in combat throughout the courtyard.

"To the gates!" Gwydion commanded. "Fly, all who can!"

With sinking heart Taran realized the little band was grievously outnumbered. Dimly, Taran saw the gates had been opened. But more of Magg's warriors had joined their fellows and the way to safety was blocked.

Suddenly a mounted figure galloped into the courtyard. It was Rhun, astride his dapple grey. The King of Mona's boyish face shone with a furious light. As the steed reared and plunged, Rhun swung his sword about his head and shouted at the top of his voice:

"Bowmen! Follow me! All of you, into the court!" He spun the mare about and beckoned with his sword. His words rang above the clash of arms. "Spearmen! This way! Make haste!"

"He's brought help!" Taran cried.

"Help?" echoed the amazed bard. "There's no one within miles!"

Rhun had not ceased to gallop back and forth amid the struggling warriors, shouting orders as if a whole army streamed behind him.

Magg's men turned to face the unseen foe.

"A ruse!" exclaimed Fflewddur. "He's a madman! It will never work!"

"But it does!" At a glance Taran saw their assailants had broken away, seeking, in confusion, to engage what they imagined to be fresh attackers. Taran brought his horn to his lips and sounded the charge. Magg's men faltered, believing the foe was now at their backs.

At that instant Llyan burst through the gates. The men who saw her shouted in terror as the huge cat leaped forwards. Llyan paid no heed to the warriors, but raced across the court while the swordsmen dropped their weapons and fled at her approach.

"She's looking for me!" Fflewddur cried. "Here I am, old girl!"

King Smoit's embattled fighting men seized this moment to press forwards with a mighty surge. Many of Magg's warriors had already flown; fear-driven, they slashed and stabbed among themselves in blind panic. Rhun galloped on and vanished into the smoke.

"He's duped them well!" Fflewddur shouted jubilantly. "For all the good those eggs and mushrooms did us – it was Rhun who turned the trick!"

The bard hastened to Llyan. Gwydion, Taran saw, was now on horseback. Golden-maned Melyngar streaked across the courtyard, as Gwydion urged the mare to overtake the retreating foe. Smoit and Coll had also leaped astride their steeds. Behind them galloped Gwystyl. Smoit's warriors, too, joined the pursuit. Taran ran to find Melynlas, but before he reached the stables, he heard Eilonwy call his name. He turned. The girl, her face smudged, her robe torn, beckoned urgently.

"Come!" she called. "Rhun is badly hurt!"

Taran raced to follow her. Near the far wall the dapple grey stood riderless. The King of Mona was sitting on the ground, his legs stretched in front of him, his back resting against a cart still smouldering from Gwystyl's fiery mushrooms. Gurgi and Glew, both unharmed, were at his side.

"Hullo, hullo!" Rhun murmured and waved a hand. His face was deathly white.

"The day is ours," Taran said. "Without you, it would have gone differently. Don't move," he cautioned, loosening the young king's bloodstained jacket. Taran frowned anxiously. An arrow had sunk deep in Rhun's side and the shaft had broken.

"Amazing!" Rhun whispered. "I've never been in battle before, and I wasn't sure of – of anything at all. But, I say, the oddest things kept running through my head. I was thinking of the seawall at Mona Haven. Isn't it surprising? Yes, your plan will work very well," Rhun murmured. His eyes wandered and suddenly he looked very young, very lost, and a little frightened. "And I think – I think I shall be glad to be home." He made an effort to raise himself. Taran bent quickly to him.

Fflewddur had come up with Llyan loping at his heels. "So there you are, old boy," he called to Rhun. "I told you we'd have more than our share of trouble. But you pulled us out of it! Oh, the bards will sing of you. . ."

Taran lifted a grief-stricken face. "The King of Mona is dead."

Silent and heavy-hearted, the companions raised a burial mound a little distance from Caer Cadarn. The warriors of Smoit joined them; and at dusk, horsemen bearing torches rode slowly circling the mound, to honour the King of Mona.

As the last flame died, Taran came to stand before the burial place. "Farewell, Rhun Son of Rhuddlum. Your seawall is unfinished," he said gently. "But I promise you your work shall not be left undone. Your fisher folk shall have their safe harbour if I must build it for you with my own hands."

Soon after nightfall Gwydion, Coll, and King Smoit returned. Magg had eluded them, and the fruitless pursuit had left them worn and haggard. They, too, mourned the death of Rhun, and did honour to all the fallen warriors. Gwydion then led the companions to the Great Hall.

"Arawn Death-Lord gives us little time for grief, and we shall mourn others, I fear, before our tasks are done," he said. "I must tell you now of a choice carefully to be weighed.

"Gwystyl of the Fair Folk has left us, and continues his journey to King Eiddileg's realm. Before we parted, he told me further of the gathering of Arawn's hosts. Magg's words were not evil boasting. Gwystyl judges, as do I, that Arawn means to defeat us in one last battle. His armies gather even now.

"There is grave risk, and perhaps fatal risk, in leaving Dyrnwyn in Arawn's grasp," Gwydion went on. "Yet we must face the more pressing danger. No longer will I seek the black sword. Whatever strength it may yield him, in my own strength I will stand against him to the death. I ride not to Annuvin but to Caer Dathyl to rally the Sons of Don."

No one spoke for some moments. At length Coll replied, "To my mind, you have chosen wisely, Prince of Don."

Smoit and Fflewddur Fflam nodded their agreement.

"Would that I were as sure of my wisdom," Gwydion replied heavily. "So be it then."

Taran rose and faced Gwydion. "Is there no way one of us can breach the Death-Lord's stronghold? Must the search for Dyrnwyn indeed be given up?"

"I read your thoughts, Assistant Pig-Keeper," Gwydion replied. "You will serve me best if you obey my commands. Gwystyl warns that a journey to Annuvin can mean only wasted life — and more than that: a loss of precious time. Gwystyl's nature is to conceal his nature, but among the Fair Folk none is shrewder or more trustworthy. I heed his warning, and so must all of you.

"Gwystyl has promised to do all in his power to gain help from the Fair Folk," Gwydion went on. "King Eiddileg has no great fondness for the race of men. Yet even he must see that Arawn's victory would blight all Prydain. The Fair Folk would suffer no less than we.

"But we dare not count too heavily on Eiddileg. Our own armies must be gathered, and our battle host raised. In this, our greatest help will come from King Pryderi of the West Domains. No lord in Prydain commands a mightier army. His allegiance to the House of Don is firm, and between us are strong bonds of friendship. I will send word to Pryderi, and pray him to join his host with ours at Caer Dathyl.

"There must we all meet," Gwydion continued. "Before then, I ask King Smoit to muster every loyal warrior in his cantrev and the dominions closest to his." He turned to the bard. "Fflewddur Fflam Son of Godo, you are a king in your own Northern Realms. Return there without delay. To you I entrust the rallying of the northern cantrevs.

"And you, Assistant Pig-Keeper," Gwydion said, seeing the question in Taran's eyes, "your own task is urgent. You are well known to the folk of the Free Commots. I charge you to raise whatever force you can among them. Lead all who will follow you to Caer Dathyl. Gurgi and Coll Son of Collfrewr will ride with you. So, too, will the Princess Eilonwy. Her safety is in your hands."

"I'm glad," Eilonwy murmured, "there's been no talk of sending me home."

"Gwystyl tells us many of Arawn's liege men are already marching," Coll said to her. "The Valley Cantrevs are too dangerous, whatever. Otherwise, Princess," he added with a grin, "you would long since have been on your way to Caer Dallben."

Well before dawn Gwydion and Fflewddur Fflam rode from Caer Cadarn, each to follow his separate path. King Smoit, girded for battle, set out from the castle, and with him went Lord Gast and Lord Goryon, who had learned belatedly of the attack on their king and now hastened to join him. Faced with the common danger, the two rivals had put aside their quarrel. Goryon declined to take insult at Gast's every word, Gast refrained from giving offence to Goryon, and neither so much as mentioned cows.

That same morning a gnarled, grey-headed farmer strode up to Taran in the castle courtyard. It was Aeddan, who had befriended him long before in Smoit's cantrev. The two clasped hands warmly, but the farmer's face was grim.

"There is no time now to speak of time past," Aeddan said. "I offer you friendship — and this," he added, unsheathing a rusted sword. "It has served once and can serve again. Say where you ride and I will go with you."

"I value the sword, and value more the man who bears it," answered Taran. "But your place is with your king. Follow him and hope that you and I will meet on a happier day."

As Gwydion had ordered, Taran and the remaining companions waited at Smoit's castle, hoping Kaw might arrive with further tidings. But when the following day brought no sign of the crow, they made ready for their own departure. Eilonwy's needlework had gone unscathed and she carefully unfolded it.

"You're a war-leader now," she said proudly to Taran, "but I've never heard of a war-leader without a battle flag."

With leather thongs she bound the still-unfinished embroidery to the end of a spear.

"There," said Eilonwy. "As an emblem Hen Wen may not be properly terrifying. And yet, for an Assistant Pig-Keeper, she's very likely the most fitting."

They rode through the gates. Gurgi, at Taran's side,

raised the spear high and the wind caught at the banner of the White Pig. Above the smoke-blackened fortress and the burial mound, whose fresh earth was already frost-covered, the clouds had grown heavy. Soon there would be snow.

CHAPTER EIGHT

The Messengers

From the moment he left Caer Dallben, Kaw had flown directly towards Annuvin. Though it was the bird's pleasure, aloft, to revel in the limitless reaches of the sky, to swoop and soar above the white sheep flocks of clouds, he now put aside all temptation to sport with the wind and held steadily to his course. Far below, Avren glinted like a long trickle of molten silver; fallow fields spread in patches; the treetops rose black and leafless, broken by dark green stretches of pine forest following the curves of the hills.

Kaw pressed ever northwestwards, resting seldom during the hours of daylight. Only at dusk, when even the crow's keen eyes could not search beyond the gathering shadows, did he drop to earth and find haven among the branches of a tree.

Days he flew high above the clouds to profit from the wind tides that bore him swiftly as a leaf in a stream. But, as he passed over the Forest of Idris, drawing closer to the harsh peaks of Annuvin, Kaw checked his gliding flight and dived earthwards, alert for any stirring among the mountain passes. Shortly he glimpsed a column of heavily armed warriors marching northwards. At closer range, he saw them to be Huntsmen of Annuvin. For a time he followed them and, when they halted amid the scrub and stunted trees, flapped to a low branch and settled there. Squatting at their cook fires, the Huntsmen prepared their midday meal. The crow cocked his head and listened intently, but their muttered speech told him little, until he heard the words "Caer Dathyl".

Kaw shifted his position and cast about for a closer branch. One of the Huntsmen, a brutish warrior garbed in bearskin, caught sight of the bird. Grinning cruelly at this chance for sport, the warrior reached for his bow and nocked an arrow to the string. Quickly he aimed, and loosed the shaft. Rapid though the Huntsman's movements were, the crow's sharp eyes followed them as quickly. Kaw flapped his wings and dodged the arrow that went rattling through the dead branches a little distance over his head. The Huntsman cursed both his lost arrow and the crow, and made to draw again. Delighted with himself, jeering raucously, Kaw sped above the trees, intending to circle back and find a safer listening post.

It was then the gwythaints appeared.

For an instant, bent on returning to the Huntsmen's camp, Kaw did not see the flight of the three huge birds. From a bank of clouds they plunged downwards in a rush of black, beating wings. Kaw's self-satisfaction vanished. The crow veered from their attack and strove desperately to climb higher, not daring to allow the deadly creatures to command the air above him.

The gwythaints, too, swiftly veered. One broke from his fellows to pursue the fleeing crow; the others, with powerful strokes of their wings, rose towards the clouds to renew their assault.

Kaw forced himself ever upwards and the gwythaint had gained only slightly when the crow burst through a sea of mist into a sunswept vastness that nearly blinded him.

The other two gwythaints were waiting. Shrieking in fury, they dropped towards him. Behind the crow his pursuer drove him closer to the oncoming creatures. Kaw glimpsed the flash of glistening beaks and blood-red eyes. The gwythaints' screams of triumph ripped the empty sky.

The crow suddenly checked his flight, feigning confusion. When the gwythaints were nearly upon him, he summoned all his strength in a single lunge that carried him beyond the talons slashing like daggers.

The crow had not gone unscathed. One of the gwythaints had struck him beneath the wing. Despite the pain that dizzied him, Kaw fluttered free of his attackers. The open sky was no refuge for him. No longer could he rely on swiftness of flight to save him. He plunged earthwards.

The gwythaints were not outwitted. The scent of blood had maddened them, and they would not be deprived of their kill. They streaked after the crow to overtake and prevent him from reaching the forest below.

The highest trees rose up towards Kaw. He avoided them to drop closer to the underbrush. The tangle of branches slowed his pursuers. Without slackening speed, Kaw skimmed above the ground, deeper and deeper into the maze of bushes. The huge wings of the gwythaints which had served so well aloft now kept them from their prize. They screamed in rage, but made no attempt to venture farther into the woods. The crow, like a fox, had gone to earth.

The day had begun to fade. Kaw settled himself painfully for the night. At dawn, he fluttered cautiously to a treetop. The gwythaints had gone, but his senses told him he had been driven far east of Annuvin. Stiffly he launched himself from the tree and flapped his way aloft. Southwards, Caer Cadarn lay beyond the reach of his ebbing strength. He must decide quickly, while life still remained to him. Kaw circled once, then flew heavily towards his new goal and his only hope.

His flight was now a constant torment. Often his wings faltered and only the wind tides held him aloft. He could no longer travel a full day's distance. Long before sundown, his wound forced him to alight and hide himself amid the trees. Nor could he fly closer to the sun's warmth, but made his way only a little above the ground, nearly brushing the treetops. Below him, the countryside was springing to life with warriors, both on horseback and afoot. During the times he halted to husband his strength, he learned their destination, like that of the Huntsmen, was the fortress of the Sons of Don. His alarm grew sharper than his pain and he flew onwards.

At length, in the numbing cold of the mountains northeast of the River Ystrad, he dimly spied what he had been seeking. Surrounded by sheer walls of cliffs, the valley was a green nest amid the snow-capped summits. A small cottage came into sight. The blue surface of a lake flashed in the sunlight. Against the protected side of a hill slope stretched a long, boatlike shape, the vessel's ribs and timbers overgrown with moss. Beating his wings feebly, Kaw dropped like a stone into the valley.

He was vaguely aware, as his eyes closed, of jaws firmly about him, lifting him from the grass; then a deep voice asking, "Now, Brynach, what have you brought us?"

The crow knew nothing more.

When he opened his eyes again, he lay upon a soft nest of rushes in a sunny chamber. He was weak, but his pain had left him; his wound had been bound up. As he feebly fluttered his wings, a pair of strong hands deftly reached to hold and calm him.

"Gently, gently," said a voice. "I fear you will be earthbound for a time."

The man's white-bearded face was as gnarled and weathered as an ancient oak in a snowdrift. White hair hung below broad, knotted shoulders, and a blue gem sparkled from the golden band circling his brow. Kaw, without his customary squawking and jabbering, humbly bowed his head. Never before had he flown to this valley, but his heart had always known such a refuge awaited him. A secret sense, like some hidden memory he shared with all the forest creatures of Prydain, had guided him unerringly; and the crow understood he had come at last into the abode of Medwyn.

"Let me see, let me see," Medwyn continued, knitting his heavy brows in search of something long stored in a corner of his mind. "You would be – yes – the family likeness is unmistakable: Kaw Son of Kadwyr. Yes, of course. Forgive me for not recognizing you immediately, but there are so many crow clans I sometimes get them mixed. I knew your father when he was a spindly-legged fledgling." Medwyn smiled at his own recollections. "The rogue was no stranger to my valley – a broken wing to be mended, a leg out of joint, one scrape after the other.

"I hope you do not follow his example," Medwyn added. "I have already heard much of your bravery and – a certain bent, shall we say, for boisterousness? It has reached my ears, as well, that you serve an Assistant Pig-Keeper at Caer Dallben. Melynlas is his name, I believe. No – forgive me. That is his steed. Of course, Melynlas Son of Melyngar. The Pig-Keeper's name escapes me at the moment. But no matter. Serve him faithfully, Son of Kadwyr, for his heart is good. Among all the race of men, he was of the few I allowed within my valley. As for you, I judge you and the gwythaints have been at close quarters. Have a care. Many of Arawn's messengers rove aloft these days. But you are safe now, and will soon be up and winging."

Perched on the back of Medwyn's chair, an enormous eagle studied the crow. Beside the old man, the wolf Brynach sat on his haunches. Lean and grey, with yellow eyes, he wagged his tail and grinned up at the crow. A moment later, another wolf, smaller and with a white blaze on her breast, trotted in and crouched beside her mate.

"Ah, Briavael," said Medwyn. "Have you come to greet our visitor? Like his father, no doubt, he will have a bold tale to tell us."

Kaw spoke then in his own tongue which Medwyn easily understood. The old man's features turned grave as he listened. When the crow had finished, Medwyn was silent for a time, deeply frowning. Brynach whined uneasily.

"It is come," Medwyn said heavily. "I should have so guessed, for I sense a strange fear among the animals. More and more find their way here, fleeing what they themselves only dimly know. They tell of Huntsmen abroad in force, and armed men. Now I understand the meaning of these tidings. The day I had ever feared has come upon us. Yet my valley cannot hold all who would seek refuge."

Medwyn's voice had begun to rise like a wrathful gale. "The race of men face the slavery of Annuvin. So, too, the creatures of Prydain. In the shadow of the Land of the Dead, the nightingale's song will choke and die. The galleries of badgers and moles will become prison houses. No beast, no bird, will roam or fly with the joy of a free heart. Those who are not slain – theirs will be the fate of the gwythaints, long ago made captive, tormented, broken, and their once gentle spirits twisted to Arawn's vile ends."

Medwyn turned to the eagle. "You, Edyrnion, fly swiftly to the mountain eyries of your kindred. Bid them rise up in all their strength and all their numbers.

"You, Brynach, and you, Briavael," he commanded, as the wolves pricked up their ears, "spread the alarm among your own brethren; among the bears, with paws to smite and arms to crush; among the sharp-antlered stags; and all forest dwellers, large and small."

Medwyn had risen to his full height. His hands clenched as tree roots clench the earth. The crow watched, awestruck and silent. Medwyn's eyes flashed and his deep voice came as a wave of thunder.

"Speak to them in my name and tell them: such are the words of one who built a ship when the dark waters flooded Prydain, of one who bore their ancient sires to safety. Now, against this flood of evil, each nest, each lair, must be a stronghold. Let every creature turn tooth, beak, and claw against all who serve Arawn Death-Lord."

Side by side, the wolves loped from the cottage. And the eagle took flight.

CHAPTER NINE

The Banner

Light snow fell before the companions had journeyed a day from King Smoit's castle, and by the time they reached the Valley of Ystrad the slopes were white-cloaked and ice had begun to sheathe the river. They forded while frozen splinters cut at the legs of their horses, and wended through the bleak Hill Cantrevs, pressing eastwards towards the Free Commots. Of all the band, Gurgi suffered most grievously from the cold. Though bundled in a huge garment of sheepskin, the unhappy creature shivered wretchedly. His lips were blue, his teeth chattered, and ice droplets clung to his matted hair. Nevertheless, he kept pace at Taran's side and his numbed hands did not loosen their grip on the banner.

Days of harsh travel brought them across Small Avren to Cenarth, where Taran had chosen to begin the rallying of the Commot Folk. But even as he rode into the cluster of thatch-roofed cottages, he saw the village thronged with men; and among them Hevydd the Smith, barrel-chested and bristle-bearded, who shouldered his way through the crowd and clapped Taran on the back with a hand that weighed as much as one of his own hammers.

"A good greeting to you, Wanderer," called the smith. "We saw you afar and gathered to welcome you."

"A good greeting to good friends," Taran replied, "but I bring a stern task in exchange for a warm welcome. Hear me well," he went on urgently. "What I ask is not asked lightly nor granted lightly: the strength of your hands and the courage of your hearts, and, if it must be, even your lives."

As the Commot folk, murmuring, pressed around him, Taran spoke of what had befallen Gwydion and of the rising of Arawn. When he had finished, the men were grim-faced, and for a long moment all stood silent. Then Hevydd the Smith lifted his voice.

"The folk of the Free Commots honour King Math and

the House of Don," he said. "But they will answer only to one they know as a friend, and follow him not in obligation but in friendship. And so let Hevydd be the first to follow Taran Wanderer."

"All follow! All!" cried the Commot men as with a single voice, and on the instant the once-peaceful Cenarth stirred like a gathering storm as each man hastened to arm himself.

But Hevydd gave Taran and the companions a hard grin. "Our will is strong but our weapons lack," he declared. "No matter, Wanderer. You toiled bravely in my smithy; now shall my smithy toil for you. And I will send word to every metalsmith in the Commot lands to labour as hard for you as I myself will do."

While the men readied their mounts and Hevydd set his forge to blazing, Taran led the companions to the neighbouring Commots. His task became quickly known and each day brought its throng of herdsmen and farmers who needed no urging to march in the growing host following the banner of the White Pig. For Taran, days and nights merged into one another. In the marshalling camps, astride unflagging Melynlas he rode among the gatherings of peaceful men turned warriors, seeing to their provisions and equipment, and by the embers of watch fires held council with the new-formed war bands.

When he had accomplished all he could at Cenarth, Hevydd rejoined Taran to serve as his master armourer.

"You have done your work well, but we still go too lightly armed," Taran said, speaking apart with the smith. "I fear all the forges in Prydain will not be enough to serve our need. Somehow I must find a way..."

"And so you shall, with luck!" called a voice.

Taran turned to see a horseman who was riding up beside him, and blinked in surprise for this was the strangest-garbed of all the Commot warriors. The man was tall, lank-haired, with legs as spindly as a stork's and so long they almost touched the ground on either side of his mount. Bits of iron and odds and ends of metal were stitched closely all over his jacket; he carried a wooden staff with a scythe blade at the end; on his head he wore what had once been a cook-pot, now worked and shaped into a makeshift helmet that sat so low on the man's forehead it nearly covered his eyes.

"Llonio!" Taran cried, warmly clasping the new arrival's hand. "Llonio Son of Llonwen!"

"None other," answered Llonio, pushing back his peculiar headpiece. "Did you not suppose I'd be along sooner or later?"

"But your wife and family," Taran began. "I would not ask you to leave them. Why, of children I remember half-a-dozen."

"And another merrily on the way," Llonio replied, grinning happily. "Perhaps twins, with my kind of luck. But my brood will be safe enough till I return. Indeed, if there is ever to be safety in Prydain I must follow the Wanderer now. But your concern is not babes in arms but men-at-arms. Hear me, friend Wanderer," Llonio went on. "I have seen pitchforks and hay-rakes among the Commot folk. Could not the tines be cut off and set in wooden shafts? Thus would you gain three, four, and even more weapons where you had only one to begin with."

"Why, so we could!" burst out Hevydd. "How did I not see that myself?"

"No more did I," admitted Taran. "Llonio sees more sharply than any of us, but calls luck what another would call keen wits. Go, friend Llonio, find what you can. I know you'll find more than meets the eye."

As Llonio, with the help of Hevydd the Smith, gleaned the Commots for sickles, rakes, fire tongs, scythes, and pruning hooks, and found ways to make even the most unlikely objects serve a new purpose, the store of weapons grew.

While each day Taran rallied followers in greater numbers, Coll, Gurgi, and Eilonwy helped load carts with gear and provisions, a task by no means to the liking of the princess, who was more eager to gallop from one Commot to the next than she was to plod beside the heavy-laden wagons. Eilonwy had donned men's garments and braided her hair about her head; at her belt hung a sword and short dagger wheedled from Hevydd the Smith. Her warrior's garb was ill-fitting, but she took pride in it and was therefore all the more vexed when Taran refused to let her go afield.

"You'll ride out with me," Taran said, "as soon as the pack animals are tended and their loads secured."

The princess reluctantly agreed; but next day, when Taran cantered past the horse lines at the rear of the camp, she furiously cried to him, "You've tricked me! These tasks will never be done! No sooner do I finish with one string of horses and carts than along come some more. Very well, I shall do as I promised. But war-leader or no, Taran of Caer Dallben, I'm not speaking to you!"

Taran grinned and rode on.

Bearing northwards through the Valley of Great Avren, the companions entered Commot Gwenith and had scarcely dismounted when Taran heard a crackling voice call out, "Wanderer! I know you seek warriors, not crones. But tarry a moment and give a greeting to one who has not forgotten you."

Dwyvach, the Weaver-Woman of Gwenith, stood in her cottage doorway. Despite her white hair and wizened features she looked as lively and untired as ever. Her grey eyes scanned Taran sharply, then turned to Eilonwy. The ancient weaver-woman beckoned to her. "Taran Wanderer I know well enough. And who you may be I can guess well enough, even though you go in the guise of a man and your hair could stand a little washing." She glanced shrewdly at the princess. "Indeed, I was sure, when the Wanderer and I first met, that he had a pretty maiden in his thoughts."

"Humph!" Eilonwy sniffed. "I'm not sure if he did then, and even less sure if he does now."

Dwyvach chuckled. "If you are not, then no one else can be. Time will tell which of us is right. But meanwhile, child," she added, unfolding a cloak she held in her withered hands and setting it about Eilonwy's shoulders, "take this as a gift from a crone to a maiden, and know there is not so much difference between the two. For even a tottering granddam keeps a portion of girlish heart, and the youngest maiden a thread of old woman's wisdom."

Taran had now come to the cottage door. He warmly greeted the weaver-woman and admired the cloak she had given Eilonwy. "Hevydd and the Commot smiths labour to make arms for us," he said. "But warriors need warmth as much as weapons. Alas, we have no garments like this."

"Do you think a weaver-woman less hardy than a metalsmith?" Dwyvach replied. "As you wove patiently at my loom, now my loom will weave the more quickly for you. And in every Commot, shuttles will fly for the sake of Taran Wanderer."

Heartened by the weaver-woman's promise, the companions departed from Gwenith. A short distance from the Commot, Taran caught sight of a small band of horsemen riding towards him at a quick pace. Leading them was a tall youth who shouted Taran's name and raised a hand in greeting.

With a glad cry Taran urged Melynlas to meet the riders. "Llassar!" Taran called, reining up beside the young man. "I did not think you and I would meet so far from your sheepfold in Commot Isav."

"Your news travels ahead of you, Wanderer," Llassar replied. "But I feared you would deem our Commot too small and pass it by. It was I," he added, with shy hesitation that could not altogether conceal his boyish pride, "it was I who led our folk to find you."

"The size of Isav is no measure of its courage," Taran said, "and I need and welcome all of you. But where is your father?" he asked, glancing at the band of riders. "Where is Drudwas? He would not let his son journey so far without him."

Llassar's face fell. "The winter took him from us. I grieve for him, but honour his memory by doing what he himself would have done."

"And what of your mother?" Taran asked, as he and Llassar trotted back to join the companions. "Was it her wish, too, that you leave home and flock?"

"Others will tend my flock," the young shepherd answered. "My mother knows what a child must do and what a man must do. I am a man," he added stoutly, "and have been one since you and I stood against Dorath and his ruffians that night in the sheepfold."

"Yes, yes!" cried Gurgi. "And fearless Gurgi stood against them, too!"

"I'm sure all of you did," Eilonwy remarked sourly, "while I was curtsying and having my hair washed on Mona. I don't know who Dorath is, but if I should ever meet him, I promise you I'll make up for lost time."

Taran shook his head. "Count yourself lucky you don't know him. I know him all too well, to my sorrow."

"He has not troubled us since that night," said Llassar. "Nor will he likely trouble us again. I have heard he has left the Commot lands and roves westwards. He has put his sword in the service of the Death-Lord, it is said. Perhaps it may be so. But if Dorath serves anyone, it is himself."

"Your service freely given counts more for us than any the Lord of Annuvin could hire," Taran said to Llassar. "Prince Gwydion will be grateful to you."

"To you, rather," said Llassar. "Our pride is not in fighting but in farming; in the work of our hands, not our blades. Never have we sought war. We come now to the banner of the White Pig because it is the banner of our friend, Taran Wanderer."

The weather worsened as the companions continued through the valley, and the growing host of Commot men forced them to travel at a slower pace. The days were too short for the work to be done, but Taran rode grimly on. Beside him galloped Coll, uncomplaining and ever cheerful. His broad face, reddened and roughened by cold and wind, was nearly hidden by the collar of a great fleece-lined jacket. A sword belt of heavy iron links bound his girth, and at his back hung a round shield of ox hide. He had found a helmet of beaten metal, but deemed it did not sit as comfortably on his bald crown as had his old leather cap.

Taran was grateful for Coll's wisdom and gladly sought his counsel. It was Coll who gave him the thought, as the marshalling camps grew crowded, to send smaller, swifter bands directly to Caer Dathyl rather than march from one Commot to the next with a force becoming ever more cumbersome. Llassar, Hevydd, and Llonio would not leave Taran's vanguard and stayed ever close at hand; but when Taran wrapped himself in a cloak and stretched on the frozen ground for rare moments of sleep, it was Coll who stood watch over him.

"You are the oaken staff I lean on," Taran said. "More than that." He laughed. "You are the whole sturdy tree, and a true warrior."

Coll, instead of beaming, looked wryly at him. "Do you mean to honour me?" he asked. "Then say, rather, I am a true grower of turnips and a gatherer of apples. No warrior whatever, save that I am needed thus for a while. My garden longs for me as much as I long for it," Coll added. "I left it unready for winter, and for that I will pay a sorry reckoning at spring planting."

Taran nodded. "We shall dig and weed together, true grower of turnips — and true friend."

The watch fires flickered in the night. The horses stirred in their lines. About them, a mass of deep shadows, dark against darkness, lay sleeping warriors. The chill wind cut at Taran's face. He was suddenly weary to the marrow of his bones. He turned to Coll.

"My heart, too, will be easier," he said, "when I am once more an Assistant Pig-Keeper."

Word reached Taran that King Smoit had raised a strong host among the cantrev lords and was now turning northwards. The companions learned, too, that certain of Arawn's liege men had sent war parties across Ystrad to harass the columns marching to Caer Dathyl. Taran's task thus grew more urgent, but he could do no more than press onwards with all haste.

The companions made their way to Commot Merin. For Taran, it had been among the fairest he had known in all his wanderings. Even now, amid the tumult of warriors arming, of neighing horses and shouting riders, the white, thatched cottages of the little village seemed to stand peaceful and apart. Taran galloped past the common fields ringed by hemlocks and tall firs. His heart laden with memories, he reined up at a familiar hut, whose smoking chimney betokened a warm fire within. The door opened and out stepped a stocky, hale old man garbed in a coarse, brown robe. His iron-grey hair and beard were cropped short; his eyes were blue and undimmed.

"Well met," he called to Taran, and raised a huge hand crusted with dried clay. "You left us a wanderer, and return to us a war-leader. As for your skill in the latter, I have heard much. But I ask: have you forgotten your skill at my potter's wheel? Or have I wasted my own to teach you?"

"Well met, Annlaw Clay-Shaper," Taran answered, swinging down from Melynlas and fondly clasping the old potter's hand. "Wasted, in truth," Taran laughed, following him into the hut, "for the master had a clumsy apprentice. My skill lacks, but not my memory. What little I could learn, I have not forgotten."

"Show me then," challenged the potter, scooping a handful of wet clay from a wooden trough.

Taran smiled sadly and shook his head. "I halted only

to give you greeting," he replied. "Now I labour with swords, not earthen bowls." Nevertheless, he paused. The hearth light glowed on shelves and rows of pottery, of graceful wine jars, of ewers handsomely and lovingly crafted. Quickly he took the cool clay and cast it upon the wheel which Annlaw had begun to spin. Time pressed him too closely, Taran knew; yet, as the work took form under his hands, for a moment he put down the burden of his other task. The days turned back and there was only the whirring of the wheel and the shape of the vessel born from the shapeless clay.

"Well done," said Annlaw in a quiet voice, then added, "I have heard how smiths and weavers throughout the Commots labour to give you arms and raiment. But my wheel cannot forge a blade nor weave a warrior's cloak, and my clay is shaped only for peaceful tasks. Alas, I can offer nothing that will serve you now."

"You have given me more than all the others," Taran answered, "and I treasure it the most. My way is not the warrior's way; yet, if I do not bear my sword now, there will be no place in Prydain for the usefulness and beauty of any craftsman's handiwork. And if I fail, I will have lost all I gained from you."

His hand faltered, for Coll's booming voice was shouting his name. Taran sprang from the wheel and, while Annlaw watched in alarm, strode out of the hut, calling a hurried farewell to the potter. Coll had already drawn his sword. In another moment, Llassar joined them. They galloped towards the camp a little way from Merin, as Coll hastily told Taran that the guard posts had sighted a band of marauders.

"They shall soon be upon us," Coll warned. "We should meet them before they attack our trains. As a grower of turnips, I advise you to rouse a company of bowmen and a troop of good riders. Llassar and I shall try to lure them with a smaller band of warriors."

Quickly they set their plans. Taran rode ahead, calling to the horsemen and foot soldiers, who hastily caught up their weapons and followed after him. He ordered Eilonwy and Gurgi to safety among the carts; without waiting to hear their protests, he galloped towards the fir forest covering the outlying hills.

The marauders were armed more heavily than Taran had expected. Swiftly they sped down from the snow-covered ridge. At a sign from Taran, the bowmen raced and flung themselves into a shallow gully, and the mounted warriors of the Commots wheeled to the charge. The riders met in a turmoil of hooves and clash of blades. Then Taran raised his horn to his lips. At the piercing, echoing signal, the bowmen rose from cover.

It was, Taran knew, little more than a skirmish, but sharply and hotly fought; only at the last, when Coll and

Llassar's band drew off many of the foe, did the marauders break and flee. Yet it was the first battle Taran had commanded as a war-leader for the Prince of Don. The Commot folk had carried the day, with none of their number slain and only a few wounded. Though weary and drained of his strength, Taran's heart pounded with the joy of victory as he led the exulting warriors from the forest and back towards Merin.

As he reached the hill crest he saw flames and black billows of smoke.

At first he thought the camp had taken fire. He spurred Melynlas at top speed down the slope. As he drew closer, as the crimson tongues wavered against the sky in a bloodstained sunset and the smoke rose and spread over the valley, he saw it was the Commot burning.

Outdistancing the troop, he galloped into Merin. Among the warriors from the camp, Taran glimpsed Eilonwy and Gurgi struggling vainly to quench the flames. Coll had reached the village before him. Taran leaped from Melynlas and ran to his side.

"Too late!" Coll cried. "The raiders circled and stormed the Commot from the rear. Merin has been put to the torch, and its folk to the sword."

With a terrible cry of grief and rage Taran ran past the blazing cottages. The thatch had burned from the roofs, and many of the walls had split and crumbled. So it was with the hut of Annlaw, which still smouldered, its ruins open to the sky. The body of the potter lay amid the rubble. Of the work of his hands, all had been shattered. The wheel was overturned, the bowl flung into pieces.

Taran dropped to his knees. Coll's hand was on his shoulder, but he drew himself away and stared up at the old warrior. "Did I shout for victory today?" he whispered hoarsely. "Small comfort to folk who once befriended me. Have I served them well? The blood of Merin is on my hands."

Later, Llassar spoke apart with Coll. "The Wanderer has not stirred from the potter's hut," the shepherd murmured. "It is harsh enough for each man to bear his own wound. But he who leads bears the wounds of all who follow him."

Coll nodded. "Leave him where he chooses to be. In the morning he will be well," he added, "though likely never healed."

By midwinter, the last of the war bands had been gathered and the Commot warriors dispatched to Caer Dathyl. In addition to a troop of horsemen, Llassar, Hevydd, and

Llonio still remained with Taran, who now led the companions northwestwards through the Llawgadarn Mountains. The force was strong enough to safeguard their progress without slowing their journey.

Twice, marauders attacked them, and twice Taran's followers beat them off, inflicting heavy losses. The raiders, having learned a bitter lesson from the war-leader who rode under the ensign of the White Pig, slunk away and dared harass the columns no further. The companions passed swiftly and unhindered through the foothills of the Eagle Mountains. Gurgi still proudly carried the banner which snapped and fluttered in the sharp winds lashing from the distant heights. In his cloak Taran bore one talisman: a shard of broken, fire-blackened pottery from Commot Merin.

At the approaches to Caer Dathyl outriders brought word of still another host. Taran galloped ahead. In a vanguard of spearmen rode Fflewddur Fflam.

"Great Belin!" shouted the bard, urging Llyan to Taran's side. "Gwydion shall rejoice! The northern lords arm in all their strength. When a Fflam commands — yes, well, I did rally them in the name of Gwydion, otherwise they might not have been so willing. But no matter, they're on the way. I've heard King Pryderi, too, has raised his armies. Then you'll see a battle host! I daresay half the western cantrevs are under his command.

"Oh, yes," Fflewddur added, as Taran caught sight of Glew perched atop a swaybacked, heavy-hoofed, grey horse, "the little fellow is still with us."

The former giant, busily gnawing a bone, gave Taran only a scant sign of recognition.

"I didn't know what to do with him," said Fflewddur in a low voice. "I hadn't the heart to send him packing, not in the midst of all the armies gathering. So, here he is. He's not stopped whining and complaining; his feet hurt one day, his head the next, and little by little all the rest of him. Then, in between meals, he goes on with his endless tales of when he was a giant.

"The worst of it is," Fflewddur went on in some dismay, "he's given my ears such a drubbing that he's made me almost feel sorry for him. He's a small-hearted weasel, always was and always will be. But as you stop and think on it — he *has* been considerably mistreated and put upon. Now, when Glew was a giant..." The bard interrupted himself and clapped a hand to his forehead. "Enough! Any more of his chatter, and I'll end by believing it! Come, join us," he cried, unslinging his harp from the tangle of bows, quivers of arrows, bucklers, and leather strapping he bore on his back. "All friends are met again. I'll play you a tune to celebrate and keep us warm at the same time!"

Cheered by the bard's music, the companions journeyed on together. Soon the high fortress of Caer

Dathyl rose golden in the winter sunlight. Its mighty bastions sprang up like eagles impatient for the sky. Beyond the walls and circling the fortress stood the camps and flag-decked pavilions of lords come in allegiance to the Royal House of Don. Yet it was not the sight of the banners or the wind-tossed emblems of the Golden Sunburst that made Taran's heart leap, but rather the knowledge that the companions and Commot warriors had come safe to the end of one journey, to warmth and rest for a little time at least. Safe — Taran halted in his own thoughts, and the memories returned: of Rhun King of Mona who slept silent before the gates of Caer Cadarn; of Annlaw Clay-Shaper. And his fingers clenched around the fragment of pottery.

CHAPTER TEN

The Coming of Pryderi

Caer Dathyl was an armed camp, where sparks like blazing snowflakes whirled from the armourers' forges. Its wide-spreading courtyards rang with the iron-shod hooves of war horses and the sharp notes of signal horns. Although the companions were now safe within its walls, the Princess Eilonwy declined to exchange her warrior's rough garb for more befitting attire. The most she agreed to do – and that reluctantly – was to wash her hair. A few ladies of the court remained, the rest having been sent to the protection of the eastern strongholds, but Eilonwy flatly refused to join them in their spinning and weaving chambers.

"Caer Dathyl may be the most glorious castle in Prydain," she declared, "but court ladies are court ladies wherever you find them, and I've had more than my share with Queen Teleria's hen flock. Listening to their giggling and gossiping – why, it's worse than having your ears tickled with feathers. For the sake of being a princess, I've been half-drowned with soapy water and that's quite enough. My hair still feels clammy as seaweed. As for skirts, I'm comfortable just as I am. I've lost all my robes, anyway, and I certainly shan't bother to be measured for others. The clothes I'm wearing will do very nicely."

"No one has considered asking *me* whether *my* clothing is suitable," Glew testily remarked, although the former giant's garments, as far as Taran could judge, were in better repair than those of the companions. "But shabby treatment is something I've grown used to. In my cavern, when I was a giant, things were much different. Generosity! Alas, gone for ever. Now, I recall when the bats and I..."

Taran had neither strength to dispute Eilonwy's words nor time to listen to Glew's. Gwydion, hearing of the companions' arrival, had summoned Taran to the Hall of Thrones. While Coll, Fflewddur, and Gurgi secured gear and provisions for the warriors who had journeyed with them, Taran followed a guard to the Hall. Finding

Gwydion in council with Math Son of Mathonwy, Taran hesitated to draw closer; but Math beckoned to him, and Taran dropped to one knee before the white-bearded ruler.

The High King touched Taran's shoulder with a hand withered but firm, and bade him rise. Not since the battle between the Sons of Don and the armies of the Horned King had Taran been in the presence of Math Son of Mathonwy, and he saw the years had borne heavily upon the monarch of the Royal House. The face of Math was even more careworn and more deeply furrowed than Dallben's; upon his brow the Gold Crown of Don seemed a cruel burden. Yet his eyes were keen and filled with stern pride. More than this, Taran sensed a sorrow so profound that his own heart grieved and he bowed his head.

"Face me, Assistant Pig-Keeper," Math commanded in a quiet voice. "Fear not to see what I myself know. The hand of death reaches towards mine and I am not loath to clasp it. I have long heard the horn of Gwyn the Hunter, that summons even a king to his barrow home.

"With a glad heart would I answer it," said Math, "for a crown is a pitiless master, harsher than the staff of a pig-keeper; while a staff bears up, a crown weighs down, beyond the strength of any man to wear it lightly. What grieves me is not my death; but at the end of my life to see blood spilled in the land where I sought only peace.

"You know the history of our Royal House; how, long ago, the Sons of Don voyaged in their golden ships to Prydain, and how men sought their protection against Arawn Death-Lord, who had robbed Prydain of its treasures and turned a rich, fair land into a fallow field. Since then the Sons of Don have stood as a shield against the ravages of Annuvin. But if the shield now be riven, then all shatters with it."

"We will gain victory," Gwydion said. "The Lord of Annuvin stakes all upon this venture, but his strength is also his weakness, for it may be that if we withstand him his power will shatter for ever.

"Good tidings, as well as bad, have reached us," Gwydion went on. "For the latter, King Smoit and his armies are embattled in the Valley of Ystrad. He cannot, for all his boldness, force his way farther northwards before the end of winter. He serves us well, nonetheless, since his warriors engage the traitors among the southern lords and keep them from joining Arawn's other battle hosts. The more distant kings in the northern realms come but slowly, for winter, to them, is a sterner enemy than Arawn.

"More heartening is word that the armies of the West Domains are but a few days' march from our stronghold. Scouts have already sighted them. It is a host greater than any ever raised in Prydain, and Lord Pryderi himself commands them. He has done all I prayed from him, and more. My only unease is that Arawn's liege men may give battle and turn him aside before he reaches Caer Dathyl. But, if so, we will have warning and our forces will march to relieve him.

"Not least among our good tidings," Gwydion added, a smile lightening his drawn and haggard features, "is the coming of Taran of Caer Dallben and the warriors led from the Commots. I have counted heavily upon him and shall ask still more."

Gwydion spoke then of the ordering of Taran's horsemen and unmounted troops. The High King listened closely and nodded his agreement.

"Go now to your task," said Math to Taran. "For the day is come when an Assistant Pig-Keeper must help bear the burden of a king."

During the days that followed, the companions served wherever need arose and as Gwydion commanded them. Even Glew shared, to some extent, in the toil — at the forceful insistence of Fflewddur Fflam and not through his own choice. Under the watchful eye of Hevydd the Smith, the former giant was set to pumping bellows at the forges, where he complained unstintingly of the blisters on his pudgy hands.

More than a stronghold of war, Caer Dathyl was a place of memory and a place of beauty. Within its bastions, in the farther reaches of one of its many courtyards, grew a living glade of tall hemlocks, and among them rose mounds of honour to ancient kings and heroes. Halls of carved and ornamented timbers held panoplies of weapons of long and noble lineage, and banners whose emblems were famed in the songs of the bards. In other buildings were stored treasures of craftsmanship sent from every cantrev and Commot in Prydain; there, Taran saw, with a twinge of heart, a beautifully fashioned wine jar from the hands of Annlaw Clay-Shaper.

The companions, when spared from their tasks, found much of wonder and delight. Coll had never before journeyed to Caer Dathyl, and he could not help staring at the archways and towers that seemed to soar higher than the snow-capped mountains beyond the walls.

"Handsome enough it all is," Coll admitted, "and skilfully worked. But the towers make me think my apple trees should have been better pruned. And left to itself, my garden will yield as much as the stones of this courtyard."

A man called out to them and beckoned from the doorway of one of the smallest and plainest of the buildings. He was tall, his face deeply weathered; white hair fell straight to his shoulders. The coarse cloak of a warrior was flung loosely about him, but neither sword nor dagger hung at his unadorned leather belt. As the companions followed, Fflewddur ran instantly to the man and, heedless of the snow, dropped to one knee before him.

"Perhaps it is I who should bow to you, Fflewddur Fflam Son of Godo," said the man, smiling, "and ask your pardon." He turned to the companions and offered his hand. "I know you better than you know me," he said, and laughed good-heartedly at their surprise. "My name is Taliesin."

"The Chief Bard of Prydain," said Fflewddur, beaming proudly and delightedly, "made me a gift of my harp. I am in his debt."

"Of that I am not altogether sure," replied Taliesin, as the companions followed him through the doorway and into a spacious chamber lightly furnished with only a few sturdy seats and benches, and a long table of curiously grained wood that glowed in the light of a cheery hearthfire. Ancient volumes, stacks and rolls of parchment crowded the walls and rose high into the shadows of the raftered ceiling.

"Yes, my friend," the Chief Bard said to Fflewddur, "I have thought often of that gift. Indeed, it has been a little on my conscience." He gave the bard a glance that was shrewd but filled with kindness and good humour. Taran at first had seen Taliesin as a man of many years; now he could not guess the Chief Bard's age. Taliesin's features, though heavily lined, seemed filled with a strange mixing of ancient wisdom and youthfulness. He wore nothing to betoken his rank; and Taran realized there was no need for such adornment. Like Adaon, his son and Taran's companion of long ago, his eyes were grey, deep-set, seeming to look beyond what they saw, and there was, in the Chief Bard's face and voice, a sense of authority far greater than a war-leader's and more commanding than a king's.

"I knew the nature of the harp when I gave it to you," the Chief Bard continued. "And, knowing your own nature, suspected that you would always have some small trouble with the strings."

"Trouble?" cried Fflewddur. "Why, not a bit of it! Never for a moment. . ." Two strings broke with such a twang that Gurgi started in alarm. Fflewddur's face turned bright red to the tip of his nose. "The fact of the matter is, as I stop and think on it, the old pot's forced me to tell the truth — ah, shall we say a little more than I normally would. But it does occur to me, telling the truth has harmed no one, least of all myself."

Taliesin smiled. "Then you have learned no small lesson. Nonetheless, my gift was in jest, yet not entirely in jest. Say, perhaps, the laughter of one heart to another. But you have borne it willingly. Now I offer you any of your choosing," he said.

Taliesin pointed to a shelf where stood a number of harps, some newer, some older, and a few even more gracefully curved than the instrument Fflewddur carried. With a joyful cry Fflewddur hastened to them, lovingly touching the strings of each, admiring the workmanship, turning from one to the next and back again.

He hesitated some while, looking dolefully at the newly broken strings of his own instrument, at the scratches and chips scarring the frame. "Ah – yes, well, you honour me," he murmured in some confusion, "but this old pot is quite good enough for me. There are times, I swear, when it seems to play of itself. None has a better tone; when the strings are fixed, that is. It sits well against my shoulder. Not to belittle these, but what I mean is that somehow we're used to each other. Yes, I'm most grateful. But I would not change it."

"So be it, then," replied Taliesin. "And you others," the Chief Bard added to the companions, "you have seen many of the treasures of Caer Dathyl. But have you seen its true pride and priceless treasure? It is here," he said quietly, gesturing around the chamber. "Stored in this Hall of Lore is much of Prydain's ancient learning. Though Arawn Death-Lord robbed men of their craft secrets, he could not gain the songs and sayings of our bards. Here they have been carefully gathered. Of your songs, my gallant friend," he said to Fflewddur, "there are not a few.

"Memory lives longer than what it remembers," Taliesin said. "And all men share the memories and wisdom of all others. Below this chamber lie even richer troves." He smiled. "Like poetry itself, the greater part is the more deeply hidden. There, too, is the Hall of Bards. Alas, Fflewddur Fflam," he said regretfully, "none but a true bard may enter it. Though one day, perhaps, you shall join our company."

"Oh, wisdom of noble bards!" cried Gurgi, his eyes popping in wonderment. "It makes humble Gurgi's poor tender head spin with whirlings and twirlings! Alas, alas, for he has no wisdom! But he would go without crunchings and munchings to gain it!"

Taliesin put a hand on the creature's shoulder. "Do you believe you have none?" he said. "That is not true. Of wisdom there are as many patterns as a loom can weave. Yours is the wisdom of a good and kindly heart. Scarce it is, and its worth all the greater.

"Such is that of Coll Son of Collfrewr," said the Chief Bard, "and added thereto the wisdom of the earth, the gift of waking barren ground and causing the soil to flourish in a rich harvest."

"My garden does that labour, not I," said Coll, his bald crown turning pink from both pleasure and modesty. "And as I recall the state I left it in, I shall wait long for another harvest, whatever."

"I was to gain wisdom on the Isle of Mona," put in Eilonwy. "That's why Dallben sent me there. All I learned was needlework, cooking, and curtsying."

"Learning is not the same as wisdom," Taliesin interrupted with a kindly laugh. "In your veins, Princess, flows the blood of the enchantresses of Llyr. Your wisdom may be the most secret of all, for you know without knowing; even as the heart itself knows how to beat."

"Alas for my own wisdom," said Taran. "I was with your son when he met his death. He gave me a brooch of great power, and while I wore it there was much I understood and much that was hidden grew clear to me. The brooch is no longer mine, if indeed it ever truly was. What I knew then I remember only as a dream lingering beyond my power to grasp it."

A shade of sorrow passed over Taliesin's face. "There are those," he said gently, "who must first learn loss, despair, and grief. Of all paths to wisdom, this is the cruellest and longest. Are you one who must follow such a way? This even I cannot know. If you are, take heart nonetheless. Those who reach the end do more than gain wisdom. As rough wool becomes cloth, and crude clay a vessel, so do they change and fashion wisdom for others, and what they give back is greater than what they won."

Taran was about to speak, but the notes of a signal horn rang from the Middle Tower and shouts rose from the guardians at the turrets. Watchers cried out the sighting of King Pryderi's battle host. Taliesin led the companions up a broad flight of stone steps where, from atop the Hall of

Lore, they could see beyond the walls of the fortress. Taran could only glimpse the gleam of the westering sun on ranks of spears across the valley. Then, mounted figures broke away from the mass and galloped across the snow-flecked expanse. Against the rolling meadow, the leading rider of the band was sharply brilliant in trappings of crimson, black, and gold, and sunlight sparkled on his golden helmet. Taran could watch no longer, for guards were shouting the names of the companions, summoning them to the Great Hall.

Catching up the banner of the White Pig, Gurgi hastened after Taran. The companions quickly made their way to the Great Hall. A long table had been placed there and at its head sat Math and Gwydion. Taliesin took his seat at Gwydion's left hand; to the right of Math stood an empty throne draped in the colours of King Pryderi's Royal House. On either side sat the Lords of Don, cantrev nobles, and war-leaders.

Circling the Hall stood the banner-bearers. Gurgi glanced about him in dismay; but, at a gesture from Gwydion, stationed himself among their ranks. The poor creature looked miserable and frightened out of his wits amid the stern warriors. But the companions turned encouraging eyes on him, and Coll gave him such a huge grin and a wink that Gurgi raised both his shaggy head and his makeshift banner more proudly than any in the Great Hall.

Taran himself felt no little awkwardness when Gwydion signalled for him and the others to take seats among the war-leaders; though Eilonwy, still in her warrior's attire, smiled happily and seemed altogether at ease.

"Humph!" she remarked. "I think Hen Wen shows up quite handsomely and, for the matter of that, better than most. You were so disagreeable about whether her eyes were blue or brown. Well, I can tell you that's not half as strange as the colours they've embroidered on some of these banners…"

Eilonwy stopped speaking, for the portals were flung open and King Pryderi entered the Great Hall. All eyes were on him as he strode towards the council table. He was as tall as Gwydion himself, and his rich raiment glittered in the torchlight. He wore no helmet; what Taran had seen was his long hair that shone like gold about his brow. At his side hung a naked sword, for it was Pryderi's custom, as Fflewddur whispered to Taran, never to sheathe his blade until the battle was won. Behind him followed falconers with hooded hawks on their gauntleted wrists; his war-leaders, with the crimson hawk emblem of the House of Pwyll broidered on their cloaks; and spearmen flanking his banner-bearer.

Gwydion, clothed like the Chief Bard in the unadorned garb of a warrior, stood to greet him, but Pryderi halted before reaching the council table and, arms folded, glanced around the Hall at the waiting cantrev kings.

"Well met, Lords," Pryderi cried. "I rejoice to see you gathered here. The threat of Annuvin makes you forget your own quarrelling. Once more you seek protection from the House of Don, like fledglings who see the hawk circling."

Pryderi's voice rang with unhidden scorn. Taran started at the king's harsh speech. The High King himself looked sharply at Pryderi, though when he spoke his words were measured and grave.

"How, then, Lord Pryderi? It is I who summoned all who will stand with us, for the safety of all hangs in the balance."

Pryderi smiled bitterly. His handsome features were flushed, whether from the cold or from anger Taran could not tell; blood tinged Pryderi's high, jutting cheekbones as he threw back his golden head and unflinchingly met the High King's stern glance.

"Would any have lingered, seeing himself threatened?" replied Pryderi. "Men answer only to an iron fist or a sword at their throats. Those who bear you allegiance bear it as it serves their own ends. Among themselves, these cantrev rulers are never at peace, but each is eager to profit from the weakness of his neighbour. In their secret hearts, are they less evil than Arawn Death-Lord?"

Shocked and angry murmurs arose from the cantrev kings. Math silenced them with a quick gesture.

Then Gwydion spoke: "It is beyond any man's wisdom to judge the secret heart of another," he said, "for in it are good and evil mixed. But these are matters to ponder over the embers of a campfire, as you and I have often done; or at the end of feasting, when the torches burn low. Our deeds now must safeguard Prydain. Come, Pryderi Son of Pwyll. Your place awaits you and we have many plans to set."

"You summoned me, Prince of Don," Pryderi answered in a hard voice. "I am here. To join you? No. To demand your surrender."

CHAPTER ELEVEN

The Fortress

For an instant, none could speak. The silver bells at the legs of Pryderi's hawks tinkled faintly. Then Taran was on his feet, sword in hand. The cantrev lords shouted in rage and drew their weapons. Gwydion's voice rang out, commanding them to silence.

Pryderi did not move. His retainers had unsheathed their blades and formed a circle about him. The High King had risen from his throne.

"You sport with us, Son of Pwyll," Math said severely,

"but treachery is no fitting matter for a jest."

Pryderi still stood with arms folded. His golden features had turned the colour of iron. "Call it no jest," he answered, "and call me no traitor. This I have pondered long and closely and with much anguish of heart. I see now that only thus can I serve Prydain."

Gwydion's face was pale and his eyes grave. "You speak in madness," he replied. "Have Arawn's false promises blinded you to reason? Would you tell me that a liege man of the Death-Lord serves any realm but Annuvin?"

"To me, Arawn can promise nothing I do not already have," answered Pryderi. "But Arawn will do what the Sons of Don failed to do: make an end of endless wars among the cantrevs, and bring peace where there was none before."

"The peace of death and the silence of mute slavery," Gwydion replied.

Pryderi glanced around him. A harsh smile was on his lips. "Do these men deserve better, Lord Gwydion? Are all their lives together worth one of ours? Crude brawlers, these self-styled cantrev lords are unfit to command even their own households.

"I choose what is best for Prydain," he continued. "I do not serve Arawn. Is the axe the woodcutter's master? At the end, it is Arawn who will serve me."

With horror, Taran listened to the words of Pryderi as he spoke to the High King.

"Lay down your arms. Abandon the weaklings who cling to you for protection. Surrender to me now. Caer Dathyl shall be spared, and yourself, and those I deem worthy to rule with me."

Math raised his head. "Is there worse evil?" he said in a low voice, his eyes never leaving Pryderi's. "Is there worse evil than that which goes in the mask of good?"

One of the cantrev lords sprang from the council table and, blade upraised, started towards Pryderi.

"Touch him not!" cried Math. "We welcomed him as a friend. He leaves as a foe, but he shall leave in safety. If any harm even a feather of his hawks, his life shall be forfeit."

"Go from here, Pryderi Son of Pwyll," Gwydion said, the coldness of his tone making his wrath the more terrible. "The anguish of my heart is no less than yours. Our comradeship is broken. Between us there can be only the lines of battle, and our only bond the edge of a sword."

Pryderi did not answer, but turned on his heel and with his retainers strode from the Great Hall. Even as he mounted his steed, word spread among the warriors, and they stared silently in their ranks. Beyond the walls, the armies of Pryderi had lit torches and the valley flamed as far as Taran's eyes could see. Pryderi rode through the gates, the crimson and gold of his raiment shimmering like the torches themselves, and galloped towards his waiting host. Taran and the Commot men watched, sick with despair; they knew, as did all in Caer Dathyl, this glittering king, like a hawk of death, had snatched their lives and now bore them away with him.

Gwydion had expected the army of King Pryderi to attack at first light, and the men in the fortress had laboured through the night making ready to withstand a siege. When dawn came, however, and the pale sun rose higher, Pryderi's battle host was seen to have advanced but little. From the wall Taran, Fflewddur, and Coll, with the other war-leaders, watched beside Gwydion, who stood scanning the valley, and the heights that dipped in raw ridges to the flatlands. Snow had not fallen for some days; gullies and rocky fissures still held streaks and patches of white, caught among the crevices like tufts of wool, but the broad meadowland was, for the most part, clear. The dead turf showed in dark brown splotches under a ragged mantle of frost.

Scouts had brought word that Pryderi's warriors held the valley in strength and barred passage through the battle lines. Nevertheless, no skirmishers or flanking columns of riders had been seen abroad; and the scouts judged, from this and the stationing of the foot soldiers and horsemen, that the attack would come in a great forward thrust, as an iron fist against the gates of Caer Dathyl.

Gwydion nodded. "Pryderi means to strike in all his might, though it will cost him dearly. He can be spendthrift of his warriors' lives, knowing we can ill afford to pay an equal price."

He frowned and rubbed his chin with the back of a gauntleted hand. His green eyes narrowed as he peered across the valley, and his lined face was that of a wolf scenting his enemies. "Lord Pryderi is arrogant," he murmured.

Gwydion turned sharply to the war-leaders. "I will not await a siege. To do so would be sure defeat. Pryderi has numbers enough to flood us like a wave. We shall give battle beyond the fortress, and we ourselves strike against the wave before it reaches its crest. Math Son of Mathonwy shall command the inner defences. Only at the last, if so it must be, shall we retreat into the fortress and make our stand there."

Gwydion looked for a long moment at the halls and towers of the castle which had now caught the early rays of the sun. "The Sons of Don raised Caer Dathyl with their own hands, and built it not only as a shield against Arawn but as safeguard for the wisdom and beauty of Prydain. As I would do all in my power to shatter Pryderi, so would I do all to spare Caer Dathyl from destruction. It may be that we shall gain both these ends, or lose both. But we must battle not as sluggish oxen but as swift wolves and cunning foxes."

The Prince of Don spoke quickly to the war-leaders, clearly setting forth the tasks of each. Taran felt uneasy. As a boy, he had dreamed of taking a man's place among men; and, as a boy, had deemed himself well fit to do so. Now, amid the grizzled, battle-wise warriors, his strength seemed feeble, his knowledge clouded. Coll, sensing Taran's thoughts, winked encouragement at him. The stout old farmer, Taran knew, had paid close heed to Gwydion's words. Yet Taran guessed that a corner of Coll's heart was distant, busily and happily occupied with his turnip patch.

For much of the morning Pryderi's host held its position while the defenders quickly formed their own battle lines. At some distance beyond the walls of Caer Dathyl, heavily armed fighting men stood ready to bear the brunt of Pryderi's assault, and there Gwydion himself would command. Fflewddur and Llyan, with Taliesin and a company of warrior-bards, held a post across the valley. The Commot horsemen would be at the flank of Pryderi's attack and it would be their task to slash into the onrushing wave, to disrupt and sap the strength from the enemy's arms.

Taran and Coll at the head of one troop, and Llassar entrusted to lead another, galloped to their stations. Gurgi, silent and shivering in his huge jacket, drove the banner of the White Pig into the frozen ground to mark a rallying point. Taran felt the eyes of the foe watching every move, and an odd impatience, mixed with fear, drew him taut as a bowstring.

Gwydion, astride Melyngar, rode up for a last glance at the ordering of the Commot men, and Taran cried out to him, "Why does Pryderi wait? Does he mock us? Are we no more than ants to him, labouring at a hill, to be crushed at his pleasure?"

"Patience," answered Gwydion in a tone that was both the reassurance of a friend and the command of a war-leader. "You are swords added to my hands," Gwydion went on. "Do not let yourselves be shattered. Move quickly, stay not overlong in one fray, but start many." He took Taran's hand and Coll's and Gurgi's. "Farewell," Gwydion said almost brusquely, then spun Melyngar about and rode swiftly to his warriors.

Taran watched him until he had disappeared, then turned towards the distant towers of Caer Dathyl. Eilonwy, along with Glew, had been commanded to remain in the fortress under the High King's protection. Taran strained his eyes in the vain hope of glimpsing her on the walls. What she might feel for him he was no more sure than he had been at Caer Dallben; but, despite his resolve, he was on the verge of speaking his own heart fully. Then, suddenly, like a man swept away in a flood, he had been caught up in the rallying of warriors, without even a moment to say his farewell. Yearning pierced him, and regret for his unspoken words was an iron hand gripping his throat.

He started and clenched the reins as Melynlas, snorting a white cloud, began to paw the ground. At a glance he saw Pryderi's host had risen and was surging into the valley. The battle was upon him.

It came quickly, not as the slow-cresting wave Taran had expected. First was a swelling sea of shouting men. The Sons of Don were not awaiting Pryderi's charge but were racing ahead to grapple with the attacking foe. He saw Gwydion on the rearing white shape of Melyngar. But Taran could not tell the instant of the first clash of arms; for in a moment, instead of two tides there was only one that spun and shifted in a great convulsion, a whirlpool of spears and swords.

Taran sounded his horn and, as an answering shout came from Llassar, clapped heels into the flanks of Melynlas. Coll and the Commot horsemen spurred their mounts after him. From a swift canter the powerful legs of Melynlas stretched to a gallop. The stallion's muscles heaved beneath him and Taran, sword raised, plunged into the sea of men. His head spun and he gasped as if drowning. He realized he was terrified.

Around him swirled the faces of friends and foes. He glimpsed Llonio flailing right and left. The man's makeshift helmet bobbed over his eyes, his long legs were drawn up high in the stirrups, and he looked like nothing so much as a scarecrow come to life; yet, where Llonio passed, attackers fell as wheat to a scythe. Hevydd's burly frame rose like a wall in the midst of the combat. Of Llassar there was no sign, but Taran thought he could hear the young shepherd's high-pitched battle cry. Then a curious roaring reached his ears and he knew Llyan, with Fflewddur, had entered the fray. In another moment, aware of nothing beyond the blade in his hand, Taran was locked in a blind madness with warriors who thrust at him and whose blows he strove to return.

Again and again Taran and the Commot horsemen slashed deep into the attackers' flanks, then wheeled to gallop free of the iron whirlpool, only to plunge back again. In a flash of clarity Taran saw glittering gold and crimson. It was King Pryderi on a black charger. Taran struggled to engage him. For an instant their eyes met, but the Son of Pwyll made no attempt to answer the challenge of a ragged horseman. Instead, he looked away and continued to press ahead. Then he was gone. And it was Pryderi's scornful glance that stung Taran more sharply than the blade which swung up from the mass of foemen to lash across his face.

Once, the swell of the armed tide flung Taran to the fringes of the battle. He caught sight of Gurgi's banner and tried to rally the horsemen around it. A trough had opened up amid Pryderi's ranks. In another moment a horse pounded towards him: Lluagor. A warrior armed with a long lance clung to the steed's back.

"Go back!" Taran shouted at the top of his voice. "Have you lost your wits?"

Eilonwy, for it was she, half-halted. She had tucked her plaited hair under a leather helmet. The Princess of Llyr smiled cheerfully at him. "I understand you're upset," she shouted back, "but that's no cause to be rude." She galloped on.

For a time, Taran could not believe he had really seen her.

Moments later, he was struggling against a band of warriors who slashed at Melynlas, threw themselves against the stallion's flanks, and strove to bear down horse and rider. Taran was vaguely aware of someone seizing his mount's bridle and dragging him to the side. Pryderi's warriors fell away. Free of the press, he turned in the saddle and blindly flung up his sword against the new attacker.

It was Coll. The stout farmer had lost his helmet. His bald crown was as scratched as if he had plunged headlong into briars. "Save your sword for your foes, not your friends!" he cried.

Taran's surprise left him speechless an instant, before he stammered, "You saved my life, Coll Son of Collfrewr."

"Why, so perhaps I did," replied Coll, as though the idea had suddenly come to him.

They looked at each other and burst out laughing like a pair of fools.

Only towards sundown, when the sky itself seemed streaked with blood, did Taran gain a new sense of the battle. Gwydion's warriors, flung across the path of Pryderi's advance, had met the full fury of their attackers. The hosts of Pryderi had faltered, as though stumbling over their own dead. The wave had crested and hung poised. Now a fresh wind surged over the valley. Taran's heart leaped as shouts of renewed strength rang from the warriors of Don. They pressed onwards, driving all before them. Taran sounded his horn and with the Commot horsemen galloped to join the sweeping tide.

The ranks of the enemy parted like a shattered wall. Taran clutched at his reins, Melynlas reared and whinnied in alarm. A shudder of horror racked the valley. Taran saw and understood why, even before the rising current of outcries reached his ears.

"The Cauldron-Born! The deathless warriors!"

The men of Pryderi fell back to let them pass, as if in fearful homage. In ghastly silence, their pace neither fast nor slow, the Cauldron-Born filled the breach and the valley rang with the tread of their heavy boots. In the crimson haze of the dying sun their faces seemed all the more livid. Their eyes were cold and dull as stones. Unfaltering, the column of deathless warriors bore towards Caer Dathyl. Among them, slung about with ropes, they carried an iron-capped battering ram.

The foemen flanking the Cauldron-Born now turned suddenly to launch a fresh attack against the Sons of Don. In horror, Taran realized why Pryderi had delayed, and understood his arrogance. Only now had the traitor king's plan reached its fulfilment. Behind the long column of Cauldron-Born fresh fighting men streamed from the heights. For Pryderi, the long day of battle had been no more than a mockery. The slaughter had begun.

At the fortress, bowmen and spearmen of the inner defences thronged the walls. The mute Cauldron-Born did not falter in the storm of arrows. Though every shaft found its mark, the foe moved steadily onwards, pausing only to rip the arrows from their unbleeding flesh. Their features showed neither pain nor anger, and no human cry, no shout of triumph, passed their lips. From Annuvin they had journeyed as though from the grave, their task only to bring death, unpitying, implacable as their own lifeless faces.

Against the pounding of the battering ram the gates of Caer Dathyl groaned and trembled. The massive hinges loosened, while echoes of the driving ram shuddered through the fortress. The portal splintered, the first breach gaped like a wound. The Cauldron-Born gathered strength once more to force the ram forwards. The gates of Caer Dathyl shattered and fell inwards. Trapped between the ranks of Pryderi's warriors, the Sons of Don fought vainly to reach the fortress. Sobbing with fury and despair, Taran, helpless, saw the Cauldron-Born stride past the broken gates.

Before them stood Math the High King. He was attired in the raiment of the Royal House, belted with links of gold, and on his brow glittered the Gold Crown of Don. About his shoulders was a cloak of fine white wool, wrapped as though it were a burial garment. Outstretched, his withered hand gripped a naked sword.

The deathless warriors of Annuvin halted as if at the faint stirring of some clouded memory. The moment passed and they strode on. The field of battle was silent now; an awed hush had fallen even upon the men of Pryderi. The High King did not turn away as the Cauldron-Born drew closer, his eyes fixed theirs as he raised his sword defiantly. Unflinching he stood in pride and ancient majesty. The first of the pallid warriors was upon him. Grasping the flashing sword in his frail hands, the High King swung it downwards in a sweeping blow. The warrior's blade turned it aside, and the Cauldron-Born struck heavily. King Math staggered and dropped to one knee. The mass of mute warriors pressed forwards, their weapons thrusting and slashing. Taran covered his face with his hands and turned away weeping, as Math Son of Mathonwy fell and the iron-shod boots of the Cauldron-Born pressed their relentless march over his lifeless body. From the dark hills then there rose the long notes of a hunting horn, trembling, echoing among the crags, and a shadow seemed to brush the sky above the fortress.

Now behind the Cauldron-Born the men of Pryderi streamed through the broken gates, while waves of attackers drove the remnants of Gwydion's army into the heights, scattering them amid snow-filled gullies. From Caer Dathyl came new claps of thunder as the ram of the Cauldron-Born turned against the walls to breach them in turn. Flames rose above the Great Hall, above the Hall of Lore, and from the Middle Tower was unfurled the crimson hawk of Pryderi.

Beside it, blotting out the dying sun, spread the black banner of Arawn Lord of Annuvin.

Caer Dathyl had fallen.

CHAPTER TWELVE

The Red Fallows

All night the destruction raged and by morning Caer Dathyl lay in ruins. Fires smouldered where once had stood the lofty halls. The swords and axes of the Cauldron-Born had levelled the hemlock grove near the mounds of honour. In the dawn light the shattered walls seemed bloodstained.

The army of Pryderi, denying even the right of burial for the slain, had driven the defenders into the hills east of Caer Dathyl. It was there, amid the turmoil of the makeshift camp, the companions found one another again.

Faithful Gurgi still bore the banner of the White Pig, though its staff had been broken and the emblem slashed almost beyond recognition. Llyan, with Fflewddur beside her, crouched in the scant shelter of a rocky outcropping; her tail twitched and her yellow eyes still glowed with anger. Hevydd the Smith built a campfire, and Taran, Eilonwy, and Coll tried to warm themselves at the embers. Llassar, though sorely wounded, had lived through the battle; but the enemy had taken cruel toll of the Commot men. Among those who lay stark and silent on the trampled battleground was Llonio Son of Llonwen.

One of the handful of survivors from the inner defences of the fortress was Glew. A warrior of Don, finding him lost and dazed outside the walls, had taken pity on his plight and brought him to the camp. The former giant was pathetically glad to rejoin the companions, though he was still too terrified and trembling to do more than mumble a few words. With a torn cloak over his shoulders, he huddled beside the fire and held his head in his hands.

Gwydion stood alone. For long, his eyes did not leave the column of black smoke staining the sky above the ruins of Caer Dathyl. At last he turned away and ordered all who had lived out the day to assemble. Taliesin came to stand before them and, taking up Fflewddur's harp, sang a lament for the slain. Amid the black pines the voice of the Chief Bard rose in deep sorrow, yet it was sorrow without despair; and while the notes of the harp were heavy laden with mourning they held, as well, the clear strains of life and hope.

As the melody died away Taliesin lifted his head and spoke quietly. "Each broken stone of Caer Dathyl shall be a mark of honour, and the whole valley a resting place for Math Son of Mathonwy and all our dead. But a High King still lives. As I honour him, so do I honour all who stand with him." He turned to Gwydion and bowed deeply. The warriors drew their swords and cried out the name of the new King of Prydain.

Gwydion then called the companions to him. "We meet only to part," he said. "Pryderi's victory gives us one choice and one hope. Though messengers bear tidings of our defeat to King Smoit and his army, and to the lords of the north, we dare not await their help. What we do must be done now. Not even a battle host ten-fold greater than Pryderi's can withstand the Cauldron-Born. Army after army can be flung against them only to swell the ranks of the slain.

"Yet here is the seed of our hope," Gwydion said. "Never in man's memory has Arawn sent his deathless warriors abroad in such strength. He has taken the greatest risk for the greatest gain. And he has triumphed. But his triumph has become his moment of greatest weakness. Without the Cauldron-Born to guard it, Annuvin lies open to attack. So must we attack it."

"Do you believe then that Annuvin is unguarded?" Taran asked quickly. "Are there none other who serve Arawn?"

"Mortal warriors, surely," replied Gwydion, "and perhaps a force of Huntsmen. But we have strength to overcome them, if the Cauldron-Born do not reach Annuvin in time to aid them."

Gwydion's blood-streaked face was hard as stone. "They must not reach Annuvin. As their power dwindles the longer they remain beyond the Death-Lord's realm, so at all cost must they be hindered, delayed, turned from every path they follow."

Coll nodded. "Indeed, this is our only hope, whatever. And it must be done quickly, for now they will seek to return quickly to their master. But can we overtake them once they are on the march? Can we hinder them and at the same time mount our own attack against Annuvin?"

"Not if we journey as one army," Gwydion said. "Instead, we must separate into two bands. The first, and smaller, shall be given as many horses as can be spared, and hasten to pursue the Cauldron-Born. The second shall make their way to the Valley of Kynvael and follow its river northwest to the coast. The valley land is gentle, and with forced marches the sea can be reached in no more than two days.

"The sea must aid our venture," Gwydion continued,

"for Pryderi can too easily forbid our army's journey overland." He turned to Taran. "Math Son of Mathonwy spoke to you of the ships that bore the Sons of Don from the Summer Country. These vessels were not abandoned. Still seaworthy, they have ever been held ready against a day of need. A faithful folk guard them in a hidden harbour near the mouth of the River Kynvael. They will carry us to the western shore of Prydain, close to the bastions of Annuvin itself.

"Two men alone have knowledge of the harbour," Gwydion added. "One was Math Son of Mathonwy. The other is myself. I have no choice but to lead the seaward march. As for the other journey," he said to Taran, "will you accept to lead it?"

Taran raised his head. "I serve as you command."

"I do not command this," replied Gwydion. "I order no man to such a task against his will. And all who follow you must do so willingly."

"Then it is my will to do so," Taran answered.

The companions murmured their assent.

"The vessels of the Sons of Don are swift," Gwydion said. "I ask you to delay the Cauldron‑Born but a little while. Yet all hangs on that little."

"If I fail," Taran said, "how shall I send word to you? Should the Cauldron warriors reach Annuvin ahead of you, your plan cannot succeed and you must turn back."

Gwydion shook his head. "There can be no turning back, for there is no further hope. Should either of us fail, all our lives are forfeit."

Llassar, Hevydd, and all the other Commot folk chose to follow Taran. With them were joined the surviving warriors of Fflewddur Fflam, and together they made the greater portion of Taran's band. To the surprise of the companions, Glew chose to ride with them.

The former giant had recovered from his fright, at least enough to regain much of his customary peevishness. He had, however, regained all of his appetite and demanded food in great quantity from Gurgi's wallet of provisions.

"I've had my fill of being dragged here and there by the scruff of the neck," said Glew, licking his fingers, "and now I'm either to be put on a ship or cast among a herd of horses. Very well, I shall take the latter, for at least it's not so wet and salty. But I assure you I would have agreed to neither, when I was a giant."

Fflewddur glowered at the former giant and spoke apart with Taran. "It seems we're doomed, on top of all our other woes, to put up with that whining weasel at every step. And I can't help feeling that in the back of that puny little mind he's hoping somehow to feather his own nest." The bard shook his head and gave Taran a sorrowful look. "But are any nests left to feather? There's not a safe place even for Glew to hide his head."

Gurgi had tied the banner of the White Pig to a new staff, but he sighed mournfully at the tattered emblem. "Poor piggy!" he cried. "None can see her now, for she is torn into threadings and shreddings!"

"I promise to sew another, " Eilonwy said. "As soon as…" She stopped abruptly and said no more as she climbed astride Lluagor. Taran saw her troubled glance. The Princess of Llyr would wait long, he feared, before her hands worked with an embroidery needle. And, unspoken but in his heart was the dread that none of them might see Caer Dallben again. At the end of their grim race, death might be the only prize.

Armed with spears and swords, the warriors were mounted and ready. With a last farewell to Gwydion, the companions rode westwards from the hills.

It was Coll's judgement that the Cauldron-Born would march directly to Annuvin, following the straightest and shortest path. At the head of the column winding its way from the snow-swept heights, Llassar rode beside Taran. The skill of the young shepherd eased their passage, and he guided them swiftly towards the lowlands, unseen by Pryderi's army which had begun to withdraw from the valley around Caer Dathyl.

For some days they journeyed, and Taran began to fear the retreating Cauldron-Born had outdistanced them. Nevertheless, they could do no more than press on as quickly as possible, southwards now, passing through long stretches of sparse woodland.

It was Gurgi who first sighted the deathless warriors. The creature's face went grey with fright as he pointed to an expanse of rock-strewn plain. Glew blinked, choked, and could barely swallow the food he was munching. Eilonwy watched silently, and the bard gave a low whistle of dismay.

Taran's heart sank at the sight of the column moving like a long serpent over the flatlands. He turned questioningly to Coll. "Can we hold them off at all?"

"A pebble can turn aside an avalanche," said Coll, "or a twig stem a flood."

"I daresay," muttered Fflewddur. "What happens to the twig or pebble afterward I should rather not think about."

Taran was about to signal the warriors to form for an attack, but Coll took his arm. "Not yet, my boy," he said. "First, I would be sure of the path these creatures of Arawn mean to follow to Annuvin. If the twig is to do its work, it must be well placed."

For the rest of that day and the morning of the next,

the companions matched their own progress with the march of the Cauldron-Born, sometimes ahead, sometimes along their flank, but never losing sight of the deathless warriors. It seemed to Taran that the Cauldron-Born had slowed their pace. The dark column moved without faltering, but heavily, as though burdened. He spoke of this to Coll, who nodded in satisfaction.

"Their strength ebbs a little," Coll said. "Time works for us, but I think we must soon work for ourselves."

They had reached a broad, winding belt of wasteland where grassless earth stretched away on either side as far as the eye could see. The dead ground was broken, rutted as though ill-ploughed, slashed with deep ditches and gullies. No tree, no shrub rose from the dull red earth, and nowhere did Taran see the faintest sign that any growing thing had ever flourished there. He looked at it uneasily, chilled not only by the bitter wind but by the silence that hovered like frozen mist about the lifeless land.

He asked, in a low voice, "What place is this?"

Coll grimaced. "The Red Fallows, it is called now. At the moment," he added wryly, "I fear it is much the way my garden looks."

"I have heard it spoken of," Taran said, "though I believed it to be no more than a traveller's tale."

Coll shook his head. "No traveller's tale, whatever. Men have long shunned it, yet once it was the fairest realm in

Prydain. The land was such that all manner of things would grow, as if overnight. Grains, vegetables, fruits — why, in size and savour the apples from the orchards here would have made mine look like shrivelled windfalls beside them. A prize it was, to be won and held, and many lords fought for its possession. But in the fighting over it, year after year, the hooves of steeds trampled the ground, the blood of warriors stained it. In time the land died, as did those who strove to claim it from their fellows, and soon its blight crept far beyond the battle grounds." Coll sighed. "I know this land, my boy, and it does not please me to see it again. In my younger days I, too, marched with the battle hosts, and left not a little of my own blood in the Fallows."

"Will they never flourish?" Taran asked, looking with dismay at the wasted expanse. "Prydain could be a rich land with the abundance they might bear. It would be a shame worse than bloodshed to leave these fields thus. Would the soil not yield again if it were laboured well?"

"Who can say?" answered Coll. "Perhaps. No man has tilled it for years long past. But for us now that is all by-the-by." He gestured towards the heights rising sharply at the distant edge of the fields. "The Red Fallows stretch along the Hills of Bran-Galedd, southwestwards almost to Annuvin. From here it is the longest but easiest path to Arawn's realm, and if I judge aright the Cauldron-Born will follow it swiftly to their master."

"We must not let them pass," Taran replied. "Here we must make our first stand and hinder them as best we can." He glanced towards the heights. "We must force them into the hills. Among rocks and broken ground, we might set snares or lure them into ambush. It is all we can hope to do."

"Perhaps," said Coll. "Though before you choose, know this: the Hills of Bran-Galedd also give a path to Annuvin, and a shorter one. They rise sharper as they go westwards and turn soon to steep crags. There stands Mount Dragon, the highest peak, guarding the Iron Portals of the Land of Death. It is a harsh passage, cruel and dangerous — more so for us than for the deathless Cauldron-Born. We can lose our lives. They cannot."

Taran frowned anxiously, then said with a bitter laugh, "Indeed, there is no happy choice, old friend. The path of the Red Fallows is easier but longer; the mountain way, harder and shorter!" He shook his head. "I have not the wisdom to decide. Have you no counsel for me?"

"The choice must be yours, war-leader," answered Coll. "Yet, as a grower of turnips and cabbages, I might say if you trust your strength, the mountains may be friend as much as foe."

Taran smiled at him sorrowfully. "Little trust do I put in the strength of an Assistant Pig-Keeper alone," he said after a long moment, "but much in the strength and wisdom of his companions. So be it. We must drive the Cauldron warriors into the hills."

"Know this, too," said Coll. "If such is your choice, it must be done at this place and at all cost. Farther southwards the Fallows widen, the plain grows broad and flat; and there is danger the Cauldron-Born may escape our reach if we fail here."

Taran grinned. "Now that is simple enough for an Assistant Pig-Keeper to understand."

Taran rode back through the column of warriors to tell them of the plan they were to follow. Though he cautioned Eilonwy and Gurgi to hold themselves as far as possible from the fray, he could judge, with little difficulty, that the Princess of Llyr had no intention of heeding his warning. As for Taran himself, the decision he had taken lay heavily on him; his doubts and fears only sharpened as the horsemen rallied at the fringe of woodland and as the moment for their advance across the Fallows drew closer. He felt cold; the wind muttering across the rutted fields seeped through his cloak like an icy flood. He caught sight of Coll, who winked at him and nodded his bald crown in a quick gesture. Taran raised the horn to his lips and signalled the warriors forwards.

At Coll's counsel the companions and each horseman had cut stout branches from the trees. Now, like ants burdened with straws, the column entered the wasteland, struggling across the ruts and gullies. To their right rose the ruins of a wall, some ancient boundary, useless now, whose broken slabs stretched over much of the Fallows' width and ended near the steep ascent of the Hills of Bran-Galedd.

It was there that Taran, with all haste, led the toiling band of warriors. The Cauldron-Born, it seemed to him, had already glimpsed them, for the dark column quickened its own pace, thrusting rapidly across the Fallows. Taran's horsemen had dismounted and raced to fling their branches between the gaps in the wall. The column of Cauldron-Born marched closer. Beside them rode mounted Huntsmen garbed in heavy jackets of wolfskin, the troop captains whose harsh commands reached Taran's ears like the snapping of a lash. Their orders rang in a language unknown to him, but Taran well understood their scornful tone and the brutal laughter that spat from their lips.

As at Caer Dathyl, the Cauldron-Born held their ranks, striding onwards, unwavering. They had drawn their swords from their belts of heavy bronze. The bronze studs covering their leather breastplates glinted dully. Their pallid faces were frozen, as empty as their staring eyes.

Suddenly the horns of the captains screamed like hawks. The Cauldron warriors stiffened, and in another moment lunged forwards at a faster gait, running heavily across the dark red earth.

The men of the Commots leaped to their makeshift barrier of rocks and branches. The Cauldron-Born flung themselves against the ruined wall and strove to clamber upwards. Fflewddur, leaving Llyan with Glew amid the other steeds, had snatched up a long branch and, shouting at the top of his voice, thrust it like a spear into the mass of climbing warriors. Beside him, Gurgi flailed a huge staff, striking desperately at the rising wave. Heedless of Taran's warning outcry, Eilonwy plied her spear and it was under her furious onslaught that the first Cauldron warrior toppled and fell, struggling to regain his footing amid the ranks that streamed silently over him. Taran's band redoubled their efforts, slashing, sweeping, fending off the mute foe with all their strength.

Others among the deathless troops lost their footing as the surging attackers threw themselves blindly against the barrier, only to be struck down by the lashing staves and spear shafts of the Commot men.

"They fear us!" cried the bard in frenzied joy. "See! They turn away! If we can't slay them, Great Belin, we can still push them back!"

In the turmoil of warriors and the shrilling of the Huntsmen's horns, Taran glimpsed the ranks of Cauldron-Born veer from the threatening hedge of spears. His heart leaped. Were the captains indeed fearful of the hindrance, of the waning power of their mute host? Even now the attacking wave seemed weaker, though he could not be sure that it was no more than his hope that made it appear so. No longer was he even sure how long they struggled at the wall. Wearied by the endless thrusts of his spear, he felt it had been for ever, although the sky was still light.

Of a sudden, he realized Fflewddur was right. The silent mass of deathless warriors had fallen back. The Huntsmen captains had taken their decision. Like beasts that find their prey too well hidden, and unworthy of their efforts, the mounted leaders sounded a long, wavering note on their horns. The ranks of Cauldron-Born swung towards the Hills of Bran-Galedd.

Cheers burst from the Commot warriors. Taran spun about to find Coll. But the old warrior was hastening farther along the wall. Taran cried out to him, then in dismay realized what Coll had seen. A band of Cauldron-Born had broken from the main force and now strove to clamber through an undefended breach.

Coll reached it as the first Cauldron warrior had begun to force himself over the stones. The old man was upon him in an instant and, dropping his spear, seized the warrior in his burly arms and flung him downwards. While other Cauldron-Born swarmed to the breach, Coll snatched out his sword and laid about him right and left, heedless of the attackers' hacking and stabbing blades. Shouting in wrath as the weapon shattered in his hands, the stout farmer cast it away and struck out with his heavy fists. The deathless warriors clung to him, striving to pull him into their midst, but he shook them off, ripped a sword from the grasp of a tottering Cauldron-Born, and swung it as if he meant to fell an oak with a single blow.

Taran was at Coll's side in a moment. The horns of the Huntsmen screamed the signal to retreat. Now Taran realized the attack had truly ended with this last convulsion. The Cauldron-Born had begun to scale the heights. The Red Fallows were barred to them.

Coll was bleeding heavily from the head; his fleece-lined coat, bloodsoaked, was slashed and tattered by the blades of the Cauldron-Born. Quickly, Taran and Fflewddur carried him between them to the bottom of the wall. Gurgi, whimpering in distress, hurried to aid them. Eilonwy had torn off her cloak to cushion the old farmer against the harsh stones.

"After them, my boy," Coll gasped. "Give them no rest. The twigs have turned the flood, but it must be turned again, and many times, if you would block the way to Annuvin."

"One stout oak tree has turned it," Taran replied. "Once again, I have leaned on it." He took Coll's work-hardened hands and gently tried to lift him.

Coll's broad face grinned and he shook his head. "I am a farmer," he murmured, "but warrior enough to know my own death wound. Go along, my boy. Carry with you no more burdens than you must."

"What then," answered Taran, "will you have me break the promise I made? That we will dig and weed together?" But the words came painfully as a dagger wound.

Eilonwy, her face drawn, looked anxiously at Taran.

"I had hoped one day to sleep in my own garden," Coll said. "The drone of bees would have pleased me more than the horn of Gwyn the Hunter. But I see the choice was not to be mine."

"The horn of Gwyn does not blow for you," said Taran. "You hear the Cauldron-Born summoned to retreat." Yet even as he spoke, the faint notes of a horn rose above the hills and its dying echoes trembled like shadows over the wasteland. Eilonwy covered her face with her hands.

"See to our plantings, my boy," said Coll.

"We shall both do so," answered Taran. "The weeds will no more stand against you than did Arawn's warriors."

The stout old farmer did not answer. It was a long moment before Taran realized that Coll was dead.

While the grieving companions gathered stones from the ruined wall, with his own hands Taran hollowed out a grave in the harsh earth, allowing none other to aid him in this

task. Even when the humble mound had risen above Coll
Son of Collfrewr, he did not move from it, but ordered
Fflewddur and the companions to press on into the Hills of
Bran Galedd, where he would join them before nightfall.

For long he stood silently. As the sky darkened, at last
he turned away and climbed heavily astride Melynlas. He
halted another moment by the mound of red earth and
rough stones.

"Sleep well, grower of turnips and gatherer of apples,"
Taran murmured. "You are far from where you longed to
be. So, too, am I."

Alone he rode across the darkening Fallows to the
waiting hills.

CHAPTER THIRTEEN

Darkness

In the days that followed, the companions strove to overtake the Cauldron-Born and again fling themselves across the path of the retreating warriors, but their progress was agonizingly slow. Taran knew Coll had spoken truly when he had called the Hills of Bran-Galedd both friend and foe: the rocky troughs and narrow defiles, the sudden drops where the ground fell away sharply into frozen gorges offered the companions their only hope of delaying the deathless host moving onwards like a river of iron. But at the same time, from the high crags of the west, gusts of snow-laden wind battered the struggling band with icy hammers. The winding trails were slippery and treacherous. The ravines held deep pits filled with snow, where horse and rider might founder beyond rescue.

In the hills, Taran's most trusted guide was Llassar. Surefooted, long used to mountain ways, the Commot youth was now shepherd to a different, grimmer flock. More than once, Llassar's keen senses kept the companions from the icy traps of snow-hidden crevices, and he discovered pathways no other eye could see. But the progress of the ragged band was nonetheless slow, and all suffered cruelly from the cold, men and animals alike. Only the great cat, Llyan, showed no concern for the bitter blasts that drove frosty needles against the faces of the companions.

"She seems to be enjoying herself," Fflewddur sighed, huddling in his cloak. He had been obliged to dismount, for Llyan had suddenly taken it into her head to sharpen her huge claws against a tree trunk. "And so should I," he added, "if I had her coat."

Gurgi ruefully agreed. Since entering the hills, the poor creature had grown more and more to resemble a drift of hairy snow. The cold had even stopped Glew's endless whining; the former giant pulled his hood over his face and little could be seen of him but the frostbitten end of his flabby nose. Eilonwy, too, was unwontedly silent. Her heart, Taran knew, was as heavy as his own.

Yet Taran forced himself, as far as he was able, to put grief aside. His dogged pursuit had at last brought his warriors within striking distance of the Cauldron-Born, and now he thought only of the means to slow their march to Annuvin. As at the Red Fallows, the companions laboured to build barriers of tree limbs, and set them across a narrow gorge, toiling until the sweat drenched their garments and froze in the bitter wind. This time the livid warriors overran them, mutely hacking away the branches with their swords. In despair, the men of the Commots clashed hand-to-hand with the oncoming foe; but the Cauldron-Born slashed mercilessly through their ranks. Taran and the Commot men sought to block the way with heavy boulders; but even with the help of Hevydd's mighty arms this labour was beyond their strength, and the toll of the slain only rose higher.

The days were a white nightmare of snow and wind. The nights were frozen with hopelessness, and like exhausted animals the companions found respite amid rocky overhangs and the scant shelter of the mountain passes. Yet concealment served little purpose, the presence of the Commot warriors was known and their movements quickly sighted by the enemy captains. At first, the Cauldron-Born had chosen to disregard the ragged band; now the deathless marchers not only quickened their pace, they swung closer to Taran's riders as though eager to join battle.

This puzzled Fflewddur, who rode beside Taran at the head of the column.

Taran frowned and shook his head grimly. "I understand it all too well," he said. "Their power had waned when they were farther from Annuvin. Closer, it returns to them, and as we grow weaker, they grow stronger. Unless we halt them, one time for all, our efforts will do no more than sap our own strength. Soon," he added bitterly, "we shall defeat ourselves more sharply than Arawn's warriors could ever hope to do."

But he said nothing of another fear that lay in all their hearts. Each passing day showed more clearly the Cauldron-Born were turning south, away from the Hills of Bran-Galedd and once again towards the swifter, easier way of the Red Fallows. With dour satisfaction, Taran judged this to mean the enemy still feared the pursuers and would strive to any lengths to be rid of them.

Snow fell that night, and the companions halted, blinded by the whirling flakes and by their own weariness. Before dawn the Cauldron-Born attacked their camp.

At first, Taran believed only one company of the mute warriors had overrun his outposts. As the Commot warriors sprang to arms amid the terrified shrieking of horses and the clang of blades, he quickly realized the entire enemy column was slashing across his lines. He spurred Melynlas into the fray. Fflewddur, with Glew clinging to his waist, was astride Llyan, who sped in great bounds to join the embattled defenders. Taran had lost sight of Eilonwy and Gurgi among the rush of warriors. Like a ruthless sword, the Cauldron-Born had split the Commot horsemen's ranks and were streaming through unhindered, crushing all who stood against them.

All day the uneven battle raged while the men of the Commots struggled vainly to rally their forces. By dusk the path of the Cauldron-Born was a bloody wake of wounded and slain. In one deadly blow, the Cauldron host had broken free of their pursuers to move swiftly and unfaltering from the hills.

Eilonwy and Gurgi were missing.

Fearful and dismayed, Taran and Fflewddur pressed their way through the shattered remnants of the war band struggling to regain their ranks. Torches had been lit to signal rallying points for the stragglers, who stumbled wounded and bewildered among the bodies of their fallen comrades. Throughout the night Taran searched frantically, sounding his horn and shouting the names of the lost companions. With Fflewddur, he had ridden beyond the battleground, hoping for some sign of either one of them. There was none, and the new snowfall, which began towards dawn, covered all tracks.

By mid-morning, the survivors had gathered. The passage of the Cauldron-Born had taken heavy toll of both mounts and men; of the Commot warriors, one out of three had fallen beneath the swords of the deathless foe; and of the steeds, more than half. Lluagor galloped empty-saddled. Eilonwy and Gurgi were among neither the slain nor the living.

Desperate now, Taran made ready to search through the farther hills. But Fflewddur, his face grave and filled with concern, took Taran's arm and drew him back.

"Alone, you can't hope to find them," warned the bard. "Neither can you spare time nor men for a search party. If we're to stop those foul brutes before they reach the Fallows, we shall have to move with all speed. Your Commot friends are ready to march."

"You and Llassar must lead them," Taran replied. "Once Eilonwy and Gurgi are found, we'll join you somehow. Go quickly. We shall meet soon again."

The bard shook his head. "If that's your command, so be it. But, as I have heard it, Taran Wanderer it was who called the Commot folk to his banner, and for the sake of Taran Wanderer they answered. They followed where you led. For none other would they have done as much."

"What, then," Taran cried, "would you have me leave Eilonwy and Gurgi in danger?"

"It is a heavy choice," Fflewddur said. "Alas, none can lighten it for you."

Taran did not reply. Fflewddur's words grieved him all
the more because of their truth. Hevydd and Llassar had
asked no more than to fight at his side. Llonio had given
his life at Caer Dathyl. There was no Commot warrior who
had not lost kinsman or comrade. If he left them to seek
Eilonwy, would she herself deem his choice good? The
horsemen awaited his orders. Melynlas impatiently pawed
the ground.

"If Eilonwy and Gurgi are slain," Taran said in an
anguished voice, "they are beyond my help. If they live, I
must hope and trust they will find their way to us." He
swung heavily into the saddle. "If they live," he murmured.

Without daring a backward glance at the silent, empty
hills, he rode towards the war band.

By the time the Commot men were on the march again, the
Cauldron-Born had well outdistanced them and were
moving without delay to the foothills of Bran-Galedd. Even
at their fastest pace, halting only for moments of fitful rest,
the Commot riders regained little of the precious time that
had been lost.

Each day Taran strained his eyes for a sign of Eilonwy
and Gurgi, hoping against hope that the princess would
find some means of reaching the war band again. But the

two companions had vanished, and Fflewddur's desperate cheerfulness and assurance that both would appear from one moment to the next rang false and hollow.

At mid-morning on the third day of their march an outrider galloped in with tidings of strange movements in the pine forest at the column's flank. Taran halted his warriors, hastily ordering them to stand ready for combat, then rode with Fflewddur to see for himself. Through the trees a little below him he could make out no more than a vague stirring, as if shadows of branches flickered across the drifts. But in another instant the bard shouted excitedly and Taran quickly sounded his horn.

From the woods tramped a long procession of short, stocky figures. Garbed in white cloaks and hoods, they were all but invisible against the snow, and not until they had begun to move across a bare stretch of rocky ground could Taran distinguish one marcher from the next. Their stout leather boots, laced and bound with thongs, barely showed below their cloaks, and looked like nothing so much as rapidly moving tree stumps. The shapes that bulked on their shoulders or at their waists were, Taran guessed, weapons or sacks of provisions.

"Great Belin!" cried Fflewddur. "If that's who I think it is..."

Taran had already dismounted and was racing down the slope, waving at the bard to follow him. At the head of the band, which seemed to number well over a hundred, trudged a familiar, stumpy figure. Though he, too, was heavily muffled in white, his crimson hair flamed out beyond the fringe of his hood. In one hand he carried a short, heavy-bladed axe, and in the other, a thick staff. He had caught sight of Taran and Fflewddur and strode to meet them.

In another instant the bard and Taran were clasping his hands, pummelling his burly shoulders, and shouting so many greetings and questions that the new arrival clapped his hands to his head.

"Doli!" Taran cried. "Good old Doli!"

"I heard you clearly the first few times," the dwarf snorted. "If I ever doubted you recognized me, you've fully convinced me that you do." He put his hands on his hips and looked up sharply, trying, as always, to appear as gruff as he could. Despite himself his bright red eyes flashed with pleasure and his features broke into a grin, which he tried, without success, to change to his usual scowl.

"You've led us a chase," Doli declared, motioning the warriors to follow Taran up the slope. "We had word you'd gone into the hills, but saw nothing of you until today."

"Doli!" Taran exclaimed, still amazed at the unexpected sight of this long-absent companion. "What good luck brings you to us?"

"Good luck?" grumbled Doli. "Do you call tramping

day and night in snow and wind good luck? All of us Fair Folk are abroad, one place or another — orders of King Eiddileg. Mine were to find you and put myself at your service. No offence, but I could guess that if anybody in Prydain needed help it would turn out to be you. So, here we are."

"Gwystyl has done his work well," Taran said. "We knew he was journeying to your realm, but we feared King Eiddileg might not heed him."

"I can't say he was overjoyed," Doli answered. "In fact, he nearly burst. I was there when our gloomy friend brought word of your plight and I thought my ears would split with Eiddileg's bellowing. Great gawks! Lumbering oafs! Giant clodpoles! All his usual opinions about humans. But he agreed willingly enough despite his bluster. He's really fond of you, no matter what he says. Above all, he remembers how you saved the Fair Folk from being turned into frogs, moles, and whatever. It was the greatest service any mortal ever did for us, and Eiddileg means to repay the debt.

"Yes, the Fair Folk are on the march," Doli continued. "Alas, we came too late to Caer Dathyl. But King Smoit has cause to thank us. There's a host of Fair Folk fighting side by side with him. The northern lords are ready for battle, and we'll take a hand in that, too, you can be sure."

Doli, for all his gruffness, was obviously proud of his own tidings. He had finished, with great relish, an account of one fray in which the Fair Folk had baffled the enemy by making an entire valley so resound with echoes that the foe fled in terror, believing themselves surrounded, and had begun another tale of Fair Folk valour, when he stopped abruptly, seeing the look of concern on Taran's face. Doli listened while Taran told what had befallen the other companions, and it was the dwarf's turn to be grave and thoughtful. When Taran finished, Doli did not reply for a time.

"As for Eilonwy and Gurgi," the dwarf said at last, "I agree with Fflewddur. They'll manage, somehow. And if I know the princess, I wouldn't be surprised to see her galloping up at the head of her own army.

"With the Cauldron‚Born, we're all in bad straits," Doli continued. "Even we Fair Folk can do little against such creatures. All the tricks that would gull a common mortal are useless. The Cauldron‚Born aren't human – I should say they're less than human. They've no memory of what they were, no fear, no hope – nothing can touch them." The dwarf shook his head. "And I see that any victory we might gain elsewhere would be wasted unless we find some way to deal with that spawn of Annuvin. Gwydion is quite right. If they aren't stopped – well, my friends, among us we'll have to do it, and that's flat."

By this time the Fair Folk band had reached Taran's lines and a murmur of wonder spread through the ranks of the Commot men. All had heard of the skill and prowess of King Eiddileg's fighting forces, but none had seen them face to face. Hevydd the Smith marvelled at their axes and short swords, pronouncing them sharper and better tempered than any he could make. For their own part, the Fair Folk seemed not the least uneasy; the tallest of Eiddileg's warriors stood barely higher than Llassar's knee, but the Fair Folk soldiers looked on their human comrades with the friendly indulgence they might show to overgrown children.

Doli patted Llyan's head and the huge animal purred happily in recognition. The sight of Glew, hunched on a rock and staring sourly at the new arrivals, brought a cry of surprise from the crimson-haired dwarf. "Whoever — or whatever — is that? It's too big for a toadstool and too small for anything else!"

"I'm glad you asked," replied Glew. "It's a tale I'm sure you will find most interesting. I was once a giant, and my present unhappy state comes, no more and no less, from a complete lack of concern from those —" he looked dourly at Taran and the bard "— who might have been expected to show at least a small amount of consideration. My kingdom — yes, I would appreciate it if you addressed me as King Glew — was the finest cavern, with the finest bats, on the Isle of Mona. A cavern so vast. . ."

Fflewddur clapped his hands to his ears. "Leave off,

giant! Enough! We've no time for your prattle about caverns and bats. We know you've been ill-used. You've told us so yourself. Believe me, a Fflam is patient, but if I could find a cavern I'd pop you into it and leave you there."

Doli's face had turned deeply thoughtful. "Caverns," the dwarf muttered. He snapped his fingers. "Caverns! Hear me well," he said quickly. "No more than a day's march from here – yes, I'm sure of it – there's a Fair Folk mine. The best gems and precious stones are gone, and Eiddileg's had no one working there as long as I can remember. But I think we can get into it. Of course! If we follow the main shaft it should bring us out almost at the edge of the Red Fallows. You'll catch up with the Cauldron-Born in no time at all. With all our warriors together we'll stop them one way or another. How, I don't know. That doesn't matter for the moment. We'll cross that bridge when we come to it."

Doli grinned broadly. "My friends, you're with Fair Folk now. When we do something, it's done right. The first half of your worries are over. The second half," he added, "might be something else again."

For the first time since leaving Caer Dallben, Glew appeared in good spirits. The idea of anything resembling a cavern seemed to cheer him, although the result of his improved temper was a further spate of rambling tales about his own feats as a giant. However, after a hard day and night of marching, when Doli halted at the sheer face of a high cliff, the former giant began glancing about fearfully. His nose twitched and his eyes blinked in dismay. The entrance to the ancient mine towards which the dwarf beckoned was no more than a fissure in the rock, barely wide enough for the horses, overhung with icicles glistening like sharp teeth.

"No, no," stammered Glew. "This doesn't compare with my realm on Mona. Not half the size. No, you can't expect me to go stumbling around a shabby den like this."

He would have drawn back had not Fflewddur taken him by the collar and dragged him along.

"Have done, giant!" cried the bard. "In you go with the rest of us." But Fflewddur himself seemed none too eager to lead Llyan through the rocky crevice. "A Fflam is valiant," he murmured, "but I've never been fond of underground passages and all such. No luck with them. Mark my words, we'll be grubbing like moles before we're through."

At the mouth of the cavern Taran halted. Beyond this point there was no hope of finding Eilonwy. Once more he battled the wish of his heart to seek her again before she would be for ever lost to him. With all his strength he fought to wrench these thoughts from his mind. But when at last he ruthlessly forced himself to follow the bard, it was as though he had left all of himself behind. He stumbled blindly into the darkness.

At Doli's orders the warriors had fashioned torches. These they now lit, and in the flickering light Taran saw the dwarf had brought them into a shaft that dipped gradually downwards. Its walls of living rock rose no higher than Taran's upraised hands. Dismounted, the Commot men led their fearful horses past sharp outcroppings and over broken stones.

This, Doli explained, was not the mine itself, but only one of many side tunnels the Fair Folk had used when carrying sacks of gems above ground. Indeed, as the dwarf foretold, the passageway soon grew much wider and the rocky ceiling soared three times Taran's height. Narrow platforms of wood, one above the other, followed the walls on either side, though many had fallen into disrepair and the beams had tumbled in a heap over the earthen floor. Lengths of half rotted timbers shored up the archways leading from one gallery to the next, but of these some had partly crumbled, forcing warriors and steeds to pick their way most cautiously over or around the piles of rubble. The air was stifling after the icy wind above ground, and hung heavy with ancient dust and decay. Echoes flitted like bats through the long abandoned chambers as the war band moved in a wavering file, with torches raised high above their heads. The twisting shadows seemed to muffle the sound of their footsteps; only the piercing whinny of a frightened steed broke the silence.

Glew, who had not left off his complaining since entering the mine, gave a sharp cry of surprise. He stooped and snatched something from the ground. In the flare of his torch, Taran saw the former giant held a glittering gem as big as a fist.

Fflewddur had seen it, too, and he sternly ordered, "Put that down, little man. This is a Fair Folk trove, not that bat-ridden cave of yours."

Glew clutched his find to his chest. "It's mine!" he squealed. "None of *you* saw it. If you had, you'd have kept it for yourselves."

Doli, who had glanced at the gem, snorted scornfully. "It's rubbish," the dwarf said to Taran. "No Fair Folk craftsman would waste his time on it. We use better quality than that to mend a roadbed. If your mushroom-faced friend wants to burden himself, he's more than welcome."

Without waiting to be told twice, Glew hastily thrust the gem into the leather pouch dangling at his side, and his flabby features took on an expression Taran had seen only when the former giant was in the midst of a meal.

From then on, as the companions progressed steadily through the mine, Glew's beady eyes darted everywhere and he strode forwards with unwonted energy and interest. The former giant was not disappointed, for soon the torchlight glinted on other gems half-buried in the ground or protruding from walls. Glew fell upon them instantly, scrabbling away with his pudgy fingers and popping the glittering crystals into his sack. With each new find he grew more excited, giggling and mumbling to himself.

The bard looked pityingly at him. "Well," he sighed, "the little weasel has at last sniffed out something to profit himself. Much good it may do him once we're above ground again. A handful of rocks! The only use I can see is if he throws them at the Cauldron-Born."

But Glew, absorbed in gathering as many gems as quickly as he could, paid no heed to Fflewddur's remarks. In little time the former giant's pouch was crammed with jewels of bright red and brilliant green, with gems clear as water or, in their glittering depths, flecked with gold and silver.

Taran's thoughts were not on the abandoned riches of the mine, although the jewels seemed to grow more plentiful as the long column of warriors made their way farther into the tunnel. As far as Taran could judge, it was no later than midday, and already the companions had journeyed a considerable distance. And, as the tunnel widened and the path straightened, their pace gained even more speed.

"Easy as whistling," declared Doli. "Another day and a half at most and we'll come above ground at the Fallows."

"It's our only hope," Taran said, "and, thanks to you, the best hope we've had. But the Fallows trouble me. If the land is barren we'll have little protection for ourselves, and little means to hinder the Cauldron-Born."

"Humph!" cried Doli. "As I told you, you're dealing with Fair Folk now, my lad. When we set to a task there's nothing paltry or small about it. You'll see. Something will come to hand."

"Speaking of paltry and small," interrupted Fflewddur, "where is Glew?"

Taran halted and quickly looked around. At first he saw nothing of the former giant. He lifted his torch and called Glew's name. A moment later he caught sight of him and ran forward in alarm.

Glew, in his search for treasure, had clambered up to one of the wooden platforms. Just above the arch leading to the next chamber a sparkling gem as big as his own head was embedded amid the rocks; Glew, having swung precariously to a narrow ledge, was trying with all his might to dislodge it.

Taran cried out to him to come down, but Glew tugged and heaved all the harder. Dropping the reins of Melynlas, Taran was about to swing up after him, but Doli seized his arm.

"Don't do it!" snapped the dwarf. "The beams won't hold you." He whistled through his teeth and signalled two of the Fair Folk warriors to climb to the platform which, under Glew's furious struggle with the gem, had begun to sway dangerously. "Hurry!" Doli shouted. "Bring that idiot down here!"

Just then Glew's pouch, already filled to bursting, tore apart. The gems streamed down in a glittering shower and Glew, with a yell of dismay, spun around to clutch at them. His foothold slipped, he clawed frantically at the platform and as he did so the arch gave way beneath him. Now shrieking not for his lost jewels but for his life, Glew flailed wildly and caught one of the swaying timbers. With a crash he toppled to earth. Behind him the archway lurched, the ceiling rumbled. Glew picked himself up and scuttled madly from the hail of falling stones.

"Back!" Doli shouted. "Back! All of you!"

The horses reared and whinnied as the warriors strove to turn them. With an earsplitting crack, the upper platforms collapsed, an avalanche of boulders and broken beams thundered into the gallery. Blinding, choking dust filled the tunnel; the mine seemed to shudder all along its length, then settle into deathly silence.

Shouting for Doli and Fflewddur, Taran stumbled to the heap of wreckage. None of the warriors or animals had been caught in it; behind them, the tunnel had held firm and kept them safe. But the way forward was hopelessly blocked.

Doli had scrambled onto the heap of stones and wood and was tugging at the end of a long beam. But after a moment he stopped, breathless, and turned a despairing face to Taran. "It's no good," he gasped. "If you want to keep on we'll have to dig our way through."

"How long?" Taran asked urgently. "How much time dare we lose?"

Doli shook his head. "Hard to say. Even with Fair Folk it will be a long task. Days, very likely. Who knows how far the damage has gone?" He snorted angrily. "You can thank that half-witted, undersized, two-legged toadstool of a giant for it!"

Taran's heart sank. "What then?" he asked. "Must we retrace our steps?" From the expression on Doli's grimy face, he feared what the dwarf's answer would be.

Doli nodded curtly. "We're badly delayed, no matter what. But if you want my advice, I say turn around and go back. Make our way to the Fallows above ground as best we can. The whole mine is weakened now; there'll be more cave-ins, or I'll miss my guess. Next time we may not be so lucky."

"Lucky!" moaned the bard, who had slumped down on a rock. He put his head in his hands. "Days wasted! The Cauldron-Born will be in Annuvin before we have another chance at them. The only luck that would suit me now would be to see that greedy weasel under a pile of his own worthless gems!"

Glew, meanwhile, had ventured to crawl from under one of the remaining platforms. His garments were torn, his pudgy face smeared with dust.

"Days wasted?" he wailed. "Cauldron-Born? Blocked-up tunnels? But has any one of you stopped to consider I've just lost a fortune? My gems are gone, all of them, and you don't give it a second thought. I call that selfish. Selfish! There's no other word for it."

CHAPTER FOURTEEN

Daylight

The Princess Eilonwy was doubly angry. First, she was lost; second, she was a prisoner. Swept away from Taran and Fflewddur during the attack, she would surely have fallen among the slain had not Gurgi dragged her from the fray. When the assault had shifted beyond them, she had stumbled blindly, with Gurgi at her side, over the darkening crags. At nightfall, when they could search no longer for Taran, Gurgi had found a shallow cave where they crouched and shivered until first light. During the next day, as the two companions sought Taran's trail, the marauders had suddenly leaped upon them.

Biting, kicking, and scratching, Eilonwy struggled vainly to free herself from the burly man who had seized her. Another had flung Gurgi to the ground and, with dagger drawn, set his knee in the small of the hapless creature's back. In a trice the two companions were bound hand and foot and hoisted like mealsacks on their assailant's shoulders. Eilonwy had no idea of the direction in which she was being carried, but in a little while she glimpsed a campfire flickering through the gathering dusk and hunched around it a ruffianly band of a dozen or more.

The man squatting nearest the fire looked up. Garbed in dirty sheepskins and a rough cloak, he was heavy-faced and stubble-bearded, his long hair yellowish and tangled.

"I sent you for game, not prisoners," he called out hoarsely. "What have you found?"

"Lean pickings," answered Eilonwy's captor, dropping his furious burden to the turf beside Gurgi. "A brace of churls, for what they may be worth."

"Nothing, very likely." The heavy-faced man spat in the fire. "You should have slit their gullets and spared yourself the burden." He climbed to his feet and strode to the companions. With a grimy, broken-nailed hand he seized Eilonwy by the throat as if he meant to throttle her. "Who are you, boy?" he demanded in a grating voice. His cold blue eyes narrowed. "Who do you serve? What ransom will you bring? Answer quickly when Dorath asks a question."

At the sound of the name Eilonwy caught her breath. Taran had spoken of Dorath. From Gurgi's terrified whimpering she judged he, too, had recognized the outlaw.

"Answer!" Dorath cried with a curse. He struck Eilonwy across the face. The girl stumbled and fell, her head singing from the blow. The golden sphere dropped from her jacket. Eilonwy strained at her bonds and tried to fling herself on top of the bauble. A booted foot kicked it from her. Dorath bent and snatched up the sphere, turning it curiously in the firelight.

"What is it?" questioned one of the ruffians, pressing closer to gape at the bauble.

"Gold it is," said another. "Come, Dorath, chop the thing apart and share it out."

"Hands off, you swine," Dorath growled. He thrust the bauble into his sheepskin. Mutters of protest rose from the band, but Dorath silenced them with a glance. He bent down to Eilonwy. "Where did you steal such a trinket, you young thief? Will you keep your head on your shoulders? Then tell me where we can find more treasure like this."

Eilonwy, though furious, kept silent.

Dorath grinned. "You will speak soon enough," he said, "and only wish you had spoken earlier. First, let me see if your fellow has a tongue looser than yours."

Gurgi, teeth chattering violently, had sunk his head deep into his sheepskin coat and tightly hunched his shoulders.

"Do you play turtle with me?" Dorath cried with a harsh laugh. He knotted his thick fingers in Gurgi's hair and jerked the creature's head upright. "Small wonder you hide your face! It's ugly as ever I've seen!"

Dorath stopped suddenly and squinted closer. "Ugly it is, and not one easily forgotten. So ho! We are old friends, you and I. You share my hospitality once more! When last we met, you were comrade to a pig-keeper." He turned his glance on Eilonwy. "But this is not the swineherd."

Dorath gripped Eilonwy's face and roughly turned it from side to side. "This beardless boy..." He grunted in surprise. "What, then? Boy? No boy at all! A wench!"

Eilonwy could no longer contain herself. "Wench indeed! I'm Eilonwy Daughter of Angharad Daughter of Regat Princess of Llyr. I don't like being tied up, I don't like being smacked. I don't like being pawed, and I'll thank you to stop doing all of that immediately!" Despite her bonds she kicked vigorously at the outlaw.

Dorath laughed and drew back a pace. "My memory is that the Lord Swineherd spoke once of you." He gave a mocking bow. "Welcome Princess Vixen. You are a choicer prize than any ransom. A long score lies between Dorath and your pig-keeper. You give me and my company the pleasure of settling a little of it."

"I'll give you the pleasure of setting Gurgi and me loose this very instant," Eilonwy flung at him. "And I shall have my bauble again."

Dorath's face had grown mottled. "You shall go free," he said between his teeth, "after a time, my pretty princess, after a time. When you shall be fitting company for pig-keepers, perhaps you may join the swineherd again. Perhaps he will even recognize your charms, whatever may be left of them."

"Have you considered what will be left of *you* when Taran finds you?" Eilonwy retorted. Until now the Princess of Llyr had kept her self-possession. But she could sense the outlaw's thoughts behind his cold eyes and for the first time she was deeply afraid.

"Lord Swineherd and I will finish our reckoning when the time comes," Dorath replied. Grinning, he bent towards her. "But your time is now."

Gurgi thrashed wildly in his bonds. "Do not harm wise and kindly princess!" he shouted. "Oh, Gurgi will make you pay for hurtful wickedness!" He flung himself against Dorath and tried to sink his teeth into the outlaw's leg.

Cursing, Dorath turned on Gurgi and snatched out his sword. Eilonwy cried aloud.

But before the outlaw could begin his downward stroke a long shape sprang suddenly from the overhanging rocks. Dorath gave a stifled shout. His weapon fell from his hand

and he toppled backwards, the furry shadow snarling and tearing at his throat. At the campfire the other outlaws leaped to their feet and screamed in terror. Grey shadows were all about, closing swiftly on them. Vainly the marauders sought to flee, but on all sides they were flung back, borne to the ground by the force of lean bodies and slashing fangs.

Gurgi began yelling fearfully. "Help, oh help! Oh, evil spirits come to slay us all!"

Eilonwy forced herself upright. Behind her she could feel something sharp gnawing and worrying at her bonds. In another moment her hands were free. She stumbled forwards while the grey shadow tore away the thongs holding her feet. In front of her lay the motionless body of Dorath. Quickly Eilonwy kneeled and drew the bauble from the outlaw's sheepskin jacket. From her cupped hand the sphere shed golden rays on a huge wolf crouching before her. By the campfire she glimpsed other wolves, withdrawing as swiftly as they had come. Behind them, all was silent. Eilonwy shuddered and looked away. The wolves had done their work well.

Gurgi had been freed by a grey she-wolf with a white blaze on her breast and, pleased though he was to be out of the warriors' clutches, he wrinkled his forehead and cast a distrustful glance at his rescuer. The wolf Briavael blinked her yellow eyes and grinned at him. Gurgi, nevertheless, chose to keep his distance.

For her own part, Eilonwy surprisingly felt no fear or uneasiness. The wolf Brynach sat on his haunches, watching her closely. Eilonwy put her hand on the animal's shaggy, muscular neck.

"I hope you know we're trying to thank you," she said, "though I'm not sure whether you understand or not. The only wolves I ever met personally lived far from here in Medwyn's valley."

At this Brynach whined and wagged his tail.

"Well, you do understand that," said Eilonwy. "Medwyn..." She hesitated. "There were two wolves..." She clapped her hands. "It must be! I don't mean to say I can tell one wolf from another, at least not at first glance. But there's something about you that reminds me... In any case, if that's who you are, we're very glad to see you again. We're obliged to you and now we'll be on our way. Though I'm not exactly sure which way our way is, if you see what I mean."

Brynach grinned and showed no sign of leaving. Instead, he remained on his haunches, opened his jaws, and gave a high-pitched bark.

Eilonwy sighed and shook her head. "We're lost and trying to find our companions, but I haven't any idea how to say Assistant Pig-Keeper in wolf speech."

Gurgi, meantime, had picked up his wallet of food and slung it over his shoulder. At last seeing the wolves meant him no harm, he drew a little closer to Brynach and Briavael and looked at them with great interest, while they studied him no less curiously.

Eilonwy turned to Gurgi. "I'm sure they're willing to help us. Oh, if I could only understand them! What good is it being half an enchantress if you can't even tell what a wolf is trying to say to you?" Eilonwy stopped short. "But – but I think I did understand! I must have! There, one of them just said 'Tell us!' I could hear – no, not *hear*; I could feel it!"

She looked at Gurgi in amazement. "It's not words at all. It's like listening without your ears or hearing with your heart. I know it, but I can't imagine how I do. And yet," she added wonderingly, "that's what Taliesin told me."

"Oh, great wisdom!" Gurgi cried. "Oh, clever listenings! Gurgi listens, too, but inside hears only rumblings and grumblings when his poor belly is empty! Oh, sorrow! Gurgi will never hear deep secret things like princess."

Eilonwy had dropped to her knees beside Brynach. Hurriedly she spoke of Taran, of all the companions and what had befallen them. Brynach pricked up his ears and barked sharply. The huge wolf rose from his haunches, shook the snow from his shaggy coat, and with his teeth gently plucked at Eilonwy's sleeve.

"He says we're to follow them," Eilonwy told Gurgi. "Come, we're in safe hands now. Or, should I say paws?"

The wolves padded silently and swiftly, following hidden trails and passages whose existence the girl would have never guessed. The two companions strove to keep up with Brynach's rapid pace; yet often, despite themselves, they were forced to halt and rest. At those times the wolves seemed satisfied to wait patiently until the companions were ready to journey once again. Brynach crouched at Eilonwy's side, his grey head between his paws, seldom drowsing, his ears alert and moving at every faint sound. Briavael, too, served as sentinel and guide, springing lightly to the rocky peaks, sniffing the air; then, with a gesture of her head, beckoning the companions to follow.

Of the rest of the pack Eilonwy saw little. Now and then, however, she would awaken from a brief slumber to find the wolves sitting in a protective circle about her. Soon the lean grey animals would vanish into the shadows while Brynach and Briavael alone remained. The girl shortly became aware the wolves were not the only creatures in the Hills of Bran Galedd. Once she glimpsed a large company of bears lumbering in single file along a ridge. They halted a moment, peered curiously, then resumed their march. In the cold, clear air she heard the barking of foxes in the distance and other sounds which might have been echoes or answers to some unknown signal.

"They're scouting all through the hills," Eilonwy whispered to Gurgi, pointing to a bare summit where a tall stag had suddenly appeared. "I wonder how many other bands of outlaws are roaming around. If the bears and wolves have anything to say about it, I somehow don't think there's very many."

The wolf Brynach glanced at her, as though he had overheard Eilonwy's words. He lolled out his tongue and blinked his yellow eyes. Around the sharp rows of gleaming teeth his lips turned slightly in an unmistakable smile.

They continued on their path. At nightfall Eilonwy lit her bauble and held it aloft. The full wolf pack, she saw, had joined them once again, moving in long files on either side of her, just beyond the circle of golden light. The bears, too, were following, and other forest creatures whose presence she sensed rather than saw.

There were, in the Hills of Bran-Galedd, many places of danger and death. Of these, the Princess of Llyr was unaware, for she and Gurgi passed them by unharmed, safe amid the watchful band of silent guardians.

Late in the morning of the next day Briavael, who had spent most of her time scouting the passages ahead, grew excited and eager. The she-wolf barked and leaped atop high-standing rocks where she faced westwards, wagging her tail briskly and urging the companions to greater speed.

"I think they've found Taran!" Eilonwy cried. "I can't quite make out what they're saying, but it sounds very much as if they have. Men and horses! A mountain cat — that must be Llyan! But what are they all doing in this direction? Are they going to the Red Fallows again?"

Neither Eilonwy nor Gurgi could check their impatience to join the companions once more; they refused to halt for food or rest and Brynach frequently had to fasten his teeth in Eilonwy's cloak to keep the girl from taking needless risks among the ever-steepening hills. Soon the travellers reached the rim of a deep mountain cup, and a cry of joy burst from Eilonwy's lips.

"I see them! I see them!" She hastily pointed downwards, into the wide valley. Gurgi had run up beside her and began to leap with excitement.

"Oh, it is kindly master!" he shouted. "Oh, yes, and brave bard! No bigger than ants, but sharp-eyed Gurgi sees them!"

Only by straining her eyes could Eilonwy distinguish the tiny figures, so distant were they. The long descent into the valley, she knew, would take the rest of the day, and she was anxious to reach the companions before nightfall. She was about to scramble down the cliff when she stopped suddenly.

"What can they be doing?" she cried. "They're going straight into that wall of rock. Is it a cave? Look, there's the last horseman. Now I can't see any of them. If it's a cave, it must be the biggest one in Prydain! I don't understand a bit of it. Is there a passage of some kind? Or a tunnel? Oh, that's vexing! You might know an Assistant Pig-Keeper would take it into his head to vanish the moment he's been found!"

Hurriedly, Eilonwy began picking her way down the steep slope. For all her haste the descent seemed endless. Even with the help of Brynach and Briavael the two had gone little more than half the distance by the time the sun had dropped westwards and the shadows had begun to lengthen. Brynach suddenly halted and growled deeply in his throat. His hackles rose and he bared his teeth. The eyes of the wolf were fixed on the valley, and his muzzle twitched uneasily. In another moment, Eilonwy saw what had made Brynach stop. A long column of warriors had appeared and was moving rapidly westwards.

Briavael whined shrilly. From the voice of the she-wolf, Eilonwy sensed fear and hatred. She understood the reason.

"Huntsmen!" the girl cried. "It looks like hundreds of them on the way back to Annuvin. Oh, I hope they don't see Taran's tracks, though he's very likely safe enough where he is."

No sooner had she said this than a movement at the distant wall of rock made her clap a hand to her mouth.

From the deepening shadows she saw, one by one, the tiny figures of Taran and his band reappear.

"No!" Eilonwy gasped. "They're coming out again!"

From her vantage point, the girl could span the valley, and it was suddenly, coldly clear to her that the Commot warriors and the Huntsmen, as yet unseen by one another, were moving closer together.

"They'll be trapped!" Eilonwy cried. "Taran! Taran!"

The echoes died in the vast, snowy expanse. Taran could neither see nor hear her. Darkness had now fallen over the valley, blinding the girl to the inevitable clash of the warrior bands. It was a nightmare in which all action was useless, in which she could only wait for the slaughter bound to come. She felt as though her hands were tied and her voice stifled.

Still calling Taran's name, Eilonwy snatched the bauble from her cloak. She lifted the sphere high. Brighter and brighter it glowed. The wolves turned away fearfully and Gurgi threw his arms over his face. The beams spread and rose towards the clouds, as though the sun itself were bursting from the mountainside. The dark cliffs and black branches of the trees were drenched in light, brilliant and clear. The whole valley had turned bright as noon.

CHAPTER FIFTEEN

The River of Ice

Under the sudden outpouring of golden light, the Huntsmen shouted in alarm and a wave of fear rippled along the marching column as they faltered and fell back into the protection of a deep gorge. Instantly Taran realized how closely he had come to leading the Commot horsemen into a fatal trap, but a cry of joy sprang from his lips.

"Eilonwy!"

He would have urged Melynlas across the valley to

the mountainside had not Fflewddur put out a restraining hand.

"Hold, hold," cried the bard. "She's found us, right enough. Great Belin, there's no mistaking the light from that girl's bauble! She's saved our lives with it. Gurgi's sure to be with her, too; but if you go galloping after them, none of you will get back. We've seen the Huntsmen, and they could hardly help seeing *us.*"

Doli had clambered atop a boulder and stood peering after the retreating Huntsmen. Eilonwy's signal winked out as quickly as it had appeared, and in another moment the winter darkness fell once more over the valley.

"A fine plight!" growled the dwarf. "Of all times to be caught above ground! The mine is useless to us, and there's no other passage within a week's march. Even if there were, we couldn't reach it with an army of Huntsmen blocking the way."

Fflewddur had drawn his sword. "I say attack! Those foul villains had a good scare. They'll have no stomach for a fight now. We'll set upon them without warning. Great Belin, that's something they won't expect!"

Doli snorted at him. "You've left your wits in the mineshaft! Set upon the Huntsmen? Slay one and make the others that much stronger? Even Fair Folk would think twice about attacking those ruffians. No, my friend, it won't answer."

"When I was a giant," put in Glew, "it would have been a simple matter for me to put them all to flight. However, through no fault of my own, times have changed, and I can hardly say they've changed for the better. On Mona, for example, one day I had decided something really had to be done about those impudent bats. It's an interesting tale..."

"Silence, you puny thing," commanded the bard. "You've said enough and done enough."

"That's right, lay all the blame on me," sniffed Glew. "It's my fault Gwydion's sword was stolen, my fault the Cauldron-Born escaped, my fault every other disagreeable thing has happened."

The bard did not deign to answer the former giant's whining outburst. Taran, having ordered the Commot warriors into the relative safety of the tunnel mouth, returned and stood beside the companions.

"I fear Doli is right," Taran said. "By attacking the Huntsmen we can only destroy ourselves. Our strength is slight enough as it is, and we dare not waste it. We have been long delayed, and already may be too late to aid Gwydion. No, we must find some means to make our way despite the Huntsmen."

Doli shook his head. "Still won't answer. They know we're here; they'll know if we try to move. All they need to do is track us. For the matter of that, I'll be surprised if we're not attacked before dawn. Look to your skins, my friends. It may be the last time you'll see them whole."

"Doli," Taran said urgently, "you're the only one who can help us now. Will you spy out the Huntsmen's camp? Learn all you can of their plans. I know how you feel about turning yourself invisible, but. . ."

"Invisible!" shouted the dwarf, clapping a hand to his head. "I knew it would come to that sooner or later. It always does! Good old Doli! Turn invisible! I'm not sure I can do it any more, I've tried to forget how. It hurts my ears. I'd sooner have my head stuffed with hornets and wasps. No, no, out of the question. Ask anything else you like, but not that."

"Good old Doli," Taran said. "I was sure you'd do it."

After a further show of reluctance, which deceived no one except perhaps Doli himself, the crimson-haired dwarf consented to do as Taran had asked. Doli wrinkled his eyes shut, took a deep breath, as though making ready to plunge into icy water, and flickered out of sight. Had it not been for a stifled sound of irritable grumbling, Taran would not have believed Doli to be there at all. Only the faint click of pebbles stirred by unseen feet told Taran that the dwarf had moved from the tunnel towards the enemy lines.

At Doli's orders the Fair Folk troop took guardposts in a wide half-circle beyond the tunnel's mouth, where their sharp eyes and ears could catch any threatening movement or sound. Taran was amazed at how still these warriors remained, silent and nearly as invisible as Doli. Their white garb made them seem no more than ice-covered stones or frosted hummocks under the moon, which had now begun to drift from behind the clouds. The horsemen drowsed among their steeds for warmth. Glew curled up nearby. Just within the tunnel Fflewddur sat with his back against the wall of rock, one hand on his harp, the other resting on the huge head of Llyan, who had stretched out beside him and was gently purring.

Muffled in his cloak, Taran gazed once more in wonder at the mountainside where first had appeared Eilonwy's signal light. "She is alive," he murmured to himself. "Alive," he whispered again and again, and his heart leaped each time he spoke the words. Gurgi would be with her, of this he was somehow sure. All his senses told him both companions had survived. Over the chill air came the baying of a wolf. There were other sounds, as of distant shouting, but they soon faded, and he gave them no thought, filled as he was with his new-found hope.

Half the night had worn away when Doli flickered back into sight. The dwarf, too excited to complain of his buzzing ears, hurriedly beckoned Taran and Fflewddur to follow him. Ordering the horsemen to stand alert, Taran hastened after the companions. The Fair Folk warriors were already jog-trotting behind Doli, silent as white shadows.

Taran at first thought the dwarf meant to lead them directly to the Huntsmen's camp; instead Doli turned off a little distance before it and began scrambling up a slope rising high above the gorge.

"The Huntsmen are still there," Doli muttered under his breath as they climbed. "No wish of their own. We have some friends we didn't know about — bears and wolves, dozens of them, all along the rim of the gorge. A band of Huntsmen tried to climb out. Good thing they couldn't see me or I wouldn't be here. But *they* were seen. The bears got to them first. Quick work they made of those villains. Bloody work, but quick."

"They slew a party of Huntsmen?" Taran frowned. "Now the others are even stronger."

"Be that as it may," replied Doli. "The bears and wolves can attend to them better than we can. I doubt the Huntsmen will attack tonight. They fear the animals. They'll stay in the gorge until morning. And that's where I want them. I think I've struck on something."

By this time they had reached the summit and had come to the rim of an ice-bound lake. At the sheer drop over the edge of the bluff, a frozen waterfall glittered under the moon; like fingers on a huge fist, vast icicles clawed at the steep slope, as though holding the lake in its frigid grip. A river of hard silver twisted downwards towards the gorge where the Huntsmen were sheltering. Taran glimpsed their campfires glowing like baleful eyes in the darkness. Though he could not be sure, it seemed to him that shadowy shapes stirred among the rocks and stunted brush of the higher ground; perhaps the bears and wolves of which the dwarf had spoken.

"There!" Doli said. "What do you think of that?"

"What do I think?" cried the bard. "My old friend, I think you're the one who left your wits in the mine. You've led us on a good climb, but I should hardly call this a moment to admire the beauties of nature."

The dwarf put his hands on his hips and looked at Fflewddur with exasperation. "Sometimes I think Eiddileg's right about you humans. Can't you see past your nose? Can't you see at all? We're nearly atop those ruffians. Free the lake! Free the waterfall! Let it go pouring down! Straight into the camp!"

Taran caught his breath. For a moment, his heart leaped hopefully. Then he shook his head. "The task is too great, Doli. The ice will defeat us."

"Then melt it!" shouted the dwarf. "Cut branches, bushes, all that will burn. Where the ice is too thick, chop it away! How many times must I tell you? You're dealing with Fair Folk!"

"Can it indeed be done?" Taran whispered.

"Would I have said it if I didn't think so?" the dwarf snapped.

Fflewddur gave a low whistle of admiration. "You think in large terms, old fellow. But it appeals to me. Great Belin, if we could pull it off we'd strike them all down at one blow! And rid ourselves of them once and for all!"

Doli was no longer listening to the bard but was passing hasty orders to the Fair Folk warriors, who unslung their axes and, with all speed, began chopping and hacking at the trees, uprooting underbrush, and racing with their burdens to the lake.

Casting his doubts aside, Taran drew his sword and hewed at the branches. Fflewddur toiled beside him. Despite the bitter cold air, their brows streamed; their panting breath hung in a white haze before their faces. At the frozen waterfall the axes of the Fair Folk rang upon the ice. Doli dashed among the warriors, adding to the pile of bushes and branches, dislodging rocks and boulders to form a straighter, swifter channel.

The night was waning quickly. Taran stumbled in exhaustion, his cold-numbed hands torn and bleeding. Fflewddur was barely able to keep his feet. But the efforts of the Fair Folk never slackened. Before dawn the lake and the watercourse were piled high, as though a forest had overgrown them. Only then was Doli satisfied.

"Now, we'll set it alight," he cried to Taran. "Fair Folk tinder burns hotter than anything you humans know. It will blaze in no time." He whistled shrilly through his teeth. All along the lake the torches of the Fair Folk flamed, then arced like shooting stars as the warriors flung them into the pyre. Taran saw the first branches catch fire, then the rest. A fierce crackling filled his ears, and over it he heard Doli shouting for the companions to race clear of the blaze. A wave of heat like the breath of a furnace caught at Taran as he struggled for a foothold among the stones. The ice was melting. He heard the hiss of quenched flames. But the fire, too high to be altogether extinguished, raged even more hotly. From the watercourse came the crack and groan of boulders shifting under the growing pressure of the rising flood. In a moment, like a gate ripped from its hinges, like a wall collapsing, the side of the bluff gave way, and through the channel burst a sheet of water carrying all before it. Huge blocks of ice thundered down the slope, bounding and rolling as if they had been no more than pebbles. The swift outpouring bore with it the flaming branches; above the streaming mass, clouds of sparks billowed and swirled, and the watercourse blazed all along its length.

In the gorge below, the Huntsmen shouted and strove to flee. It was too late. The rushing waters and careening boulders flung back the warriors as they sought to scramble up the ravine. Screaming and cursing, they fell beneath the cascade or were tossed in the air like chips, to be dashed against the sharp rocks. A few gained higher ground, but as they did, Taran saw dark shapes spring to grapple with them, and now it was the turn of the waiting animals to take vengeance on those who had ever mercilessly hunted and slaughtered them.

Silence fell over the gorge. In the dawn light Taran saw the glint of the dark water that had flooded the ravine. Some of the branches still burned, others smouldered, and a grey mist of smoke hung in the air. A rattle of stones behind him made Taran spin about and snatch his blade from the scabbard.

"Hullo!" said Eilonwy. "We're back again!"

"You have an odd way of welcoming people," Eilonwy went on, as Taran, his heart too full to speak, stared speechless at her. "You might at least say something."

While Gurgi, yelping joyfully, tried to greet everyone at once, Taran stepped quickly to Eilonwy's side, put his arms about her, and drew the princess close to him. "I had given up hope..."

"A silly thing to do," Eilonwy answered. "*I* never did. Though I admit having a few uneasy moments with that ruffian Dorath, and I could tell you tales you wouldn't believe about wolves and bears. I'll save them for later, when you can tell me all that's been happening to you. As for the Huntsmen," she continued, as the reunited companions made their way to the tunnel, "I saw the whole thing. At first I hadn't any idea what you were up to. Then I understood. It was wonderful. I should have known Doli had a hand in it. Good old Doli! It looked like a river of burning ice..." The princess stopped suddenly and her eyes widened. "Do you realize what you've done?" she whispered. "Don't you see?"

"Know what we've done?" laughed Fflewddur. "Indeed we do! We've rid ourselves of the Huntsmen, and a good job it was. A Fflam couldn't have done better. As for what I see, I'm more pleased with what I *can't* see, if you take my meaning, namely, not a sign of those villains."

"Hen Wen's prophecy!" Eilonwy cried. "Part of it's come true! Have all of you forgotten? *'Night turn to noon and rivers burn with frozen fire ere Dyrnwyn be regained.'* Well, you've burned a river, or so it seems to me. Frozen fire could just as well mean all that ice and flaming branches, couldn't it?"

Taran looked closely at the princess. His hands trembled as the words of the prophecy echoed in his memory. "Have you seen what we ourselves did not see? But have you not done as much as we did? Without realizing it yourself? Think! *'Night turn to noon.'* Your bauble made daylight of darkness!"

It was Eilonwy's turn to be surprised. "So it did!" she exclaimed.

"Yes, yes!" shouted Gurgi. "Wise piggy told the truth! Mighty blade will be found again!"

Fflewddur cleared his throat. "A Fflam is always encouraging," he said, "but in this case I should remind you, the prophecy also said Dyrnwyn's flame would be quenched and its power would vanish, which leaves us no better off than we were, even if we did manage to find it. And I also recall something about asking mute stones to speak. So far I've heard not a word from any of the stones here, though in the matter of boulders and rocks, there's hardly a short supply. The only message they've given me is that they're hard to sleep on. Moreover, if you want my opinion, I'd say don't trust prophecies in the first place. It's been my experience they're as bad as enchantments and lead only to one thing: trouble."

"I do not understand the meaning of the prophecy myself," Taran said. "Are these signs of hope, or do we deceive ourselves by wishing them to be? Only Dallben or Gwydion has wisdom to interpret them. And yet I can't help feeling there is some hope at last. But it is true. Our task is no easier than it was."

Doli grimaced. "No easier? It's impossible now. Do you still mean to gain the Red Fallows? I warn you the Cauldron-Born are far out of reach." He snorted. "Don't talk to me about prophecies. Talk about time. We've lost too much of it."

"I have thought long about this, too," Taran answered. "It has been in my mind ever since the tunnel fell. I believe our only chance is to go straight across the mountains and try to hold back the Cauldron-Born as they turn northwest to Annuvin."

"Slim hope," Doli replied. "The Fair Folk can't venture that far. It's forbidden land. That close to Arawn's realm, Fair Folk would die. Gwystyl's way post was nearest to the Land of Death, and you've seen what it did to his digestion and disposition. The best we could do is to put you well on your way. One of us might go with you," he added. "You can imagine who that is. Good old Doli! I've spent so much time above ground with you humans that being in Annuvin can't harm me.

"Yes, I'll go with you," Doli went on, scowling furiously. "I see nothing else for it. Good old Doli! Sometimes I wish I didn't have such an agreeable temper. Humph!"

CHAPTER SIXTEEN

The Enchanter

Like a weary child, the old man hunched over the book-strewn table, his head upon his arm. Across his bony shoulders he had flung a cloak; the fire still flickered in the hearth, but the chill of this winter sank into him more deeply than any other he could remember. At his feet, Hen Wen stirred restlessly and whimpered in a high, plaintive voice. Dallben, who was neither altogether asleep nor awake, reached down a frail hand and gently scratched her ear.

The pig would not be calmed. Her pink snout twitched, she snorted and muttered unhappily and tried to hide her head in the folds of his robe. The enchanter at last roused himself.

"What is it, Hen? Is our time upon us?" He gave the pig a reassuring pat and rose stiffly from the wooden stool. "Tut, it is a moment to pass, no more than that, whatever the outcome."

Without haste he took up a long ash-wood staff and, leaning on it, hobbled from the chamber. Hen Wen trotted at his heels. At the cottage door, he pulled the cloak tighter about him and stepped into the night. The moon was at its full, riding distant in a deep sky. Dallben stood, listening carefully. To another's ears, the little farm would have seemed silent as the moon itself, but the old enchanter, his brow furrowed, his eyes half closed, nodded his head. "You are right, Hen," he murmured. "I hear them now. But they are still far. What then," he added, with a wrinkled smile, "must I wait long for them and freeze the little marrow left in my bones?"

Nevertheless, he did not return within the cottage but moved a few paces across the dooryard. His eyes, which had been heavy with drowsiness, grew bright as ice crystals. He peered sharply past the leafless trees of the orchard, as though to see into the shadows entwining the circling forest like black ivy tendrils. Hen Wen stayed behind, sitting uneasily on her haunches and watching the enchanter with much concern on her broad, bristly face.

"I should say there are twenty of them," Dallben remarked, then added wryly, "I do not know whether to be insulted or relieved. Only twenty? It is a paltry number. Yet more than that would be too cumbersome for the long journey, especially through the fighting in the Valley of Ystrad. No, twenty would be deemed ample and well chosen."

For some time the old man stood quietly and patiently. At last, through the clear air, a faint sound of hoofbeats grew more insistent, then stopped, as if the riders had dismounted and were walking their steeds.

Against the dark tangle of trees where the forest rose at the edge of the stubble field, the darting shapes could have been no more than shadows cast by the bushes. Dallben straightened, raised his head, and blew out his breath as gently as if he were puffing at thistledown.

In an instant a biting gale shrieked across the field. The farm was calm, but the wind ripped with the force of a thousand swords into the forest, where the trees clashed and rattled. Horses whinnied, men shouted as branches suddenly lashed against them. The gale beat against the warriors, who flung up their arms to shield themselves from it.

Still, the war band pressed on, struggling through the

wind-whipped forest and at last gaining the stubble field. At the onset of the gale, Hen Wen, squealing fearfully, had turned tail and dashed into the cottage. Dallben raised a hand and the wind died as quickly as it had risen. Frowning, the old man smote his staff on the frozen turf.

Deep thunder muttered, the ground shuddered; and the field heaved like a restless sea. The warriors staggered and lost their footing, and among the attackers many fled to the safety of the forest, hastening to escape, fearful the earth itself might open and swallow them. The rest, urging each other on, drew their swords and stumbled across the field, racing towards the cottage.

With some vexation Dallben thrust out his arm with fingers spread as though he were casting pebbles into a pond. From his hand a crimson flame spurted and stretched like a fiery lash, in blinding streaks against the black sky.

The warriors cried out as ropes of crackling flame caught at them and twined about their arms and legs. The horses broke loose and galloped madly into the woods. The attackers threw down their weapons and tore frantically at their cloaks and jackets. Howling in pain and terror, the men reeled and plunged in full flight back to the forest.

The flames vanished. Dallben, about to turn away, glimpsed one figure which still pressed across the empty field. Alarmed, the old man gripped his staff and hobbled as quickly as he could into the cottage. The warrior was striding past the stables and into the dooryard. With footfalls pounding behind him, Dallben hurried across the threshold, but the old man had no sooner gained the refuge of his chamber than the warrior burst through the doorway. Dallben spun about to face his assailant.

"Beware!" cried the enchanter. "Beware! Take no step closer."

Dallben had drawn himself up to his full height, his eyes flashed, and his voice rang with such a commanding tone that the warrior hesitated. The man's hood had fallen back and the firelight played over the golden hair and proud features of Pryderi Son of Pwyll.

Dallben's eyes never faltered. "I have long awaited you, King of the West Domains."

Pryderi made as if to take a step forwards. His hand dropped to the pommel of the naked sword at his belt. Yet the old man's glance held him. "You mistake my rank," Pryderi said mockingly. "Now I rule a larger realm. Prydain itself."

"What then," replied Dallben, feigning surprise, "is Gwydion of the House of Don no longer High King of Prydain?"

Pryderi laughed harshly. "A king without a kingdom? A king in rags, hunted like a fox? Caer Dathyl has fallen, the Sons of Don are scattered to the wind. This you already know, though it seems the tidings have reached you swiftly."

"All tidings reach me swiftly," Dallben said. "Swifter, perhaps, than they reach you."

"Do you boast of your powers?" Pryderi answered scornfully. "At the last, when you most needed them, they failed. Your spells did no more than frighten a handful of warriors. Does the crafty Dallben take pride in putting churls to flight?"

"My spells were not meant to destroy, only to warn," Dallben replied. "This is a place of danger to all who enter against my will. Your followers heeded my warning. Alas, Lord Pryderi, that you did not. These churls are wiser than their king, for it is not wisdom that a man should seek his own death."

"Again you are mistaken, wizard," Pryderi said. "It is your death I seek."

Dallben tugged at the wisps of his beard. "What you may seek and what you may find are not always one, Son of Pwyll," he said quietly. "Yes, you would take my life. That is no secret to me. Has Caer Dathyl fallen? That victory is hollow so long as Caer Dallben stands and so long as I live. Two strongholds have long stood against the Lord of Annuvin: a golden castle and a farmer's cottage. One lies in ruins. But the other is still a shield against evil, and a sword ever pointed at Arawn's heart. The Death-Lord knows this, and knows as well that he cannot enter here, nor can his Huntsmen and Cauldron-Born.

"Thus have you come," Dallben added, "to do your master's bidding."

A flush of anger spread over Pryderi's face. "I am my own master," he cried. "If power is given me to serve Prydain, shall I fear to use it? I am no Huntsman, who kills for the joy of killing. I do what must be done, and shrink not from it. My purpose is greater than the life of a man, or a thousand men. And if you must die, Dallben, then so be it."

Pryderi ripped the sword from his belt, and in a sudden movement struck at the enchanter. But Dallben had taken a firmer grip on his staff and raised it against the blow. Pryderi's blade shattered upon the slender wood, and the shards fell ringing to the ground.

Pryderi cast the broken hilt from him. Yet it was not fear that filled his eyes, but scorn. "I have been warned of your powers, wizard. I chose to prove them for myself."

Dallben had not moved. "Have you been truly warned? I think not. Had you been, you would not have dared to face me."

"Your strength is great, wizard," Pryderi said, "but not so great as your weakness. Your secret is known to me. Strive against me as you will. At the end it is I who must conquer. Of all powers, one is forbidden you on pain of your own death. Are you master of winds? Can you make the earth tremble? This is useless toying. You cannot do what the lowest warrior can do: you cannot kill."

From his cloak Pryderi had drawn a short black dagger whose pommel bore the seal of Annuvin. "No such ban is laid upon me," he said. "As I have been warned, so have I been armed. This blade comes from the hand of Arawn himself. It can be wielded despite all your spells."

A look of pity and deep sorrow had come over Dallben's wrinkled face. "Poor foolish man," he murmured. "It is true. This weapon of Annuvin can take my life and I cannot stay your hand. But you are blind as the mole that toils in the earth. Ask now, Lord Pryderi, which the master and which the slave. Arawn has betrayed you.

"Yes, betrayed you," Dallben said, his voice sharp and cold. "You thought to make him serve you. Yet all unwitting you have served him better than any of his hirelings. He sent you to slay me, and gave you the means to do it. Indeed, perhaps you shall slay me. But it will be Arawn's triumph, not yours. Once you have done his bidding, you are a useless husk to the Lord of Annuvin. He knows full well that never will I let you depart alive from Caer Dallben. You are a dead man, Lord Pryderi, even as you stand here."

Pryderi raised the black dagger. "With words you seek to ward off your death."

"See from the window," Dallben answered.

As he spoke, a crimson glow poured through the casement. A broad belt of flames had sprung up to circle

Caer Dallben. Pryderi faltered and stepped back. "You have believed half-truths," Dallben said. "No man has ever suffered death at my hands. But those who scorn my spells do so at their own peril. Slay me, Lord Pryderi, and the flames you see will sweep over Caer Dallben in an instant. There is no escape for you."

Pryderi's golden features were drawn in a look of disbelief, mingled with growing fear at the enchanter's words. "You lie," he whispered hoarsely. "The flames will die, even as you will die."

"That, Lord, you must prove for yourself," Dallben said.

"I have my proof!" Pryderi cried. "Arawn would not destroy what he seeks most. There were two tasks! In all your wisdom you did not guess them. Your death was only one. The other, to gain *The Book of Three.*"

Dallben shook his head sadly and glanced at the heavy, leather-bound tome. "You have been doubly betrayed, then. This book will no more serve Arawn than it will serve any evil end. Nor will it serve you, Lord Pryderi."

The force of the old man's voice was like a cold wind. "You have steeped your hands in blood, and in your pride sought to pass judgement on your fellow men. Was it your concern to serve Prydain? You chose an evil means to do it. Good cannot come from evil. You leagued yourself with Arawn for what you deemed a noble cause. Now you are a prisoner of the very evil you hoped to overcome, prisoner and victim. For in *The Book of Three* you are already marked for death."

Dallben's eyes blazed and the truth of his words seemed to grip Pryderi's throat. The king's face had turned ashen. With a cry, he flung away the dagger and clutched at the huge book. Desperately his hands reached out as if they would rip it asunder.

"Touch it not!" Dallben commanded.

But Pryderi had already seized it. As he did so a blinding bolt of lightning sprang like a blazing tree from the ancient tome. Pryderi's death shriek rang through the chamber.

Dallben turned away and bowed his head as though some heavy grief had come upon him. Beyond the little farm the circle of fire dwindled and faded in the quiet dawn.

CHAPTER SEVENTEEN

The Snowstorm

The Fair Folk warriors, all save Doli, had turned back at the line of treeless crags marking the westernmost edge of the Hills of Bran-Galedd, for beyond that point the land lay under the sway of Arawn Death-Lord. For some days now the companions had toiled painfully through a wilderness of stone, where not even moss or lichen flourished. The sky was grey, and the few thin clouds no more than shreds of darker grey. It was as though an evil mist had seeped from the stronghold of Annuvin, stifling all living things and leaving only this rocky waste.

The companions spoke little, husbanding their strength. From the first day within the borders of the Land of Death, they had been obliged to dismount and go on foot, leading the weary horses through the treacherous passes. Even the stallion Melynlas showed signs of fatigue; the steed's powerful neck drooped and his gait sometimes faltered. Llyan, however, padded skilfully along the narrowest and most dangerous of ledges. Often, while the companions laboured down one sharp descent to clamber up an even sharper slope, the enormous cat leaped from one crag to the next, and they would come upon her sitting with her tail coiled about her haunches, waiting for Fflewddur to scratch her ears, after which she would bound off once more.

Doli, firmly gripping his staff, his white hood pulled well down over his face, trudged at the head of the little band. Taran had never ceased to wonder at the tireless dwarf who found, as though by secret sense, hidden footpaths and narrow ways that helped speed the harsh journey.

Yet, after a time, Doli's pace seemed to flag. Taran saw with growing concern and uneasiness that from time to time the dwarf would lose his footing and his step turn suddenly unsure. When Doli staggered and dropped to one knee, Taran ran to his side, alarmed, and tried to lift up the dwarf. The companions hurried to join him.

Doli's usually ruddy face had grown mottled and he

breathed only in painful gasps. He struggled to regain his feet.

"Curse this evil realm," he muttered. "Can't stand it as well as I thought. Don't gawk! Give me a hand up."

Stubbornly, the dwarf refused to mount one of the horses, insisting he felt better when his feet were on the ground. When Taran urged him to rest, Doli angrily shook his head. "I said I'd find a passage for you," he snapped. "And I mean to. Can't stand a botched job. When the Fair Folk set about a task, they do it right, and don't dawdle over it."

Nevertheless, after a short while Doli reluctantly consented to climb astride Melynlas. He fumbled with the stirrups but grumbled irritably when Fflewddur helped him into the saddle.

Even this relief was not long lasting. The dwarf's head soon dropped weakly forward, he swayed unsteadily and, before Taran could reach him, lurched from the stallion's back and pitched to the ground.

Taran quickly signalled a halt. "We'll go no farther today," he told the dwarf. "By morning you'll have your strength again."

Doli shook his head. His face was white, his crimson eyes had turned dull. "No use waiting," he gasped. "I've been too long here. It will grow worse. Must keep on while I can still guide you."

"Not at the cost of your life," Taran said. "Hevydd the

Smith will ride with you to the border. Llassar Son of
Drudwas will help the rest of us find our way."

"Won't do," muttered the dwarf. "Take too long without
Fair Folk skill. Tie me to the saddle," he commanded.

He strove to raise himself from the ground, but fell back
and lay motionless. His breathing grew rasping and violent.

Taran cried out in alarm, "He's dying. Hurry, Fflewddur.
Help me put him on Llyan. She is the swiftest mount. Ride
back with him. There may still be time."

"Leave me here," Doli gasped. "You can't spare Fflewddur.
His sword is worth ten. Or six, at least. Go quickly."

"That I will not do," replied Taran.

"Fool!" choked the dwarf. "Heed me!" he commanded. "It
must be done. Are you a war-leader or an Assistant Pig-Keeper?"

Taran kneeled by the dwarf, whose eyes were half-
closed, and gently put a hand on Doli's shoulder. "Need you
ask, old friend? I'm an Assistant Pig-Keeper."

Taran rose to meet the bard, who had hastened up with
Llyan, but when he turned back to the dwarf, the ground
was empty. Doli had vanished.

"Where has he gone?" shouted Fflewddur.

An irritable voice came from somewhere near a boulder.
"Here! Where else do you think?"

"Doli!" cried Taran. "You were close to your death,
and now..."

"I've turned invisible, as any clodpole with half an ounce

of sense can plainly see," snorted Doli. "Should have thought of it before. Last time in Annuvin, I was invisible most of the way. Never realized how it protected me."

"Can it serve you now?" asked Taran, still a little bewildered. "Dare you keep on?"

"Of course," the dwarf retorted. "I'm better already. But I'll have to stay invisible. As long as I can stand it, that is! Invisible! Hornets and wasps in my ears!"

"Good old Doli!" Taran cried, seeking vainly to pump the dwarf's unseen hand.

"Not that again!" snapped the dwarf. "I'd not do this willingly – oh, my ears – for any mortal in Prydain – oh, my head – but you! And don't shout! My ears won't stand it!"

Doli's staff, which had dropped to the ground, seemed to rise of itself, as the invisible dwarf picked it up. From the motion of the staff Taran could see that Doli had once more begun trudging ahead.

Guiding themselves by the length of wood, the companions followed. Yet even without sight of the staff they could have found their way, led by the sound of loud and furious grumbling.

Fflewddur was first to sight the gwythaints. In the distance, above a shallow ravine three black-winged shapes soared and circled. "What have they found?" the bard cried. "Whatever it is, I hope we're not the ones to be found next!"

Taran sounded his horn and signalled the war band to find whatever protection they could among the huge boulders. Eilonwy, disregarding Taran's orders, scrambled to the top of a high, jutting stone and shaded her eyes.

"I can't tell for sure," Eilonwy said, "but it looks to me as though they've cornered something. Poor creature. It will not last long against them."

Gurgi crouched fearfully against a rock and tried to make himself as flat as a fish. "Nor will Gurgi, if they see him," he wailed. "They will seize his poor tender head with gashings and slashings!"

"Pass on! Pass on!" Glew shouted, his little face puckered in fright. "They're busy with their prey. Don't stop here like fools. Get as far away as we can. Oh, if I were a giant again, you'd not find me lingering!"

The gwythaints narrowed their circle and had begun to swoop downwards, seeking their kill. But suddenly what appeared to be a black cloud, with a dark shape leading it, streaked down from the eastern quarter of the sky. Before the surprised companions could follow its swift movement overhead, the cloud shattered as if at its leader's command into winged fragments that drove straight upon the huge birds. Even at this distance Taran could hear the furious screams of the gwythaints as they veered aloft to face these strange assailants.

Fflewddur had leaped up beside Eilonwy and, as Taran and Doli clambered to a vantage point, the bard shouted excitedly: "Crows! Great Belin, I've never seen so many!"

Like great black hornets, the crows swarmed over their enemy; it was not a single combat of bird against bird, but a battle in which whole troops of crows grappled and clung to the gwythaints' lashing wings, heedless of sharp beaks and talons, forcing the creatures earthwards. When, by sheer strength, the gwythaints shook off their attackers, a new troop would form and renew the charge. The gwythaints sought to break free of their burden by plunging downwards, scraping as closely as they dared against the sharp stones. But as they did, the crows pecked furiously at them and the gwythaints spun and fluttered dizzily, losing their course and falling once again victim to the relentless onslaught.

In a last burst of power, the gwythaints beat their way aloft; they turned and sped desperately northwards, with the crows in hot pursuit. They vanished over the horizon, all save a solitary crow that flew swiftly towards the companions.

"Kaw!" Taran shouted and held out his arm.

Jabbering at the top of his voice, the crow swooped down. His eyes glittered in triumph and he flapped his shiny wings more proudly than a rooster. He gabbled, croaked, squawked, and poured forth such a torrent of yammering that Gurgi clapped his hands over his ears.

From his perch on Taran's wrist, Kaw bobbed his head and clacked his beak, thoroughly delighted with himself and never for a moment ceasing his chatter.

Taran, trying vainly to interrupt the crow's raucous and boastful clamour, had despaired of learning any tidings from the roguish bird when Kaw flapped his wings and sought to fly off again.

"Achren!" Kaw croaked. "Achren! Queen!"

"You've seen her?" Taran caught his breath. He had given little thought to the once-powerful queen since her flight from Caer Dallben. "Where is she?"

The crow fluttered a little distance away, then returned, his beating wings urging Taran to follow him. "Close! Close! Gwythaints!"

Eilonwy gasped. "That's what we saw. The gwythaints have slain her!"

"Alive!" Kaw answered. "Hurt!"

Taran ordered the Commot horsemen to await him, then leaped to the ground to follow after Kaw. Eilonwy, Doli, and Gurgi hastened to join him. Glew refused to budge, remarking that he had already skinned himself on enough rocks and had no intention of going out of his way for anyone.

Fflewddur hesitated a moment. "Yes, well, I suppose I shall go along, too, should you need help in carrying her.

But it doesn't sit well with me. Achren was eager enough to go her own way, and I rather think we shouldn't meddle. Not that I fear her, not for a moment — ah, the truth of it is," he hurriedly added, as the harp strings tensed, "the woman makes me shudder. Since the day she threw me into her dungeon, I've noticed something unfriendly about her. She has no fondness for music, I can tell you. Nevertheless," he cried, "a Fflam to the rescue!"

Like a tattered bundle of black rags the still form of Queen Achren lay in the fissure of a massive rock where she had, in her last hope, pressed to escape the gwythaints' vicious beaks and talons. Yet her refuge, Taran saw pityingly, had offered the queen scant protection. Achren moaned faintly as the companions carefully lifted her from the crevice. Llyan, who had followed along with the bard, crouched silently nearby, and lashed her tail uneasily. Achren's face, drawn and deathly pale, had been badly slashed, and her arms bore many deep and bleeding wounds. Eilonwy held the woman and tried to revive her.

"Llyan shall carry her back with us," Taran said. "She will need more healing herbs than I have brought; more than her wounds, a fever has weakened her. She has gone long without food or drink."

"Her shoes are in ribbons," Eilonwy said. "How far must she have wandered in this awful place? Poor Achren! I can't say I'm fond of her, but it makes my toes curl up just imagining what could have happened."

Fflewddur, after helping move the unconscious queen to more level ground, had stayed a few paces away. Gurgi, too, chose to keep some distance between Achren and himself. Nevertheless, at Taran's bidding they drew closer and the bard, with many soothing words, held Llyan steady while the other companions lifted Achren to the great cat's back.

"Hurry along," called the voice of Doli. "It's starting to snow."

White flakes had begun drifting from the heavy sky; within little time a biting wind swirled around the companions and snow drove against them in an ever-thickening cloud. Needles of ice stung their faces, it grew more and more difficult to see, and as the storm gained in fury even Doli could no longer be sure of the path. The companions staggered blindly in a file, each clutching the other, with Taran gripping an end of Doli's staff. Kaw, almost entirely covered with snow, hunched up his wings and tried desperately to keep his perch on Taran's shoulder. Llyan, burdened with the motionless queen, bent her great head against the gale and plodded onwards; but the surefooted cat often stumbled over hidden boulders and snow-filled pits. Once Gurgi yelled in terror and vanished as suddenly as if the earth had swallowed him. He had tumbled into a deep crevice and by the time the companions were able to haul him out, the hapless creature had nearly turned into a shaggy icicle. He trembled so violently he could scarcely walk, and between them, Taran and Fflewddur bore him along.

The wind did not slacken, the snow fell in an impenetrable curtain; and the cold, already bitter, grew even more intense. Breathing was painful and with each laboured gasp Taran felt the frigid draught like daggers in his lungs. Eilonwy half-sobbed with cold and exhaustion, and she clung to Taran, striving to keep her footing as Doli led them through drifts that now had risen more than knee-high.

"We can't go on," the dwarf shouted above the wind. "Find shelter. Make our way to the horsemen when the snow lets up."

"But the warriors, how shall they fare?" Taran replied anxiously.

"Better than we!" the dwarf cried. "Where they are, there's a good-sized cave I noticed along the cliff wall. Your young shepherd is bound to find it, never fear. Our trouble is finding something for ourselves."

However, even after long and painful searching, the dwarf discovered nothing more than a shallow gully below an overhanging ledge. The companions stumbled gratefully into it; here they were protected against the worst battering of the wind and snow. But the cold still gripped them, and no sooner had they halted than their bodies seemed to stiffen and they moved arms and legs only with the greatest difficulty. They clung together for warmth and pressed against Llyan's thick coat of fur. Even this gave them little comfort for, as night fell, the chill deepened. Taran stripped off his cloak and covered Eilonwy and Achren; Gurgi insisted on adding his sheepskin jacket and he crouched with his shaggy arms wrapped around himself, his teeth chattering loudly.

"I fear that Achren will not live the night," Taran murmured to Fflewddur. "She was too close to death when we found her. She will not have strength to stand such cold."

"Will any of us?" answered the bard. "Without a fire, we might just as well say farewell to each other right now."

"I don't know what you're complaining about," Eilonwy sighed. "I've never been so comfortable in all my life."

Taran looked at her in alarm. The girl did not stir under the cloak. Her eyes were half-shut, her voice faltered with drowsiness.

"Quite warm," she rambled on happily. "What a lovely goosefeather quilt I have. How odd. I dreamed we were all caught in a terrible storm. It wasn't pleasant at all. Or am I still dreaming? No matter. When I wake up, it will all be gone away."

Taran, his face drawn with anxiety, shook her roughly. "Don't sleep!" he cried. "If you sleep it will be your death."

Eilonwy did not answer him, but only turned her head away and closed her eyes. Gurgi had curled up beside her and could not be roused. Taran himself felt a fatal drowsiness spreading over him. "Fire," he said, "we must build a fire."

"From what?" Doli brusquely replied. "There's not a twig to be found in this wilderness. What will you burn? Our boots? Our cloaks? We'll freeze all the faster." He flickered back into sight. "And if I'm going to freeze, I won't do it with hornets buzzing in my ears."

Fflewddur, who had been silent this while, reached behind him and unslung his harp. At this, Doli gave a furious shout.

"Harp music!" he cried. "My friend, your wits are frozen solid as ice!"

"It shall give us the tune we need," replied Fflewddur.

Taran dragged himself to the side of the bard. "Fflewddur, what do you mean to do?"

The bard did not answer. For a long moment he held the harp lovingly in his hands and gently touched the strings, then with a quick motion raised the beautiful instrument and smashed it across his knee.

Taran cried out in anguish as the wood shattered into splinters and the harp strings tore loose with a discordant burst of sound. Fflewddur let the broken fragments drop from his hands.

"Burn it," he said. "It is wood well-seasoned."

Taran seized the bard by the shoulders. "What have you done?" he sobbed. "Gallant, foolish Fflam! You have destroyed your harp for the sake of a moment's warmth. We need a greater fire than this wood can ever give us."

Doli, however, had quickly taken flint from his pouch and had struck a spark into the pitiful heap of splinters. Instantly, the wood blazed up and sudden warmth poured over the companions. Taran stared amazed at the rising flames. The bits of wood seemed hardly to be consumed, yet the fire burned all the more brightly. Gurgi stirred and raised his head. His teeth had ceased their chattering and colour was returning to his frost-pinched face. Eilonwy, too, sat up and looked about her as though waking from a dream. At a glance she understood what fuel the bard had offered, and tears sprang to her eyes.

"Don't give it a second thought," cried Fflewddur. "The truth of the matter is that I'm delighted to be rid of it. I could never really play the thing, and it was more a burden than anything else. Great Belin, I feel light as a feather without it. Believe me, I was never meant to be a bard in the first place, so all is for the best."

In the depths of the flame several harp strings split in two and a puff of sparks flew into the air.

"But it gives a foul smoke," Fflewddur muttered, though the fire was burning clear and brilliant. "It makes my eyes water horribly."

The flames had now spread to all the fragments, and as the harp strings blazed a melody sprang suddenly from the heart of the fire. Louder and more beautiful it grew, and the strains of music filled the air, echoing endlessly among the crags. Dying, the harp seemed to be pouring forth all the songs ever played upon it, and the sound shimmered like the fire.

All night the harp sang, and its melodies were of joy, sorrow, love, and valour. The fire never abated, and little by little new life and strength returned to the companions. And as the notes soared upwards a wind rose from the south, parting the falling snow like a curtain and flooding the hills with warmth. Only at dawn did the flame sink into glowing embers and the voice of the harp fall silent. The storm had ended, the crags glistened with melting snow.

Wordless and wondering, the companions left their shelter. Fflewddur lingered behind for a moment. Of the harp, nothing remained but a single string, the one unbreakable string which Gwydion had given the bard long ago. Fflewddur kneeled and drew it from the ashes. In the heat of the fire the harp string had twisted and coiled around itself, but it glittered like pure gold.

CHAPTER EIGHTEEN

Mount Dragon

As Doli had foretold, Llassar had led the warriors to shelter in a cave and had saved them from the full fury of the snowstorm. The companions now made ready to continue their journey. The sharp crags that were their last obstacle lay not far distant. The crest of Mount Dragon loomed dark and forbidding. With the help of Taran's healing potions and Eilonwy's care, Achren had regained consciousness. Fflewddur was still reluctant to come within fewer than three paces of the black-robed queen, but Gurgi had finally taken enough courage to open his wallet and offer food to the half-starved woman — although the creature's face wrinkled uneasily and he held out the morsels at arm's length, as if fearful of being bitten. Achren, however, ate sparingly; Glew, for his part, lost no time in snatching up what remained, popping it into his mouth and glancing about to see whether more might be forthcoming.

Achren's fever had left her weakened in body, yet her face had lost none of its haughtiness; and after Taran had briefly recounted what had brought the companions so close to Annuvin it was with ill-disguised scorn that she answered him.

"Does a pig-keeper and his shabby followers hope to triumph where a queen failed? I would have reached Annuvin long since, had it not been for Magg and his warriors. By chance, his war band came upon me in Cantrev Cadiffor." Her broken lips drew back in a bitter grimace. "They left me for dead. I heard Magg laugh when they told him I had been slain. He, too, shall know my vengeance.

"Yes, I lay in the forest like a wounded beast. But my hatred was sharper than their sword thrusts. I would have crept after them on hands and knees and given my last strength to strike them down, though indeed I feared that I would die unrevenged. But I found refuge. There are still those in Prydain who pay homage to Achren. Until I could journey once again, they sheltered me; and for that service they shall be rewarded.

"Yet I failed even within sight of my goal. The gwythaints were more ruthless than Magg. They would have made certain of my death – I, who once commanded them. Sharp will be their punishment."

"I have the awful feeling," Eilonwy whispered to Taran, "that Achren sometimes thinks she's still Queen of Prydain. Not that I mind, so long as she doesn't take it into her head to try to punish *us*."

Achren, overhearing Eilonwy's remarks, turned to the girl. "Forgive me, Princess of Llyr," she said quickly. "I spoke half in a rambling dream and the cold comforts of memory. I am grateful to you for my life and shall repay you far beyond its worth. Hear me well. Would you pass the mountain bastions of Annuvin? You follow the wrong path."

"Humph!" Doli cried, popping visible for a moment. "Don't tell one of the Fair Folk he's on the wrong path."

"Yet it is true," Achren replied. "There are secrets unknown even to your people."

"It's no secret that if you cross mountains you choose the easiest way," Doli snapped back. "And that's what I plan. I'm taking my bearings from Mount Dragon, but you can believe me, once we're closer, we'll turn aside and find a passage through the lower slopes. Do you think I'm such a fool as to do otherwise?"

Achren smiled contemptuously. "In so doing, dwarf, you would indeed be a fool. Of all the peaks surrounding Annuvin, Mount Dragon alone can be breached. Heed me," she added, as Taran murmured in disbelief. "The crags are lures and traps. Others have been deceived, and their bones lie in the pitfalls. The lower mountains beckon with promise of easier passage, but no sooner are they crossed than they fall away into sheer cliffs. Does Mount Dragon warn you to shun its heights? The western descent is a very roadway to the Iron Portals of Annuvin. To reach it there is a hidden trail, where I shall guide you."

Taran looked closely at the queen. "Such are your words, Achren. Do you ask us to stake our lives on them?"

Achren's eyes glittered. "In your heart you fear me, Pig-Keeper. But which do you fear the more — the path I offer you or the certain death of Lord Gwydion? Do you seek to overtake Arawn's Cauldron warriors? This you cannot do, for time will defeat you unless you follow where I lead. This is my gift to you, Pig-Keeper. Scorn it if you choose, and we shall go our separate ways."

Achren turned and muffled herself with her ragged cloak. The companions drew away from her and spoke among themselves. Doli, thoroughly vexed and disgruntled by Achren's judgement of his skill, nonetheless admitted that he could have unwittingly led them astray. "We Fair Folk have never dared to journey here, and I can't prove what she says one way or the other. But I've seen mountains that look sheer on one side — and on the other you could roll down without so much as a bump. So she could be telling the truth."

"And she could be trying to get rid of us the fastest way she knows," the bard put in. "Those pitfalls with bones in them make my flesh creep. I think Achren would be delighted if some of those bones were ours. She's playing her own game, you can be sure of that." He shook his head uneasily. "A Fflam is fearless, but with Achren, I prefer being wary."

Taran was silent a moment, searching for the wisdom to choose one way or the other, and again felt the weight of the burden Gwydion had set upon him to be more than he could bear. Achren's face was a pallid mask; he could read nothing of her heart in it. More than once the queen would have taken the lives of the companions. But, as he knew, she had served Dallben well and faithfully after her own powers had been shattered. "I believe," he said slowly, "that we can do no less than trust her until she gives us clear reason to doubt. I fear her," he added, "as do all of us. Yet I will not let fear blind me to hope."

"I agree," said Eilonwy, "which makes me think in this case, at least, your judgement is quite right. I admit that trusting Achren is like letting a hornet sit on your nose. But sometimes you only get stung when you try to brush it off — the hornet, I mean."

Taran went to Achren's side. "Lead us to Mount Dragon," he said. "We will follow you."

Another day's travel brought the companions across a harsh, uneven valley that lay within the shadow of Mount Dragon itself. The summit had been well named, for Taran saw its peak was in the rough shape of a monstrous, crested head with gaping jaws, and on either side the lower slopes spread like outflung wings. The great blocks and shafts of stone that rose to form its jagged bulk were dark, mottled with patches of dull red. Before this last barrier, poised as though to swoop downwards and crush them, the companions fearfully halted. Achren strode to the head of the waiting column and beckoned them onwards.

"There are other, easier paths," Achren said, as they entered a narrow defile that twisted between towering walls of sheer cliffs, "but they are longer and those who travel them can be seen before they reach the stronghold of Annuvin. This one is known only to Arawn and his most trusted servants. And to me, for it was I who showed him the secret ways of Mount Dragon."

Taran, however, soon began to fear Achren had deceived them, for the path rose so steeply that men and horses could barely keep their footing. Achren seemed to be leading them deep into the heart of the mountain. Mighty shelves of overhanging rocks rose like arches above the toiling band, blotting the sky from their sight. At times, the path skirted yawning chasms and more than once Taran stumbled, buffeted by a sudden chill blast that flung him against the walls. His heart pounded and his head reeled at the sight of the deep gorges opening at his feet, and terrified he clung to the sharp edges of jutting rocks. Achren, whose step did not falter, only turned and silently glanced at him, a mocking smile on her ravaged face.

The path continued to rise, though not so abruptly, for it no longer followed the slope of the mountain but seemed almost to double back on itself, and the companions gained the higher reaches of the trail only by small degrees. The huge stone jaws of the dragon's head loomed above. The trail that for some of its course had been hidden by grotesque formations of rocks now lay exposed, and Taran could see most of the mountain slope dropping sharply below him. They were almost at the highest ridge of the dragon's shoulder, and it was there that Kaw, scouting ahead, returned to them and clacked his beak frantically.

"Gwydion! Gwydion!" the crow jabbered at the top of his voice. "Annuvin! Haste!"

Taran sprang past Achren and raced to the ridge, clambering upwards among the rocks, straining his eyes for a glimpse of the stronghold. Had the Sons of Don already begun their attack on Annuvin? Had Gwydion's warriors themselves overtaken the Cauldron-Born? His heart pounding against his ribs, he struggled higher. Suddenly the dark towers of Arawn's fastness were below him. Beyond the high walls, beyond the massive Iron Portals, ugly and brooding, he glimpsed the spreading courtyards, the Hall of Warriors where once the Black Cauldron had stood. Arawn's Great Hall rose, glittering like black, polished marble, and above it, at the highest pinnacle, floated the Death-Lord's banner.

The sight of Annuvin sickened him with the chill of death that hung over it, his head spun and shadows seemed to blind him. He pressed higher. Struggling shapes filled the courtyard, the clash of blades and shouted battle cries struck his ears. Men were scaling the western wall; Dark Gate itself had been breached, and Taran believed he saw the flash of Melyngar's white flanks and golden mane, and the tall figures of Gwydion and Taliesin.

The Commot men had not failed! Arawn's deathless host had been held back and victory was in Gwydion's hands. But even as Taran turned to shout the joyous tidings, his heart froze. Southwards he glimpsed the hastening army of Cauldron-Born. Their iron-shod boots rang and clattered as the mute warriors raced towards the heavy gates and the horns of the troop captains shrieked for vengeance.

Taran leaped from the ridge to join the companions. The shelf of stone crumbled at his feet. He pitched forward. Eilonwy's scream rang in his ears, and the sharp rocks seemed to whirl upwards against him. Desperately he clutched at them and strove to break his fall. With all his strength he clung to the sheer side of Mount Dragon, while jagged stones bit like teeth into his palms. His sword, ripped from his belt, clattered into the gorge.

He saw the horrified faces of the companions above him and knew he was beyond their reach. His muscles trembling, his lungs bursting with his efforts, he fought to climb upwards to the path.

His foot slipped and he twisted about to regain his balance. It was then that he saw, plunging from the peak of Mount Dragon, the gwythaint speeding towards him.

CHAPTER NINETEEN

The Death-Lord

The gwythaint, greater than any Taran had ever seen, screamed and beat its wings, churning a wind like a gale of death. Taran saw the curved, gaping beak and blood-red eyes, and in another instant the gwythaint's talons sank into his shoulders, seeking to grip the flesh beneath his cloak. The relentless bird pressed so closely that the reek of its feathers filled Taran's nostrils. Its head, deeply scarred by an old wound, thrust against him.

Taran turned his face away and waited for the beak to

rend his throat. Yet the gwythaint did not strike. Instead, it was pulling him from the rocks with a strength Taran could not resist. The gwythaint no longer screamed, but made soft keening sounds, and the bird's eyes fixed upon him not in fury but in a strange gaze of recognition.

The bird seemed to be urging him to loosen his grasp. A sudden memory from his boyhood flooded Taran, and again he saw a fledgling gwythaint in a thornbush – a young bird wounded and dying. Was this the ragged bundle of feathers he had nursed back to life? Had the creature come at last to pay a debt so long remembered? Taran dared not hope, yet as he clung, weakening, to the side of Mount Dragon, it was his only hope. He relaxed his grip and let himself fall free.

The weight of its burden made the gwythaint falter and drop earthwards for a moment. Below Taran, the crags reeled. With all its strength, the huge bird beat its wings and Taran felt himself borne upwards, higher and higher, as the wind whistled in his ears. Its black wings heaving and straining, the gwythaint pressed steadily aloft until at last its talons opened and Taran fell to the stone-crested peak of Mount Dragon.

Achren had spoken the truth. The short, downward slope lay before him, clear and unhindered to the Iron Portals, which now swung open as the hastening army of Cauldron-Born streamed into Annuvin. The deathless host had drawn their swords. Within the stronghold, Gwydion's warriors had seen the foe, and shouts of despair rose from the embattled Sons of Don.

A troop of Cauldron-Born, sighting the lone figure of Taran atop the mountain's summit and the companions who now had crossed the ridge, broke from the main body of the host and turned their attack upon Mount Dragon. Brandishing their weapons, they sped up the slope.

The gwythaint, circling overhead, screamed a war cry. Sweeping its wings, the giant bird flew straight to the onrushing warriors and plunged into their ranks, striking out with beak and claws. Under the violence of the gwythaint's unexpected charge, the first rank of Cauldron-Born fell back and stumbled to the ground, but one of the mute warriors lashed out with his sword, striking again and again until the gwythaint dropped at his feet. The huge wings fluttered and trembled, then the battered body lay still.

Three of the Cauldron-Born had leaped past their comrades and raced towards Taran, who read his own death in their livid faces. His eyes darted about the summit, vainly seeking a last means of defence.

At the highest peak of the dragon's crest rose a tall rock. Time and tempest had gnawed it into a grotesque shape. The wind, blowing through the eroded crannies and hollows, set up a baleful keening, and the stone shrieked and moaned as if with human tongue. The weird wail seemed to command, to beseech, to draw Taran closer. Here was his only weapon. He flung himself against the rock and wrestled against the unyielding bulk, struggling to uproot it. The Cauldron-Born were nearly upon him.

The stone crest seemed to move a little as Taran redoubled his efforts. Then suddenly it rolled from its socket. With a final heave Taran sent it crashing amid his assailants. Two of the Cauldron-Born tumbled backwards and their blades spun from their hands, but the third warrior did not falter in his upward climb.

Driven by despair, as a man casts pebbles at the lightning that would strike him down, Taran groped for a handful of stones, of loose earth, even a broken twig to fling in defiance of the Cauldron warrior who strode closer, blade upraised.

The socket from which the dragon's crest had been torn was lined with flat stones, and in it, as in a narrow grave, lay Dyrnwyn, the black sword.

Taran snatched it up. For an instant, his mind reeling, he did not recognize the blade. Once, long before, he had sought to draw Dyrnwyn and his life had been almost forfeit to his rashness. Now, heedless of the cost, seeing no more than a weapon come to his hand, he ripped the sword from its sheath. Dyrnwyn flamed with a white and blinding light. It was only then, in some distant corner of his mind,

Taran dimly understood that Dyrnwyn was blazing in his grasp and that he was still alive.

Dazzled, the Cauldron-Born dropped his sword and flung his hands to his face. Taran leaped forward and with all his strength drove the blazing weapon deep into the warrior's heart.

The Cauldron-Born stumbled and fell; and from lips long mute burst a shriek that echoed and re-echoed from the Death-Lord's stronghold as though rising from a thousand tongues. Taran staggered back. The Cauldron-Born lay motionless.

Along the path and at the Iron Portals the Cauldron warriors toppled as one body. Within the stronghold the deathless men locked in combat with the Sons of Don screamed and crumpled to earth even as Taran's foe had fallen. A troop hastening to fill the breach at Dark Gate pitched headlong at the feet of Gwydion's warriors, and those who strove to slay the soldiers at the western wall dropped in mid-stride and their weapons clattered on the stones. Death at last had overcome the deathless Cauldron-Born.

Shouting for the companions, Taran raced from the peak of Mount Dragon. The Commot horsemen leaped to their saddles and urged their steeds to a gallop, plunging after Taran and into the fray.

Taran sped across the courtyard. At the death of the Cauldron-Born, many of Arawn's mortal guards threw down their weapons and sought vainly to flee the stronghold. Others fought with the frenzy of men whose lives were already lost; and the remaining Huntsmen, who had gained new strength as their comrades fell under the blades of the Sons of Don, still shouted their war cry and flung themselves against Gwydion's warriors. One of the Huntsmen troop captains, his branded face twisted in rage, slashed at Taran, then shouted in horror and fled at the sight of the flaming sword.

Taran fought his way through the press of warriors that swirled about him and raced towards the Great Hall where he had first glimpsed Gwydion. He burst through the portals and as he did so, sudden fear and loathing plucked at him. Torches flared along the dark, glittering corridors. For a moment he faltered, as though a black wave had engulfed him. From the far end of the corridor Gwydion had seen him and he strode quickly to Taran's side. Taran ran to meet him, shouting triumphantly that Dyrnwyn had been found.

"Sheathe the blade!" Gwydion cried, shielding his eyes with a hand. "Sheathe the blade, or it will cost your life!"

Taran obeyed.

Gwydion's face was drawn and pale, his green-flecked eyes burned feverishly. "How have you drawn this blade, Pig-Keeper?" Gwydion demanded. "My hands alone dare touch it. Give me the sword."

The voice of Gwydion rang harsh and commanding, yet Taran hesitated, his heart pounding with a strange dread.

"Quickly!" Gwydion ordered. "Will you destroy what I have fought to win? Arawn's treasure trove lies open to our hands, and power greater than any man has dreamed awaits us. You will share with me in it, Pig-Keeper. I trust no other.

"Shall some base-born warrior keep these treasures from us?" Gwydion cried. "Arawn has fled his realm, Pryderi is slain and his army scattered. None has strength to stand against us now. Give me the sword, Pig-Keeper. Half a kingdom is in your grasp, seize it now before it is too late."

Gwydion reached out his hand.

Taran flung himself back, his eyes wide with horror. "Lord Gwydion, this is not the counsel of a friend. It is betrayal..."

Only then, as he stared bewildered at this man he had honoured since boyhood, did he understand the ruse.

In another instant Taran ripped Dyrnwyn from its sheath and raised the glittering blade.

"Arawn!" Taran gasped, and swung the weapon downwards.

Before the blade struck home, the Death-Lord's disguised shape blurred suddenly and vanished. A shadow writhed along the corridor and faded away.

The companions now pressed into the Great Hall and Taran hurried towards them, crying the warning that Arawn still lived and had escaped.

Achren's eyes blazed with hatred. "Escaped you, Pig-Keeper, but not my vengeance. The secret chambers of Arawn are no secret to me. I shall seek him out wherever he has taken refuge."

Without waiting for the companions, who ran to follow her, Achren set off with all speed down the winding halls. She sprang past a heavy portal which bore the Death-Lord's seal branded deeply in the iron-studded wood. At the far end of the long chamber Taran glimpsed a hunched, spidery figure scuttling to a high, skull-shaped throne.

It was Magg. The Chief Steward's face was ghastly white, his lips trembled and slavered, and his eyes rolled in his head. He stumbled to the foot of the throne, snatched at an object that lay on the flagstones, clutched it to him, and whirled to face the companions.

"No closer!" shrieked Magg, in such a tone that even Achren halted and Taran, about to draw Dyrnwyn from its scabbard, was gripped in horror at Magg's contorted features.

"Will you keep your lives?" Magg cried. "To your knees, then! Humble yourselves and beg mercy. I, Magg, shall favour you by making you my slaves."

"Your master has abandoned you," replied Taran. "And your own treachery has ended." He strode forwards.

Magg's spidery hands thrust out in warning, and Taran saw that the Chief Steward held a strangely wrought crown.

"I am master here," Magg shouted. "I, Magg, Lord of Annuvin. Arawn pledged that I should wear the Iron Crown. Has it slipped from his fingers? It is mine, mine by right and promise!"

"He has gone mad," Taran murmured to Fflewddur, who stared in revulsion as the Chief Steward raised high the crown and gibbered to himself. "Help me take him prisoner!"

"No prisoner shall he be," cried Achren, drawing a dagger from her cloak. "His life is mine for the taking, and he shall die as all who have betrayed me. My vengeance begins here, with a treacherous slave, and next, his master."

"Harm him not," commanded Taran, as the queen struggled to make her way past him to the throne. "Let him find justice from Gwydion."

Achren fought against him, but Eilonwy and Doli hastened to hold the raging queen's arms. Taran and the bard strode towards Magg, who flung himself to the seat of the throne.

"Do you tell me Arawn's promises are lies?" the Chief Steward hissed, fondling and fingering the heavy crown. "It was promised I should wear this. Now it is given into my hands. So shall it be!" Quickly, Magg lifted the crown and set it on his brow.

"Magg!" he shouted. "Magg the Magnificent! Magg the Death-Lord!"

The Chief Steward's triumphant laughter turned to a shriek as he clawed suddenly at the iron band circling his forehead. Taran and Fflewddur gasped and drew back.

The crown glowed like red iron in a forge. Writhing in agony, Magg clutched vainly at the burning metal which now had turned white hot, and with a last scream toppled from the throne.

Eilonwy cried out and turned her face away.

Gurgi and Glew had lost track of the companions and were now pelting through the maze of winding corridors trying vainly to find them. Gurgi was terrified at being in the heart of Annuvin and at every step shouted Taran's name. Only the echoes from the torch-lit halls came back to him. Glew was no less fearful. Between gasps, the former giant also found enough breath to complain bitterly.

"It's too much to bear!" he cried. "Too much! Is there no end to the wretched burdens put upon me? Thrown aboard a ship, hustled off to Caer Dallben, half frozen to death, dragged through mountains at the risk of my life, a fortune snatched from my hands! And now this! Oh, when I was a giant I'd not have stood for such high-handed treatment!"

"Oh, giant, leave off pinings and whinings!" replied Gurgi, miserable enough at being separated from the companions. "Gurgi is lost and lorn, but he tries to find kindly master with seekings. Do not fear," he added reassuringly, though it was all he could do to keep his voice from trembling, "bold Gurgi will keep plaintful little giant safe, oh, yes."

"You're not doing very well at it," snapped Glew. Nevertheless, the pudgy little man clung to the side of the shaggy creature and, his stubby legs pumping, matched him stride for stride.

They had come to the end of one corridor where a squat and heavy iron portal stood open. Gurgi fearfully halted. A bright cold light poured from the chamber. Gurgi took a few cautious paces and peered within. Beyond the doorway stretched what seemed to be an endless tunnel. The light came from heaps of precious stones and golden ornaments. Farther on, he glimpsed strange objects half-hidden by shadows. Gurgi drew back, his eyes popping in wonder and terror.

"Oh, it is treasure-house of evil Death-Lord," he whispered. "Oh, glimmerings and shimmerings! This is a very secret place and fearsome, and not wise for bold Gurgi to stay."

Glew, however, pressed forwards, and at the sight of the gems his pale cheeks twitched and his eyes glittered.

"Treasure, indeed!" he said, choking in his excitement. "I've been cheated of one fortune, but now I'll be repaid. It's mine!" he cried. "All of it! I spoke first! No one shall deprive me of it!"

"No, no," protested Gurgi. "It cannot be yours, greedy giant! It is for mighty prince to give or take. Come with hastenings and seek companions even faster. Come with tellings and warnings, for Gurgi also fears snappings and trappings. Costly treasures without guardings? No, no, clever Gurgi sniffs evil enchantments."

Heedless of the creature's words, Glew thrust him aside. With an eager cry the former giant sprang past the threshold and into the tunnel, where he plunged his hands into the largest heap of jewels. Gurgi, seizing him by the collar, tried vainly to drag him back, as flames burst from the walls of the treasure trove.

Before the Great Hall of Annuvin, Gwydion rallied the last survivors of the Sons of Don and the Commot horsemen. There the companions, with Kaw squawking jubilantly overhead, joined them. For a moment, Taran stared searchingly at Gwydion, but his doubts vanished when the tall warrior strode quickly to him and clasped his hand.

"We have much to tell each other," Gwydion said, "but

no time for the telling. Though Annuvin is in our hands the Death-Lord himself has escaped us. He must be found and slain, if it is in our power to do so."

"Gurgi and Glew are lost in the Great Hall," Taran said. "Give us leave to find them first."

"Go quickly, then," answered Gwydion. "If the Death-Lord is still in Annuvin, their lives are in as much danger as ours."

Taran had unbuckled Dyrnwyn from his belt and held out the sword to Gwydion. "I understand now why Arawn sought possession of it – not for his own use but because he knew it threatened his power. Only Dyrnwyn could destroy his Cauldron-Born. Indeed, he dared not even keep it in his stronghold, and believed it harmless buried atop Mount Dragon. When Arawn disguised himself in your shape, he nearly tricked me into giving him the weapon. Take it now. The blade is safer in your hands."

Gwydion shook his head. "You have earned the right to draw it, Assistant Pig-Keeper," he said, "and thus the right to wear it."

"Indeed so!" put in Fflewddur. "It was magnificent the way you struck down that Cauldron-Born. A Fflam couldn't have done better. We're rid of those foul brutes for ever."

Taran nodded. "Yet I hate them no longer. It was not their wish to bend in slavery to another's will. Now they are at peace."

"In any case, Hen Wen's prophecy came true after all," Fflewddur said. "Not that I ever doubted it for a moment." He glanced instinctively over his shoulder, but this time there came no jangling of harp strings. "But she did have a curious way of putting things. I still haven't heard any stones speaking."

"I have," answered Taran. "Atop Mount Dragon, the sound from the crest was like a voice. Without it, I'd have paid no heed to the stone. Then, when I saw how hollowed and eaten away it was, I believed I might be able to move it. Yes, Fflewddur, the voiceless stone spoke clearly."

"I suppose so, if you think about it in that way," Eilonwy agreed. "As for Dyrnwyn's flame being quenched, Hen was quite mistaken. Understandably. She was very upset at the time..."

Before the girl could finish, two frightened figures burst from the Great Hall and raced to the companions. Much of Gurgi's hair had been singed away in ragged patches; his shaggy eyebrows were charred and his garments still smouldered. The former giant had fared worse, for he seemed little more than a heap of grime and ashes.

Taran had no time to welcome the lost companions, for the voice of Achren rose in a terrible cry.

"Do you seek Arawn? He is here!"

Achren flung herself at Taran's feet. Taran gasped and froze in horror. Behind him coiled a serpent ready to strike.

Taran sprang aside. Dyrnwyn flashed from its scabbard. Achren had clutched the serpent in both hands, as though to strangle or tear it asunder. The head of the snake darted towards her, the scaly body lashed like a whip, and the fangs sank deep into Achren's throat. With a cry she fell back. In an instant, the serpent coiled again; its eyes glittered with a cold, deadly flame. Hissing in rage, jaws gaping and fangs bared, the serpent shot forwards, striking at Taran. Eilonwy screamed. Taran swung the flashing sword with all his strength. The blade clove the serpent in two.

Flinging Dyrnwyn aside, Taran dropped to his knees beside Gwydion, who held the limp body of the queen. The blood had drained from Achren's lips and her glazed eyes sought Gwydion's face.

"Have I not kept my oath, Gwydion?" she murmured, smiling vaguely. "Is the Lord of Annuvin slain? It is good. My death comes easily upon me." Achren's lips parted as though she would speak again, but her head fell back and her body sagged in Gwydion's arms.

A horrified gasp came from Eilonwy. Taran looked up as the girl pointed to the cloven serpent. Its body writhed, its shape blurred. In its place appeared the black-cloaked figure of a man whose severed head had rolled face downwards on the earth. Yet in a moment this shape too lost its form and the corpse sank like a shadow into the earth; and where it had lain was seared and fallow, the ground wasted, fissured as though by drought. Arawn Death-Lord had vanished.

"The sword!" cried Fflewddur. "Look at the sword!"

Quickly, Taran caught up the blade, but even as he grasped the hilt the flame of Dyrnwyn flickered, as though stirred by a wind. The white brilliance dimmed like a dying fire. Faster then the glow faded, no longer white but filled with swirling colours which danced and trembled. In another moment, Taran's hand held no more than a scarred and battered weapon whose blade glinted dully, not from the flame that once had burned within it but only from the mirrored rays of the setting sun.

Eilonwy, hurrying to his side, called out, "The writing on the scabbard is fading, too. At least I think it is, unless it's just the dim light. Here, let me see better."

She drew the bauble from her cloak and brought it closer to the black scabbard. Suddenly, in the golden rays, the marred inscription glittered.

"My bauble brightens the lettering! There's more than what used to be there!" cried the surprised girl. "Even the part that was scratched out – I can see most of it now!"

The companions hastily gathered and, while Eilonwy held the bauble, Taliesin took the scabbard and scanned it closely.

"The writing is clear, but fading quickly," he said. "Indeed, Princess, your golden light shows what was hidden.

'*Draw Dyrnwyn, only thou of noble worth, to rule with justice, to strike down evil. Who wields it in good cause shall slay even the Lord of Death.*'"

In another moment the inscription had vanished. Taliesin turned the black scabbard back and forth in his hands. "Perhaps now I understand what was only hinted in the lore, that once a mighty king came upon great power and strove to use it for his own advantage. I believe Dyrnwyn was that weapon, turned from its destiny, long lost and found again."

"Dyrnwyn's task is ended," Gwydion said. "Let us leave this evil place."

In death the face of Achren, no longer bitterly haughty, was at last tranquil. Shrouding the woman in her tattered black cloak, the companions bore the body to rest in the Great Hall, for she who had once ruled Prydain had died not without honour.

At the pinnacle of the Death-Lord's tower, the dark banner suddenly burst into flames and fell away in blazing shreds. The walls of the Great Hall trembled, and the stronghold shuddered deep within itself.

The companions and the warriors rode from the Iron Portals, behind them the walls shattered and the mighty towers crumbled. A sheet of flame reached skywards from the ruins where Annuvin had stood.

CHAPTER TWENTY

The Gift

They were home again. Gwydion had led the companions westwards to the coast where the golden ships waited. From there, with Kaw proudly perched on the highest mast, the great vessels with their gleaming sails bore them to Avren harbour. Word of Arawn's destruction had spread swiftly; and even as the companions disembarked, many cantrev lords and their battle hosts gathered to follow the Sons of Don, to do homage to King Gwydion, and to cry greetings to the Commot folk and Taran Wanderer. Gurgi unfurled

~ 271 ~

what remained of the banner of the White Pig and raised it triumphantly.

Yet Gwydion had been strangely silent. And Taran, as the little farm came into sight, felt more heartache than joy. The winter had broken; thawing earth had begun to stir, and the first, hardly visible traces of green touched the hills like a faint mist. But Taran's eyes went to Coll's empty garden, and he grieved afresh for the stout grower of turnips, far distant in his lonely resting place.

Dallben hobbled out to greet them. The enchanter's face had grown even more deeply lined, his brow seemed fragile, the wrinkled skin almost transparent. Seeing him, Taran sensed that Dallben already knew Coll would not return. Eilonwy ran to his outstretched arms. Taran, leaping from the back of Melynlas, strode after her. Kaw flapped his wings and gabbled at the top of his voice. Fflewddur, Doli, and Gurgi, who looked more than ever patchy and scraggly, hastened to add their greetings, attempting to tell Dallben, all at the same time, what had befallen them.

Hen Wen was squealing, grunting, and wheezing, and very nearly climbing over the bars of the pen. As Taran jumped into the enclosure to fling his arms about the delighted pig, he suddenly heard shrill squeakings and his jaw dropped in surprise.

Eilonwy, who had hurried to the enclosure, gave a joyful cry. "Piglets!"

Six small pigs, five white as Hen Wen and one black, stood squealing on their hind legs beside their mother. Hen Wen chuckled and grunted proudly.

"We have had visitors," said Dallben. "One of them a very handsome boar. During the winter, when there was much stirring among the forest creatures, he came seeking food and shelter, and found Caer Dallben more to his liking than the woods. He is roaming about somewhere now, for he is still a little wild and unused to so many new arrivals."

"Great Belin!" cried Fflewddur. "Seven oracular pigs! Taran, my friend, your tasks will be harder than they were in the Hills of Bran-Galedd."

Dallben shook his head. "Sturdy and healthy they are, and as fine a litter as I have seen, but their powers are no greater than those of any other pig — which should be quite enough to satisfy them. Hen Wen's own gift began to fade when the letter sticks shattered and now is gone past recall. It is for the best; such power is a heavy burden, for men as well as pigs, and I daresay she is much happier now."

For two days, the companions rested, grateful and content to be together in the peacefulness of the little farm. The sky had never seemed clearer, filled with happier promise of spring or greater joy. King Smoit had arrived with his guard of honour, and through a night's feasting the cottage rang with merriment.

Next day Dallben summoned the companions to his chamber, where Gwydion and Taliesin already waited. He peered deeply and kindly at all gathered there, and when he spoke his voice was gentle.

"These have been days of welcome," he said, "but also days of farewell."

A questioning murmur rose from the companions. Taran, with alarm, looked searchingly at Dallben. Fflewddur, however, clapped a hand to his sword and exclaimed, "I knew it would be so! What task remains to be done? Have the gwythaints returned? Is a band of Huntsmen still abroad? Have no fears! A Fflam stands ready!"

Gwydion smiled sadly at the excited bard. "Not so, gallant friend. Like the Huntsmen, the gwythaints have been destroyed. Yet it is true: one task remains. The Sons of Don, their kinsmen and kinswomen, must board the golden ships and set sail for the Summer Country, the land from which we came."

Taran turned to Gwydion as though he had not grasped the High King's words. "How then," he quickly asked, not daring to believe he had heard aright, "the Sons of Don leave Prydain? Must you sail now? To what purpose? How soon shall you return? Shall you not first rejoice in your victory?"

"Our victory is itself the reason for our voyage," Gwydion answered. "This is a destiny long ago laid upon us: when the Lord of Annuvin shall be overcome, then must the Sons of Don depart for ever from Prydain."

"No!" Eilonwy protested. "Not now, of all times!"

"We cannot turn from this ancient destiny," Gwydion replied. "King Fflewddur Fflam, too, must join us, for he is kin to the House of Don."

The bard's face filled with distress. "A Fflam is grateful," he began, "and under ordinary circumstances I should look forward to a sea voyage. But I'm quite content to stay in my own realm. Indeed, dreary though it is, I've found myself rather missing it."

Taliesin spoke then. "It is not for you to choose, Son of Godo. But know that the Summer Country is a fair land, fairer even than Prydain, and one where all heart's desires are granted. Llyan shall be with you. A new harp you shall have. I myself shall teach you the playing of it, and you shall learn all the lore of the bards. Your heart has always been the heart of a true bard, Fflewddur Fflam. Until now, it was unready. Have you not given up that which you loved most for the sake of your companions? The harp that awaits you shall be all the more precious, and its strings shall never break.

"Know this, too," Taliesin added. "All men born must die, save those who dwell in the Summer Country. It is a land without strife or suffering, where even death itself is unknown."

"There is yet another destiny laid upon us," Dallben said. "As the Sons of Don must return to their own land, so must there come an end to my own powers. I have long pondered the message Hen Wen's last letter stick might have given us. It is clear to me now why the ash rods shattered. They could not withstand such a prophecy, which could only have been this: not only shall the flame of Dyrnwyn be quenched and its power vanish, but all enchantments shall pass away, and men unaided guide their own destiny.

"I, too, voyage to the Summer Country," Dallben continued. "I do so with sorrow but with even greater joy. I am an old man and weary, and for me there shall be rest and a laying down of burdens which have grown all too heavy upon my shoulders.

"Doli, alas, must return to the realm of the Fair Folk, and so must Kaw," the enchanter went on. "The way posts are being abandoned. King Eiddileg will soon command the barring of all passages into his kingdom, just as Medwyn has already closed his valley for ever to the race of men, allowing only the animals to find their way to him."

Doli bowed his head. "Humph!" he snorted. "It's about time to stop dealing with mortals. Only leads to trouble. Yes, I'll be glad enough to go back. I've had my fill of good-old-Doli this and good-old-Doli that, and good-old-Doli would you mind turning invisible just once more!" The dwarf strove to look as furious as he could, but there were tears in his bright red eyes.

"Even the Princess Eilonwy Daughter of Angharad must voyage to the Summer Country," Dallben said. "So it must be," he went on, as Eilonwy gasped in disbelief. "At Caer Colur, the princess gave up only the usage of her magical powers. They are still within her, as they have been handed down to all daughters of the House of Llyr. Therefore must she depart. However," he went on quickly, before Eilonwy could interrupt, "there are others who have well-served the Sons of Don: faithful Gurgi; Hen Wen, too, in her own fashion; and Taran of Caer Dallben. It is their reward that they may journey with us."

"Yes, yes!" shouted Gurgi. "All go to land of no sighings and no dyings!" He bounded joyously and waved his arms in the air, shedding a good portion of what hair remained to him. "Yes, oh yes! All together for ever! And Gurgi, too, will find what he seeks. Wisdom for his poor tender head!"

Taran's heart leaped as he cried out Eilonwy's name and hastened to the side of the princess to take her in his arms. "We shall not part again. In the Summer Country we shall be wed —" He stopped short. "If — if that is your wish. If you will wed an Assistant Pig-Keeper."

"Well, indeed," replied Eilonwy, "I wondered if you'd

ever get round to asking. Of course I will, and if you'd given half a thought to the question you'd have already known my answer."

Taran's head still spun from the enchanter's tidings, and he turned to Dallben. "Can this be true? That Eilonwy and I may voyage together?"

Dallben said nothing for a moment, then he nodded. "It is true. No greater gift lies in my power to grant."

Glew snorted. "That's all very well, bestowing never-ending life right and left. Even on a pig! But no one's given a thought to me. Selfishness! Lack of consideration! It's plain that if that Fair Folk mine hadn't come tumbling down – robbing me of my fortune, I might add – we'd have taken a different path, we'd never have gone to Mount Dragon, Dyrnwyn would never have been found, the Cauldron-Born never slain..." For all his indignation, however, the former giant's brow puckered wretchedly and his lips trembled. "Go, by all means! Let me stay this ridiculous size! I assure you, when I was a giant..."

"Yes, yes!" Gurgi shouted. "Whining giant, too, has served, even as he says. It is not fair to leave him lone and lost in smallness! And in treasure-house of evil Death-Lord, when all rich treasures fall in flames, a life was saved from hot and hurtful blazings!"

"Yes, even Glew has served, though all unwitting," Dallben replied. "His reward shall be no less than yours.

In the Summer Country he may grow, if he so desires, to the stature of a man. But do you tell me," Dallben said, looking sternly at Gurgi, "that he saved your life?"

Gurgi hesitated a moment. Before he could answer, Glew quickly spoke. "Of course he didn't," said the former giant. "A life was saved. Mine. If he hadn't pulled me out of the treasure‚house I'd be no more than a cinder in Annuvin."

"At least you've told the truth, giant!" cried Fflewddur. "Good for you! Great Belin, I think you've already grown a little taller!"

Gwydion stepped forward and gently put his hand on Taran's shoulder. "Our time is soon upon us," he said quietly. "In the morning, we shall depart. Make ready, Assistant Pig‚Keeper."

That night Taran drowsed fitfully. The joy that so lightened his heart had strangely flown, fluttering out of reach like a bird of brilliant plumage he could not lure back to his hand. Even thoughts of Eilonwy, of happiness awaiting them in the Summer Country, could not regain it.

At last he rose from his pallet and stood, uneasy, by the chamber window. The campfires of the Sons of Don had burned to ashes. The full moon turned the sleeping fields to a sea of silver. From far beyond the hills a voice began to lift in song, faint but clear; another joined it, then still others. Taran caught his breath. Only once, long ago in the Fair Folk realm, had he heard such singing. Now, more beautiful than he remembered, the song swelled, in a long flood of melody shimmering brighter than the moonbeams. Suddenly it ended. Taran cried out in sorrow, knowing he would never hear its like again. And, perhaps in his own imaginings there echoed from every corner of the land the sound of heavy portals closing.

"What, sleepless, my chicken?" said a voice behind him.

He turned quickly. Light filling the chamber dazzled him, but as his vision cleared he saw three tall and slender figures; two garbed in robes of shifting colours, of white, gold, and flaming crimson; and one hooded in a cloak of glittering black. Gems sparkled in the tresses of the first, at the throat of the second hung a necklace of shining white beads. Taran saw their faces were calm, beautiful to heartbreak, and though the dark hood shadowed the features of the last, Taran knew she could be no less fair.

"Sleepless and speechless, too," said the middle figure. "Tomorrow, poor dear, instead of dancing with joy he'll be yawning."

"Your voices — I know them well," Taran stammered, barely able to speak above a whisper. "But your faces — yes, once have I seen them, a time long past, in the Marshes of

Morva. Yet you cannot be the same. Orddu? Orwen, and –
Orgoch?"

"Of course we are, my gosling," Orddu replied, "though
it's true whenever you met us before we were hardly at
our best."

"But good enough for the purpose," Orgoch muttered
from the depths of her hood.

Orwen giggled girlishly and toyed with her beads. "You
mustn't think we look like ugly old hags *all* the time," she
said. "Only when the circumstances seem to require it."

"Why have you come?" Taran began, still baffled at the
familiar tones of the enchantresses coming from such fair
shapes. "Do you, too, journey to the Summer Country?"

Orddu shook her head. "We are journeying, but not
with you. Salt air makes Orgoch queasy, though it's very
likely the only thing that does. We travel to – well –
anywhere. You might even say everywhere."

"You shall see no more of us, nor we of you," added
Orwen, almost regretfully. "We shall miss you. As much,
that is, as we can miss anyone. Orgoch especially would
have loved to – well, best not to dwell on that."

Orgoch gave a most ungentle snort. Orddu, meanwhile,
had unfolded a length of brightly woven tapestry and held
it out to Taran.

"We came to bring you this, my duckling," she said.
"Take it and pay no heed to Orgoch's grumbling. She'll have

to swallow her disappointment — for lack of anything better."

"I have seen this on your loom," Taran said, more than a little distrustful. "Why do you offer it to me? I do not ask for it, nor can I pay for it."

"It is yours by right, my robin," answered Orddu. "It does come from our loom, if you insist on strictest detail, but it was really you who wove it."

Puzzled, Taran looked more closely at the fabric and saw it crowded with images of men and women, of warriors and battles, of birds and animals. "These," he murmured in wonder, "these are of my own life."

"Of course," Orddu replied. "The pattern is of your choosing and always was."

"My choosing?" Taran questioned. "Not yours? Yet I believed..." He stopped and raised his eyes to Orddu. "Yes," he said slowly, "once I did believe the world went at your bidding. I see now it is not so. The strands of life are not woven by three hags or even by three beautiful damsels. The pattern indeed was mine. But here," he added, frowning as he scanned the final portion of the fabric where the weaving broke off and the threads fell unravelled, "here it is unfinished."

"Naturally," said Orddu. "You must still choose the pattern, and so must each of you poor, perplexed fledglings, as long as thread remains to be woven."

"But no longer do I see mine clearly," Taran cried. "No longer do I understand my own heart. Why does my grief shadow my joy? Tell me this much. Give me to know this, as one last boon."

"Dear chicken," said Orddu smiling sadly, "when, in truth, did we really give you anything?"

Then they were gone.

CHAPTER TWENTY-ONE

Farewells

Through the remainder of the night, Taran did not move from the window. The unfinished weaving lay at his feet. By dawn, a still greater number of Commot folk and cantrev nobles came to throng the fields and hillsides around Caer Dallben, for it had become known the Sons of Don were departing Prydain, and with them the Daughters of Don who had journeyed from the eastern strongholds. At last Taran stirred and made his way to Dallben's chamber.

The companions were already gathered, even Doli, who

had flatly refused to set out for the Fair Folk realm without taking a last leave of each and every friend. Kaw, quiet for once, perched on the dwarf's shoulder. Glew seemed excited and pleased to be on his way. Taliesin and Gwydion stood near Dallben, who had donned a heavy travel cloak and bore an ash-wood staff. Under his arm the enchanter carried *The Book of Three*.

"Kindly master, hasten!" shouted Gurgi, as Llyan at Fflewddur's side twitched her tail impatiently. "All are ready for floatings and boatings!"

Taran's eyes went to the faces of the companions; to Eilonwy, who was watching him eagerly; to the weathered features of Gwydion, and the face of Dallben, furrowed with wisdom. Never had he loved each of them more than at this moment. He did not speak until he came to stand before the old enchanter.

"Never shall I have greater honour than the gift you offer me," Taran said. The words came slowly, yet he forced himself to continue. "Last night my heart was troubled. I dreamed that Orddu — no, it was not a dream. She was indeed here. And I have seen for myself your gift is one I cannot take."

Gurgi's yelping stopped short and he stared at Taran with wide and unbelieving eyes.

The companions started and Eilonwy cried out, "Taran of Caer Dallben, do you have any idea what you're saying?

Has the flame of Dyrnwyn scorched your wits?" Suddenly her voice caught in her throat. She bit her lips and turned quickly away. "I understand. In the Summer Country we were to be wed. Do you still question my heart? It has not changed. It is your heart that has changed towards mine."

Taran dared not look at Eilonwy, for his grief was too keen in him. "You are wrong, Princess of Llyr," he murmured. "I have long loved you, and loved you even before I knew that I did. If my heart breaks to part from our companions, it breaks twice over to part from you. Yet, so it must be. I cannot do otherwise."

"Think carefully, Assistant Pig-Keeper," Dallben said sharply. "Once taken, your choice cannot be recalled. Will you dwell in sorrow instead of happiness? Will you refuse not only joy and love but never-ending life?"

Taran did not answer for a long moment. When at last he did, his voice was heavy with regret, yet his words were clear and unfaltering.

"There are those more deserving of your gift than I, yet never may it be offered them. My life is bound to theirs. Coll Son of Collfrewr's garden and orchard lie barren, waiting for a hand to quicken them. My skill is less than his, but I give it willingly for his sake.

"The seawall at Dinas Rhydnant is unfinished," Taran continued. "Before the King of Mona's burial mound I vowed not to leave his task undone."

From his jacket Taran drew the fragment of pottery. "Shall I forget Annlaw Clay-Shaper? Commot Merin and others like it? I cannot restore life to Llonio Son of Llonwen and those valiant folk who followed me, never to see their homes again. Nor can I mend the hearts of widows and orphaned children. Yet if it is in my power to rebuild even a little of what has been broken, this must I do.

"The Red Fallows once were a fruitful place. With labour, perhaps they shall be so again." He turned and spoke to Taliesin. "Caer Dathyl's proud halls lie in ruins, and with them the Hall of Lore and the treasured wisdom of the bards. Have you not said that memory lives longer than what it remembers? But what if memory be lost? If there are those who will help me, we will raise the fallen stones and regain the treasure of memory."

"Gurgi will help! He will not voyage, no, no!" Gurgi wailed. "He stays always. He wants no gift that takes him from kindly master!"

Taran put a hand on the creature's arm. "You must journey with the others. Do you call me master? Obey me, then, in one last command. Find the wisdom you yearn for. It awaits you in the Summer Country. Whatever I may find, I must seek it here."

Eilonwy bowed her head. "You have chosen as you must, Taran of Caer Dallben."

"Nor will I gainsay you," Dallben said to Taran, "but

only warn you. The tasks you set yourself are cruelly difficult. There is no certainty you will accomplish even one, and much risk you will fail in all of them. In either case, your efforts may well go unrewarded, unsung, forgotten. And at the end, like all mortals, you must face your death; perhaps without even a mound of honour to mark your resting place."

Taran nodded. "So be it," he said. "Long ago I yearned to be a hero without knowing, in truth, what a hero was. Now, perhaps, I understand it a little better. A grower of turnips or a shaper of clay, a Commot farmer or a king — every man is a hero if he strives more for others than for himself alone. Once," he added, "you told me that the seeking counts more than the finding. So, too, must the striving count more than the gain.

"Once, I hoped for a glorious destiny," Taran went on, smiling at his own memory. "That dream has vanished with my childhood; and though a pleasant dream it was fit only for a child. I am well-content as an Assistant Pig-Keeper."

"Even that contentment shall not be yours," Dallben said. "No longer are you Assistant Pig-Keeper, but High King of Prydain."

Taran caught his breath and stared with disbelief at the enchanter. "You jest with me," he murmured. "Have I been prideful that you would mock me by calling me King?"

"Your worth was proved when you drew Dyrnwyn from

its sheath," Dallben said, "and your kingliness when you chose to remain here. It is not a gift I offer you now, but a burden far heavier than any you have borne."

"Then why must I bear it?" cried Taran. "I am an Assistant Pig-Keeper and such have I always been."

"It has been written in *The Book of Three*," Dallben answered, and raised his hand for silence before Taran could speak again. "I dared not tell you this. To give you such knowledge would have defeated the prophecy itself. Until this very moment, I was not sure you were the one chosen to rule. Indeed, yesterday I feared you were not."

"How then?" Taran asked. "Could *The Book of Three* deceive you?"

"No, it could not," Dallben said. "The book is thus called because it tells all three parts of our lives: the past, the present, and the future. But it could as well be called a book of 'if'. If you had failed at your tasks; if you had followed an evil path; if you had been slain; if you had not chosen as you did – a thousand 'ifs', my boy, and many times a thousand. *The Book of Three* can say no more than 'if' until at the end, of all things that might have been, one alone becomes what really is. For the deeds of a man, not the words of a prophecy, are what shape his destiny."

"I understand now why you kept my parentage a secret," Taran said. "But shall I never be given to know it?"

"I did not keep it secret from you entirely through my own wish," Dallben answered. "Nor do I keep it so now. Long ago, when *The Book of Three* first came into my hands, from its pages I learned that when the Sons of Don departed from Prydain the High King would be one who slew a serpent, who gained and lost a flaming sword, who chose a kingdom of sorrow over a kingdom of happiness. These prophecies were clouded, even to me; and darkest was the prophecy that he who would come to rule Prydain would be one of no station in life.

"Long did I ponder these things," Dallben continued. "At last, I left Caer Dallben to seek this future king and to hasten his coming. For many years I searched, yet all whom I questioned well knew their station, whether shepherd or war-leader, cantrev lord or Commot farmer.

"The seasons turned; kings rose and fell, wars turned to peace, and peace to war. Indeed, on a certain time, so many years ago as you yourself have years, a grievous war was upon the land, and I despaired of my quest and turned my steps once more towards Caer Dallben. On that day I chanced to pass a field where a battle had raged. Many lay slain, noble as well as humble folk; even the women and children had not been spared.

"From the forest nearby I heard a piercing cry. An infant had been hidden among the trees, as though his mother had sought, at the last, to keep him safe. From his wrappings I could judge nothing of his parentage and only sensed with certainty that both mother and father lay upon that field of the slain.

"Here, surely, was one of no station in life, an unknown babe of unknown kin. I bore the child with me to Caer Dallben. The name I gave him was Taran.

"I could not have told you of your parentage, even had I wished to," Dallben continued, "for I knew it no more than you did. My secret hope I shared only with two others: Lord Gwydion and Coll. As you grew to manhood, so our hopes grew, though never could we be certain you were the child born to be High King.

"Until now, my boy," said Dallben, "you were always a great 'perhaps'."

"What was written has come to pass," Gwydion said. "And now in truth we must say farewell."

The chamber was silent. Llyan, sensing the bard's distress, nuzzled him gently. The companions did not move. It was Glew who stepped forward and spoke first.

"I've been carrying this with me ever since I was so shabbily hustled away from Mona," he said, drawing from his jacket a small blue crystal which he pressed into Taran's hand. "It reminded me of my cavern and those grand days when I was a giant. But for some reason I don't want to be reminded of them any longer. Since I don't want it – here, take it as a small remembrance of me."

"He's still hardly the most generous spirit in the world," muttered Fflewddur, "but I've no doubt it's the first time he's ever given anybody anything. Great Belin, I swear the little fellow's actually grown another inch!"

Doli had taken the handsomely crafted axe from his belt. "You'll need this," he told Taran, "and it should serve you well in many tasks. It's Fair Folk quality, my lad, and you'll not blunt it easily."

"It can serve me no better than did its owner," Taran replied, clasping the dwarf's hand, "and its metal cannot be as true as your own heart. Good old Doli..."

"Humph!" The dwarf snorted furiously. "Good old Doli! I've heard that somewhere before."

Kaw, on Doli's shoulder, bobbed up and down while Taran gently ran a finger over the crow's sleek feathers.

"Farewell," Kaw croaked. "Taran! Farewell!"

"Farewell to you," Taran answered, smiling. "If I have despaired of teaching you good manners, I have rejoiced in your bad ones. You are a rogue and a scamp, and a very eagle among crows."

Llyan had padded up to rub her head affectionately against Taran's arm, which she did so vigorously that the enormous cat nearly knocked him off his feet.

"Bear my friend good company," Taran said, stroking Llyan's ears. "Cheer him with your purring when his spirits are low, as I wish you might cheer me. Stray not far from him, for even such a bold bard as Fflewddur Fflam is no stranger to loneliness."

Fflewddur himself had drawn near, and in his hand held the harp string he had taken from the fire. The heat of the flame had caused the string to curl and twine in a curious pattern that seemed without beginning or end, constantly changing as from one melody to another even as Taran looked at it.

"I'm afraid it's all that's left of the old pot," Fflewddur said, offering the string to Taran. "Truthfully, I'm just as well pleased. It was forever jangling and going out of tune..." He paused, glanced behind him nervously, and cleared his throat. "Ah — what I meant to say was that I shall miss those snapping strings."

"No more than I shall miss them," Taran said. "Remember me as well and fondly as I remember you."

"Have no fear!" cried the bard. "There's still songs to be sung and tales to be told. A Fflam never forgets!"

"Alas, alas!" wailed Gurgi. "Poor Gurgi has nothing to give kindly master for fond rememberings. Woe and misery! Even wallet of crunchings and munchings now is empty!"

The tearful creature suddenly clapped his hands together.

"Yes, yes! Forgetful Gurgi has one gift. Here, here it is. From burning treasure-house of wicked Death-Lord, bold Gurgi seized it with catchings and snatchings. But his poor tender head was so filled with fearful spinnings that he forgot!"

With this, Gurgi drew from his leather pouch a small, flame-scarred, battered coffer of unknown metal and held it out to Taran, who took it, studied it curiously, then broke the heavy seal which kept it locked.

The coffer held no more than a number of thin, closely written parchments. Taran's eyes widened as he scanned them, and he turned quickly to Gurgi.

"Do you know what you have found?" he whispered. "Here are the secrets of forging and tempering metals, of shaping and firing pottery, of planting and cultivating. This is what Arawn stole long ago and kept from the race of men. This knowledge is itself a priceless treasure."

"Perhaps the most precious of all," said Gwydion, who had come to study the parchments in Taran's hand. "The flames of Annuvin destroyed the enchanted tools that laboured of themselves and would have given carefree idleness. These treasures are far worthier, for their use needs skill and strength of hand and mind."

Fflewddur gave a low whistle. "Who owns these secrets is truly master of Prydain. Taran, old friend, the proudest cantrev lord will be at your beck and call, begging for anything you choose to grant him."

"And Gurgi found it!" shouted Gurgi, springing into the air and madly whirling about. "Yes, oh yes! Bold, clever, faithful, valiant Gurgi always finds things! Once he found a lost piggy and once he found evil black cauldron! Now he finds mighty secrets for kindly master!"

Taran smiled at the excited Gurgi. "Indeed, you have found many mighty secrets. But they are not mine to keep. These will I share with all in Prydain, for by right they belong to all."

"Then share this, as well," said Dallben, who had been listening closely and now held out the heavy, leather-bound volume he had kept under his arm.

"*The Book of Three?*" Taran said, looking wonderingly and questioningly at the enchanter. "I dare not..."

"Take it, my boy," Dallben said. "It will not blister your fingers, as once it did with an over-curious Assistant Pig-Keeper. All its pages are open to you. *The Book of Three* no longer foretells what is to come, only what has been. But now can be set down the words of its last page."

The enchanter took a quill from the table, opened the book, and in it wrote with a bold, firm hand:

"*And thus did an Assistant Pig-Keeper become High King of Prydain.*"

"This, too, is a treasure," said Gwydion. "*The Book of Three* is now both history and heritage. For my own gift, I could give you nothing greater. Nor do I offer you a crown, for a true king wears his crown in his heart." The tall warrior clasped Taran's hand. "Farewell. We shall not meet again."

"Take Dyrnwyn, then, in remembrance of me," Taran said.

"Dyrnwyn is yours," Gwydion said, "as it was meant to be."

"Yet Arawn is slain," Taran replied. "Evil is conquered and the blade's work done."

"Evil conquered?" said Gwydion. "You have learned much, but learn this last and hardest of lessons. You have conquered only the enchantments of evil. That was the easiest of your tasks, only a beginning, not an ending. Do you believe evil itself to be so quickly overcome? Not so long as men still hate and slay each other, when greed and anger goad them. Against these even a flaming sword cannot prevail, but only that portion of good in all men's hearts whose flame can never be quenched."

Eilonwy, who had been standing in silence, now drew close to Taran. The girl's eyes did not waver from his as she held out the golden sphere.

"Take this," she softly said, "though it does not glow as brightly as the love we might have shared. Farewell, Taran of Caer Dallben. Remember me."

Eilonwy was about to turn away, but suddenly her blue eyes flashed furiously and she stamped her foot. "It's not fair!" she cried. "It's not my fault I was born into a family of enchantresses. I didn't ask for magical powers. That's worse than being made to wear a pair of shoes that doesn't fit! I don't see why I have to keep them!"

"Princess of Llyr," said Dallben. "I have waited for you yourself to say those words. Do you truly wish to give up your heritage of enchantment?"

"Of course I do!" Eilonwy cried. "If enchantments are what separates us, then I should be well rid of them!"

"This lies within your power," Dallben said, "within your grasp, and, for the matter of that, upon your finger. The ring you wear, the gift Lord Gwydion gave you long ago, will grant your wish."

"What?" Eilonwy burst out, in both surprise and indignation. "Do you mean to say that all the years I've worn my ring I could have used it to have a wish granted? You told me nothing of it! That's worse than unfair. Why, I could simply have wished to destroy the Black Cauldron! Or to find Dyrnwyn! I could have wished Arawn conquered! Without the least danger! And I never knew!"

"Child, child," Dallben interrupted, "your ring can indeed grant you a wish, and one wish alone. But evil cannot be conquered by wishing. The ring will serve only you, and grant only the deepest wish of your own heart. I did not tell you before because I was uncertain that you truly knew what you longed for.

"Turn the ring once upon your finger," Dallben said. "Wish with all your heart for your enchanted powers to vanish."

Wondering and almost fearful, Eilonwy closed her eyes and did the enchanter's bidding. The ring flared suddenly, but only for a moment. The girl gave a sharp cry of pain. And in Taran's hand the light of the golden bauble winked out.

"It is done," Dallben murmured.

Eilonwy blinked and looked around her. "I don't feel a bit different," she remarked. "Are my enchantments truly gone?"

Dallben nodded. "Yes," he said gently. "Yet you shall always keep the magic and mystery all women share. And I fear that Taran, like all men, shall be often baffled by it. But, such is the way of it. Come, clasp hands the two of you, and pledge each other your troth."

When they had done so, the companions pressed around the wedded couple to wish them happiness. Then Gwydion and Taliesin went from the cottage and Dallben took up his ash-wood staff.

"We can tarry no longer," the enchanter said, "and here our ways must part."

"But what of Hen Wen?" Taran asked. "Shall I not see her one last time?"

"As often as you please," answered Dallben. "Since she was free to go or stay, I know she will choose to remain with you. But I suggest you first let those visitors trampling about the fields see there is a new High King in Prydain, and a new queen. Gwydion will have proclaimed the tidings and your subjects will be impatient to hail you."

The companions following, Taran and Eilonwy left the chamber. But at the cottage door, Taran drew back and turned to Dallben. "Can one such as I rule a kingdom? I remember a time when I jumped headfirst into a thornbush and I fear kingship will be no different."

"Very likely more nettlesome," put in Eilonwy. "But should you have any difficulties, I'll be happy to give you my advice. Right now, there's only one question: Are you going in or out of this doorway?"

In the waiting throng beyond the cottage, Taran glimpsed Hevydd, Llassar, the folk of the Commots, Gast and Goryon side by side near the farmer Aeddan, King Smoit towering above them, his beard bright as flame. But many were the well-loved faces he saw clearly only with his heart. A sudden burst of cheering voices greeted him as he took Eilonwy's hand tightly in his own and stepped through the door.

And so they lived many happy years, and the promised tasks were accomplished. Yet long afterwards, when all had passed away into distant memory, there were many who wondered whether King Taran, Queen Eilonwy, and their companions had indeed walked the earth, or whether they had been no more than dreams in a tale set down to beguile children. And, in time, only the bards knew the truth of it.

Prydain Pronunciation Guide

Achren	~	*AHK-ren*
Adaon	~	*ah-DAY-on*
Aeddan	~	*EE-dan*
Angharad	~	*an-GAR-ad*
Annuvin	~	*ah-NOO-vin*
Arawn	~	*ah-RAWN*
Arianllyn	~	*ahree-AHN-lin*
Briavael	~	*bree-AH-vel*
Brynach	~	*BRIHN-ak*
Caer Cadarn	~	*kare KAH-darn*
Caer Colur	~	*kare KOH-loor*
Caer Dathyl	~	*kare DA-thil*
Coll	~	*kahl*
Dallben	~	*DAHL-ben*
Doli	~	*DOH-lee*
Don	~	*dahn*
Dwyvach	~	*DWIH-vak*
Dyrnwyn	~	*DUHRN-win*

Edyrnion	~	*eh-DIR-nyon*
Eiddileg	~	*eye-DILL-eg*
Eilonwy	~	*eye-LAHN-wee*
Ellidyr	~	*ELLI-deer*
Fflewddur Fflam	~	*FLEW-der flam*
Geraint	~	*GHER-aint*
Goewin	~	*GOH-win*
Govannion	~	*go-VAH-nyon*
Gurgi	~	*GHER-ghee*
Gwydion	~	*GWIH-dyon*
Gwythaint	~	*GWIH-thaint*
Islimach	~	*iss-LIM-ahk*
Llawgadarn	~	*law-GAD-arn*
Lluagor	~	*lew-AH-gore*
Llunet	~	*LOO-net*
Llyan	~	*lee-AHN*
Llyr	~	*leer*

Melyngar	~	*MELLIN-gar*
Melynlas	~	*MELLIN-lass*
Oeth-Anoeth	~	*eth-AHN-eth*
Orddu	~	*OR-doo*
Orgoch	~	*OR-gahk*
Orwen	~	*OR-wen*
Prydain	~	*prih-DANE*
Pryderi	~	*prih-DAY-ree*
Rhuddlum	~	*ROOD-lum*
Rhun	~	*roon*
Smoit	~	*smoyt*
Taliesin	~	*tally-ESS-in*
Taran	~	*TAH-ran*
Teleria	~	*tell-EHR-ya*

Author's Note

Despite their shortcomings, no books have given me greater joy in the writing than *The Chronicles of Prydain*. I come sadly to the end of this journey, aware of the impossibility of commenting objectively on a work which has absorbed me so long and so personally.

I must, however, warn readers of this fifth chronicle to expect the unexpected. Its structure is somewhat different, its range wider. If there is more external conflict, I have tried to add more internal content; if the form follows that of the traditional hero tale, the individuals, I hope, are genuinely human. And although it deals with a battle on an epic scale, where Taran, Princess Eilonwy, Fflewddur Fflam, even the oracular pig Hen Wen, are pressed to the limits of their strength, it is a battle whose aftermath is deeper in consequences than the struggle itself. The final choice, which even faithful Gurgi cannot avoid, is almost too hard to bear. Fortunately, it is never offered to us in the real world — not, at least, in such unmistakeable terms. In another sense, we face this kind of choice again and again, because for us it is never final. Whether the Assistant Pig-

Keeper chose well, whether the ending is happy, heartbreaking, or both, readers must decide for themselves.

Like the previous tales, this adventure can be read independently of the others. Nevertheless, certain long-standing questions are resolved here. Why was that sneering scoundrel, Mag, allowed to escape from the Castle of Llyr? Whatever became of the small-hearted giant, Glew? Can Achren really be trusted in Caer Dallben? And, of course, the secret of Taran's parentage. Readers who have been asking me these questions will see why I could not, until now, answer them fully without spoiling the surprises.

As for Prydain itself, part Wales as it is, but more as it never was: at first, I thought it a small land existing only in my imagination. Since then, for me it has become much larger. While it grew from Welsh legend, it has broadened into my attempt to make a land of fantasy relevant to a world of reality.

The first friends of the Companions are as steadfast today as they were at the beginning; many I thought were new have turned out to have been old friends all along. I owe all of them considerably more than they suspect; and, as always, I offer these pages to them fondly, hoping they will find the result not too far below the promise. If time has tried their patience with me, it has only deepened my affection for them.

Lloyd Alexander

LLOYD ALEXANDER is one of the most respected and best-loved of American authors, with a huge following worldwide. He has written over forty books for adults and children. *The Chronicles of Prydain* have won many awards, including the highly prestigious Newbery Medal for *The High King*, as well as the Newbery Honour for *The Black Cauldron* and the ALA Notable Book for *The Book of Three*. He is best known for his tales of high fantasy and adventure, and in 2003 he was awarded a Life Achievement Award by the World Fantasy Convention.

Lloyd was born in Pennsylvania and still lives a few blocks away from his childhood home. He met his future wife, Janine, while attending the University of Paris. After they married, Lloyd wrote novel after novel but it was seven years before his first book was published. His magical stories have now sold millions of copies and have been translated into thirteen languages.

"I never became a world traveller, an explorer, an adventurer. But I did become a writer, which is pretty much the same thing."

Lloyd Alexander

THE CHRONICLES
of PRYDAIN

by

LLOYD ALEXANDER

THE BOOK OF THREE
THE BLACK CAULDRON
THE CASTLE OF LLYR
TARAN WANDERER
THE HIGH KING

THE CHRONICLES *of* PRYDAIN
BOOK ONE
THE BOOK OF THREE

Being an Assistant Pig-Keeper just isn't exciting and Taran longs for adventure. But he gets more than he bargained for when the magical pig, Hen Wen, disappears and Taran has to set off on a death-defying quest to save her from the evil Horned King.

His perilous adventures lead him on an incredible journey across the land of Prydain. Along the way he makes many new friends: an irritable dwarf, an impulsive bard, a strange hairy beast and the hot-headed Princess Eilonwy. Together, they face many dangers from the deathless Cauldron-Born warriors, dragons, witches, and the terrifying Horned King himself.

Taran learns much about his identity, but the mysterious *Book of Three* is yet to reveal his true destiny.

"...offers a blend of mythology and Welsh legend, and describes exciting adventures and battles between good and evil..."
Los Angeles Times

0 7460 6038 6   £5.99

THE CHRONICLES *of* PRYDAIN
BOOK TWO
THE BLACK CAULDRON
A Newbery Honour Book

Once again, the peaceful land of Prydain is being threatened by evil. Arawn, Lord of Annuvin, is harnessing the dark magic of the black cauldron and creating a terrifying army of deathless warriors from the stolen bodies of the slain.

Fresh from rescuing the magical pig, Hen Wen, from the clutches of the Horned King, Taran must face even more danger as he sets off to destroy the black cauldron. He and his faithful friends face constant peril as they journey into the nightmare world beyond the Dark Gate. When they finally come face-to-face with the three evil enchantresses who are guarding their enemy's evil prize, Taran realizes he will have to pay the high price they demand... But will that be enough?

"This is a book to pass down the family and keep for the next generation of children... The plot is first class...utterly absorbing."   *Children's Book News*

0 7460 6039 4   £5.99

THE CHRONICLES *of* PRYDAIN
BOOK THREE
THE CASTLE OF LLYR

Princess Eilonwy is distraught at the news that she must leave her friends and travel to the Island of Mona to learn how to be a proper princess. But a princess needs special skills to be part of the royal household and as it turns out, the Island of Mona isn't boring at all. Especially when Eilonwy discovers that she possesses magical powers. But soon her life is under threat from Achren, the most evil enchantress in all Prydain, and the wicked Chief Steward.

Then Taran learns that Eilonwy has disappeared, and, with his faithful companions, he undertakes a bold mission to rescue the princess.

"Mr. Alexander tells his tale in prose that is clear and fresh. There is a classic ring about it."

Times Educational Supplement

0 7460 6040 8   £5.99

THE CHRONICLES of PRYDAIN
BOOK FOUR
TARAN WANDERER

Taran is in turmoil. The Assistant Pig-Keeper's many adventures have seen him become a hero and fall in love with a princess, but he is yet to discover the truth about himself. Taran aches to know who his parents were and to prove himself worthy in the eyes of Princess Eilonwy, and so he sets off on a quest for knowledge of his birthright.

Accompanied by his loyal friends, Taran meets the three witches in the Marshes of Morva, who send him to consult the mysterious Mirror of Llunet. During his adventurous journey, he loses his horse and his sword and narrowly escapes being transformed into a worm. But he also meets Craddoc, the shepherd, and other people of Prydain, and with their help he finally learns the secret of the Mirror, and of himself – and finds not an ending but a beginning.

"It is rare that high excitement yields such quiet wisdom."

New York Times

0 7460 6839 5   £5.99

Also by Lloyd Alexander

The Fantastical Adventures
of the Invisible Boy

David hates being The Invisible Boy, ignored by his eccentric family because he's considered too young to understand anything. But right now he's happy to be forgotten. Signed off school to recover from a bout of pneumonia, David is looking forward to plenty of time for his imaginary swashbuckling adventures as The Sea-Fox, buccaneer captain and terror of the sea lanes.

Then his dry-as-dust aunt volunteers as his tutor and David is devastated. This is worse than school! But it turns out that Aunt Annie has some secrets to share, and together they set off on an exciting fantastical voyage.

"This book is delightful, a warm homage to creativity and the power of imagination."   *TES Teacher*

An ALA Notable Book
A *School Library Journal* Best Book of the Year

0 7460 6041 6   £5.99